I0760293

DISCOVERING ME

book 1

dating NASHVILLE

ANN MAREE CRAVEN

MICHELLE MACQUEEN

DATING NASHVILLE: Discovering Me book 1

By: Ann Maree Craven & Michelle MacQueen
Twin Rivers Press LLC
Atlanta, Georgia

For more information contact: Hello@Melissaacraven.com or visit the authors' websites at Melissaacraven.com or MichelleLynnAuthor.com

Cover design by: Daqri Bernado at Covers by Combs
Edited by: Kelly Hartigan at Xterraweb
Interior design by: Melissa A. Craven

ISBN 978-1-970052-03-9 Hardcover
ISBN 978-1-688611-46-7 Paperback
First edition for print by Twin Rivers Press LLC: September 25, 2019

Printed in the United States of America

DISCOVERING ME

book 1

ANN MAREE CRAVEN

MICHELLE MACQUEEN

ALSO BY ANN MAREE CRAVEN

(Pen Name: Melissa A. Craven)
Emerge: The Awakening (Book 1)
Emerge: The Edge (Book 1.5)
Emerge: The Scholar (Illustrated Character Journal)
Emerge: The Judgment (Book 2)
Emerge: The Volunteer (An Emerge Short Story)
Emerge: The Catalyst (An Emerge Short Story)
Emerge: The Captive (Book 3)
Emerge: The Heir (Book 4)
Emerge: The Betrayal (Book 5)

ALSO BY MICHELLE MACQUEEN

Choices: New Beginnings book 1
Promises: New Beginnings book 2
Dreams: New Beginnings book 3
Confessions: New Beginnings book 4

We Thought We were Invincible book 1
We Thought We Knew it All book 2

BY ANN MAREE CRAVEN & MICHELLE MACQUEEN

Dating My Best Friend (Redefining Me Book 1)
Dating the Boy Next Door (Redefining Me Book 2)
Dating My Nemesis (Redefining Me Book 3)

Dating Nashville (Discovering Me Book 1)
Dating Washington (Discovering Me Book 2)
Dating Texas (Discovering Me Book 3)

BONUS CHAPTERS

Don't forget your free Bonus Chapters! Download now at http://bit.ly/DNBonus. Along with the chapters, you'll receive occasional emails with special deals, giveaways, and new release alerts for all of our upcoming Twin Rivers books.

For the readers who wanted more Becks. We're so glad you asked for this book.

1

Nicky:

"Nicky St. Germaine." Principal Stevens' voice drifted over the crowd.

"Finally." Nicky stepped from the rows of Twin Rivers High graduates, eager to receive his diploma and get out of there. Grinning from ear to ear, Nicky made the short walk to the stage, and a cheer roared from the crowd—not that Nicky was popular; he just had a few really loud friends. Well, in reality, they were mostly his brother Avery's friends, but he loved them. It was good to see their familiar faces beaming up at him. Avery and his girlfriend, Nari, Wylder, Julian and Addison, and even Beckett Anderson showed up for his graduation. Becks was dressed in the most obvious disguise. Large, dark sunglasses covered half his face, and his ridiculous blond wig was swept back into a man-bun. The people of Twin Rivers pretended to let him blend in. They were used to his antics—and they were proud of their homegrown rising country music sensation.

God, I've missed him. Nicky accepted his diploma and a hug from Principal Stevens before returning to his seat. He'd missed his older friends over the last two years since they all graduated. It was strange, going back to school for his junior year without them. It hadn't occurred to Nicky until then that he didn't have any friends his age. The only one left to brave the halls of Twin Rivers High was Becks' little sister Wylder, who was a year younger than Nicky. They'd bonded over the shared demise of their social lives with the departure of their older siblings.

And then there was Kenny. Nicky's eyes swept the crowd, looking for his Defiance Academy boyfriend, also a year younger than Nicky. The last two years with Kenny had been rocky at times, but they were doing well—and looking forward to their last summer together before Nicky left for Vanderbilt University in the fall. Kenny still wasn't completely out of the closet, but he was trying, and Nicky was patient. With his conservative politician parents, Nicky understood how much harder it was for Kenny to come to terms with his sexuality than it had been for Nicky. Sure, his own father hadn't always made it easy, but that was nothing compared to Kenny's parents.

Nicky's heart stopped when he found his boyfriend among the crowd. He somehow managed to be both adorable and sizzling hot in his suit and tie with his sunglasses shielding his eyes. But that wasn't the source of his heart's distress this time. It was the gorgeous brunette girl hanging on his arm. Seeing his boyfriend with a Defiance Academy girl always gave Nicky reason to freak out. This was the same girl Kenny had cheated on him with two years ago.

Surprise. Nicky had trust issues with his boyfriend. It was no secret Kenny wished he wasn't bi. He felt his life would be easier if he could be the future politician his parents wanted him to be with a smart Jackie O. at his side to conqueror Washington as a power couple.

But he loved Nicky. That much Nicky knew. Sometimes he wondered if that was enough.

As Kenny draped his arm around the girl's waist, Nicky knew the end was near. He couldn't take much more of this. In a perfect world, Kenny would be the guy he wanted him to be. But this was never a perfect world.

"Trust me, Nicky, if anyone gets in trouble for this, it's going to be me, and I've already been expelled, and you graduated a few hours ago, so it's a win-win." Wylder finished picking the lock, moving to hold the door open for him.

"There's still the legal matter of breaking and entering." Nicky shouldered past her, carrying a huge box of party supplies.

"Nothing's broken." Wylder shrugged. "We're just borrowing the venue." She darted down the main hall of Twin Rivers High where she'd already spent hours setting up the most legendary party Twin Rivers would ever see.

"How did you do this?" Nicky dropped the box he was carrying. White fairy lights draped from the ceiling to cascade over the lockers, transforming the wide school hallway into a fantasy world. "It's beautiful."

"Principal Stevens left for her annual cruise right after the graduation ceremony, and I hacked into the alarm system and changed the phone number. I disabled the alarm, but if it happens to go off, the alarm company will just call me, and I'll tell them it's a false alarm. I found the code word they'll ask for the last time I was in Stevens' office. Then we'll lock up when we leave, and I'll change the call list back to the way it was. When summer school starts up next week, they'll be in for a huge surprise and think it was an epic senior prank. Come on, let me show you the rest." She tugged Nicky back down the hall to the school lobby she'd set up for the buffet and bar area.

"I can't hire caterers, so we're having a pizza and taco bar courtesy of Uber Eats delivery, and we'll have a couple of kegs at the bar." The whole lobby was set up like a sports bar, decked out in the school colors and sports team logos.

"You didn't do all of this by yourself in the last three hours?" Nicky looked at her like she might have magic he didn't know about.

"I have minions." She tossed her dreadlocks over her shoulder and beckoned him to follow her.

"There's more?"

"We have multiple forms of entertainment planned for the evening." Wylder led him to the junior hall, lit with tiki lanterns and unlit torches he hoped would stay unlit.

"What the?" Nicky stared down at his feet covered in sand. "What did you do, Wylder?" his voice rose a few octaves.

"I brought the beach inside." The long hallway was buried in at least two feet of sand, and the classroom doors stood open. Nicky peeked inside the nearest classrooms to see they were all covered in sand too, "We're having a sandcastle contest in the classrooms, but the hallway is for the waterslide. And the pool is in the last room on the left."

"Pool? Waterslide? Wylder, you're insane." Nicky ran a hand through his carefully styled hair, worried his best friend was going to jail this time.

"It's a slip and slide." She pointed to the end of the hall where the long yellow slide of death waited for a bunch of drunken teenagers to probably kill themselves. The slip and slide ended in a kiddie pool, and a huge hill of sand would likely keep most from really hurting themselves.

"It's definitely epic." Nicky sighed.

"Come see the cafeteria. It's the dance club for the night. We moved all the tables out and hung a bunch of disco balls and black lights. It's going to be amazing."

"It will be a miracle if we don't all get arrested before the night is over."

"I've set up escape routes for that possibility. When everyone comes in at the front, they'll get a colored bracelet and instructions on what to do when the cops show up. I've already sent parking instructions to the whole student body so the lot doesn't fill up with more than a few cars. Exit routes will take the students out in all different directions to get to their cars and out of the area before the cops know where to look."

"You've thought of everything." There was no doubt this party would be legendary. Just a few weeks ago, Wylder was caught stealing the final exam answers for all of her classes. It was a desperate attempt to improve her grades enough so she could pass her junior year. Not only did she end up flunking the whole year, but she'd been expelled for cheating.

"This party is my swan song to Twin Rivers High. No one will ever forget it."

Nicky stuck to the lobby-slash-sports bar, waiting for Kenny to arrive. Nothing would get him back to the "beach" hall tonight. That place was dangerous. Kids in bathing suits, beer, and a waterslide were a bad combination. The cafeteria-slash-dance club was the place to be. Wylder and her minions had outdone themselves on the décor. Nicky couldn't wait to get on the dance floor and celebrate with his boyfriend.

"There you are," Kenny said, clapping him on the shoulder. "This place is nuts."

Nicky turned to greet him, but his smile faltered when he saw the brunette clinging to his boyfriend again.

"Penny." Nicky nodded, the tension he'd felt all day returning with a vengeance. The muscles in his jaw ticked as he turned to face Kenny.

"I'll just let you two talk." Penny darted across the lobby to get herself a drink.

"Are you even serious right now?" Nicky glared at Kenny.

"What, she's a friend from school." Kenny shrugged, shoving his hands into his pockets, refusing to meet Nicky's furious gaze.

"That girl has never been just a friend, Ken. What are you doing to us?"

"Me?" Kenny returned his glare. "You're the one leaving."

"I'm going to college, Kenny! It's just a few hours away, and I'm not leaving for three months."

"I know." Kenny's shoulders sagged.

"Your parents are home, aren't they?" For the last two years, his parents had spent so much of their time in Washington DC that Kenny had moved to the dorm rooms at Defiance Academy. It was one of the main reasons their relationship had flourished. Without his parents' influence, Kenny was free to be himself in a way he'd never had before, as long as no one found out.

"Yeah. Mom's home for the summer, and Dad wants me traveling to Washington with him as like an intern or something when I'm not at hockey camp."

"So what, you're straight now?" Nicky snapped, hating himself for falling into this same old argument with a boy who would likely never come to terms with his sexuality.

"It's not as black and white for me as it is for you, Nicky." Kenny's voice dropped to a hush. "You know, I still like girls. And I don't know what that means yet."

"So we're done? You're going back to your old ways to please your dad and what? I'm just a casualty."

"It's not like that, Nicky. You know I still love you. But—"

"You know what, Ken. I'm done with the buts. Go be happy with Penny if that's what you want. I just hope for your sake some day you figure out who you are." Nicky stumbled away before the tears he choked back found their way into his eyes.

The steady beat of the bass matched the rhythm of Nicky's heart as he sipped a bottle of water—wishing for the first time in ages it was something stronger. But Nicky didn't drink. His father was an alcoholic who'd finally managed to get his shit together. Nicky never wanted to go down that road and had given up booze after one particularly bad night a few years ago. It was an ironically similar night. After walking in on Kenny and Penny making out, Nicky had spent the night hitting the hard stuff only to arrive home to find his father in worse shape. Nicky hadn't touched a drink since that night, but it didn't escape him that his boyfriend's drama was what made him want to drink in the first place.

Nicky watched Wylder make her way around the dance floor, dancing with everyone and having the time of her life. But he felt like going home to wallow in misery. This should be one of the happiest nights of his life. He just graduated high school, and his life stood like an open road in front of him, just waiting for him to ride out of town and never look back.

Maybe that's what I should do. Maybe he should leave Twin Rivers now and move in with Avery and Nari a few months early to start his new life in Nashville—a single life in a city with more options. In a small town like Twin Rivers, the gay dating pool was pretty small. But in Nashville? Maybe Nicky's real love story awaited him there?

"Becks, Becks, Becks!" The crowd chanted, taking Nicky's attention away from his personal drama.

There he was in the middle of his adoring fans, the big bad country music star, and Nicky's onetime friend. But Nicky hadn't seen or spoken to Becks since he left Twin Rivers two years ago after his own graduation. Becks ate up the crowd's attention, no surprise there. Nari was with him, garnering a lot of attention herself. She was just as famous, but she was a lot more down to earth about it. And Nari came home often so she wasn't quite the anomaly Becks was.

Once upon a time, Nicky counted Becks among his closest friends. Seeing him now, and how much he'd changed in some ways and how little he'd changed in others, just made him sad.

Get over yourself, Nicky! You were on cloud nine earlier today. He needed to stop letting other people dictate his happiness. It was time Nicky grabbed his future in his fist and made decisions for himself, taking what he wanted out of life. That was what everyone around him seemed to do.

The music came to a screeching halt, and Wylder's voice sounded over the PA system. "Party's over, guys. The cops are on the way. Please proceed to your exit and get home safe. I have Ubers waiting in every lot to take anyone home who's too drunk to drive."

Kids scattered in every direction, following Wylder's instructions to the letter. But Becks and Nari stood in the center of the cafeteria, looking confused.

"Come on, you two oldies. Follow me." Nicky grabbed Nari's hand in his left and Becks' in his right. He pretended not to notice the warmth of Becks' skin against his or the way his large hand engulfed Nicky's with a firm and familiar grip. "The last thing you two need is to get caught crashing a high school party. Your fans will die of embarrassment for you."

"Lead the way, Nick-Nick." Becks ran with him down the hall lit with fairy lights into the gym. At least a dozen other students rushed through the back doors to the small lot behind the gym. Nicky shoved Nari and Becks into the waiting Uber and sent them home to Nari's house.

"Just great." Nicky watched them leave. "Even after two years, I still have a crush on my brother's best friend."

Becks:

Home sweet home. Well, not home exactly for Beckett Anderson, current rising country star and future music legend—at least in his mind. No, this Cincinnati crowd wouldn't resemble the small groups of people who'd once flocked to see him play as a part of the band *Anonymous* two towns over. But that was two years ago, a lifetime in the music industry. He'd seen stars rise and fall in that short time, ending with a crash.

And each time the lights of Nashville dimmed, he just had to hope and pray he wouldn't follow in their footsteps.

Anyone who knew Beckett would probably claim it was his confidence that got him where he currently stood atop a wide stage with a sea of expectant faces stretching out before him.

What would they do if they knew it was all a lie?

A grin slid across Beckett's face as he leaned into the microphone. They'd finished the first set and were due for a break. He already liked the festival setup more than any concert where he had to sweat through hours of playing before he got to rest.

"Thank ya'll for coming today." He did his best to keep his fake Southern accent even. His public relations team insisted on it, and what they wanted, they got. They'd gotten him this far, so he rarely questioned their ideas.

"Do you know I used to come to this festival every year with my little sister? I grew up right around the corner in Twin Rivers." This next move was another idea from the brain trust that was his PR team. "This sister of mine plays music too. She was in my high school band." He shot a glance over his shoulder where Nari stood behind her keyboard shaking her head, whispering, "No, Becks."

She was right. Beckett was about to be a dead man.

But he didn't care. His eyes found Wylder standing to the side of the stage with Avery and Nicky, her eyes wide.

"Who wants my sister to come up here?" A roar rose from the crowd. This was why Beckett had been able to climb the ladder to fame so quickly. He had people eating out of the palm of his hand.

Wylder shook her head. Funny, she hadn't seemed so shy about attention when she'd thrown an epic party in the freaking school halls. God, he loved his sister. She'd always been cooler than him.

"Come on, sis!" Becks yelled over the noise of the waiting crowd. Wylder wasn't the same girl who'd hammered on her drums every time *Anonymous* took the stage. There was something sad about her now. All Becks wanted was to see his sister smile up on stage. Music had always been their language. He wanted to prove to her she hadn't forgotten the words.

Becks pulled the guitar strap over his head and set it on the ground before running to the side of the stage. He took Wylder's arm and pulled.

Nari Won Song, Becks' keyboardist and favorite person in the world because of her next actions, lifted her hands and started to clap, slow and rhythmic. She leaned in to her mic. "Wylder. Wylder." The crowd picked up her chant. "Wylder. Wylder."

"I hate you for this," Wylder mumbled under her breath as she gave in and let Becks led her to the center of the stage.

He winked at her. "Do you know 'About a Boy'?"

She sighed. "You mean the chart-topping, insipid song you remind me is amazing every time we talk?"

"It was one time, Wylder." Becks was the one person who never got offended by his sister's attitude or harsh words. She didn't have to tell him she was proud or that she loved him, because he already knew. "About a Boy" was the story of a girl who waited her whole life for someone who could love her like she deserved. It had been called heartbreaking, but that didn't stop every radio station across the country from using it to turn Beckett into a household name.

Nari set her hands on the keyboard, but Becks shook his head. "No instruments."

He pushed Wylder toward the mic and took his position next to her.

"Hush now," Becks told the crowd with a wink. "My sister is about to steal your hearts, and you don't want to miss a word." He wrapped an arm around her shoulders, knowing how happy his PR people would be at how much he'd played up the siblings angle. Girls around the country would watch this on YouTube tomorrow and swoon. It was the Beckett power. But Wylder... Most people discounted her. With her blond dreadlocks and a constant scowl, she was suited to the drums she loved, rarely stepping forward to show anyone the voice Becks knew she had. She'd shocked him the night before as she'd danced and laughed in the very school that didn't want her anymore. Becks wanted to hate Twin Rivers High for kicking her out even with the constant trouble she found herself in. He wanted to burn the place down for not allowing his sister to pass her junior year after she'd struggled through some hard times.

The first verse started and Becks' voice covered the crowd like a blanket, cloaking them in solitary comfort. When Wylder joined him and eventually Nari, he wondered why they ever needed instruments. Tears built in the corners of his eyes as he hit the final verse.

I waited my whole life
To be set free
I waited my whole life
For you and me

Nari's voice faded out, and Becks let his drop as well even though he normally sang the last lines alone. Wylder's sweet voice carried them to the end.

And what if you never come
I waited my whole life
Dreaming of the day I let you go

As the crowd cheered, some wiped tears from their eyes. Becks hugged Wylder to his side and kissed the top of her head. In the two years he'd been gone from Ohio, he hadn't returned home, but he still loved his family and constantly begged them to come to Nashville. They'd visited a few times. Wylder needed him. He hadn't realized how much until the day before when she'd told him about the expulsion. He'd make sure she had everything. Dropping out wasn't an option. It would cost a lot, but he'd get her into Defiance Academy. Whatever it took.

Wylder ducked out of his embrace and sprinted off stage. Becks leaned back in to the microphone. "I am Beckett Anderson, and we'll be back this evening. Enjoy the other bands while I'm sleeping off all the beer ya'll have been throwing at me." With a final wink, he pulled out his earpiece, letting the cord hang around his neck. The noise from the crowd was deafening, but he loved it.

Some people complained about fame, but Beckett embraced it. What was the point of being a country star if you didn't have girls screaming your name and men buying you drinks everywhere you went?

Arms slipped around Beckett's waist from behind, and he shot Nicky and Avery a grin before turning to face Sofie, assistant extraordinaire.

"Oops." She laughed. "Didn't mean to get so close to you." She held out a bottle of water, her face the picture of innocence. He took the water and uncapped it before swigging it back. Leveling her with a gaze again, his lips ticked up. "You mean you didn't want your hand caressing my abs?"

"Babe, if you think that was a caress, you need to get out more."

"No one got me any water," Nari grumbled as she wiped her face with a towel. Their other two band members, Quinn and Harrison, both looked ready to jump at Nari's command.

But Nari didn't seem to want their help. She approached Sofie. "You're not Beckett Anderson's assistant. Your official title is assistant to Becket and the band." She pointed from herself to Quinn and Harrison. "We're the band part of that title."

Sofie suppressed a grin and lifted her hand in mock salute. "Aye-aye, Captain." She marched toward a table piled high with food and drinks, grabbing three bottles of water and lobbing them at each band member. Nari ducked hers, and it hit Avery.

Wanting to keep everything under control as he always did, Beckett nodded toward the back of the stage. "Uh, Sof… I think we need to talk logistics for tonight's concert."

She nodded. "Yes. We do." They left the others staring after them.

"Logistics, my ass." It was Nicky's voice that followed them, and something about that didn't sit well with Becks. But he didn't have time to think about it before Sofie pulled him into a dark corner, pressing him against the wall.

"So," she whispered. "About these logistics."

He kissed her as he'd done a million times over the last two years. She'd been assigned to Beckett at the same time the label brought Quinn and Harrison on board. They stole their first moments together later that same day.

Only this time, half an hour away from Twin Rivers and all the memories associated with the place, he couldn't turn his mind off and get lost in Sofie. Not when he couldn't help but think he should be sharing this homecoming with Nari and Avery who'd grown up there as well. And Nicky? Avery's little brother was all grown up now, a man. He'd always been smarter than the rest of them, but now, something else lived in his eyes. Some secret Becks wanted, needed, to know.

He pushed away from Sofie.

"Everything okay, baby?" She'd started calling him that lately, and he didn't like it. It reeked of a relationship title, and Beckett Anderson didn't do commitment.

But he didn't want to hurt her, so he kept his mouth shut.

Because he was Becks: a good-time guy who never rocked the boat. And if he was going to survive life in the spotlight, he had to stay that way.

How could the rest of the band nap?

The adrenaline from the concert continued to buzz through Becks long after they returned to the hotel. Last night, they'd stayed in Twin Rivers, but the label claimed a hotel was more suitable for the two-day festival. Luckily, the Beckett Anderson band only had to play on day one.

But that meant two performances within twenty-four hours.

Becks leaned back in his chair at the hotel's rooftop bar overlooking the city. The bar was closed, but the manager was a big fan and had let him sit on the deck. He'd always loved coming to Cinci when he was a kid. The rolling hills and rivers felt like home. A home that wasn't his anymore.

Now, he found himself missing the streets of Nashville that teemed with musicians who needed to make music just to get through the day.

Becks' knee shook. He always got this way after a performance. It took a long time for the excitement to wear off. He glanced down at the notebook in his lap and tapped the pencil against the wiry spine.

He needed Nari. She'd been with him since the first time he stepped onto a stage years ago. Nowadays, he wrote most of his songs with her and hated that he'd somehow lost the ability to do it on his own. Did he have nothing left to say?

Footsteps approached him, but he figured it was only Avery being nosy as usual. They'd been friends since high school, even moving to Nashville together, but every time Avery took one of his psych classes at Vanderbilt, he suddenly thought he could see inside Becks' head.

But no one knew what Becks was feeling. Ever. It was something he'd perfected over the years—hiding any shred of emotion behind a layer of humor.

He scratched out the last line he'd written as someone took a seat across from him.

"Shouldn't you be resting?" Nicky's voice was the last thing Becks expected to hear.

He met his gaze. "You sound like your brother."

Nicky groaned. "Take that back."

"No."

"Fine." Nicky leaned forward. "Then I'll just have to take a peek here." He snatched Becks' notebook.

Becks jumped toward him, tackling him back into his chair. "Come on, Nick-Nick. We're practically brothers. Don't be a dick."

Nicky froze, pushing Becks off him. "We aren't brothers, Beckett. My brother has actually kept in contact since leaving two years ago."

Becks flinched. "Yeah." He rubbed the back of his neck. "Uh…sorry. I've been—"

"Busy. I get it, Becks. I do. I shouldn't have brought that up." Nicky shifted his eyes away, and Becks cursed himself.

The last thing he ever wanted to do was hurt Avery's brother. If he were honest, he'd become friends with Nicky outside of his friendship with Avery. Leaving him had sucked as much as leaving Becks' own family, but Nashville was a new world full of new people. He wouldn't lie and say he hadn't gotten lost in it.

Leaning back in his chair, he held his notebook to his chest. "I guess I need to thank you for getting me out of the party last night. My PR team would've freaked if I'd been arrested." He paused to study his old friend. "How have you been, Nicky?"

Nicky shrugged. "You don't really want to know. I've spent the last two years in Twin Rivers. That's boring compared to your new life."

"But I do. Want to know, I mean."

Nicky sighed. "Fine. You asked for it. I've spent the past two years back in a closet of someone else's making, hiding my relationship with him because his parents are assholes, only to learn that the real asshole was him. My life in a nutshell. Next question?"

Something tightened in Becks' gut. "Nicky, you better not tell me you've spent the last two years dating that Defiance Academy douche bag."

"Okay, I won't tell you then."

Becks blew out a frustrated breath. "Why? Kenny is and always will be a tool. You shouldn't give any of yourself to someone like that."

Nicky scrubbed a hand over his face and tilted his head back to look up at the brilliant blue sky. "Don't go all big brother on me, Becks. I've heard it enough from Avery."

"I'm not concerned as a brother. Just a friend. Why, Nicky?"

Nicky shrugged. "I liked him."

"That's not a good enough answer."

"Maybe I didn't want to be alone."

"Nicky, you don't need to date a jerk just because he's there. There are other people out there."

Nicky shot to his feet, towering over Becks. Two years ago, he'd been shorter and considerably less muscular. Some things were bound to change, but others never did. "That's rich coming from someone whose assistant probably spends more time in his bed than on the job."

"That's not fair, Nick." He didn't know how this had turned into an argument.

"I'm gay, Becks. In case you haven't noticed. Twin Rivers isn't exactly swimming in gay men. You think I have options? Some of us have to just make do with what's there. Kenny was a jerk, but not all the time. He was never mean to me." He lifted his shoulders. "He was the best I could do, maybe the best I'll ever do." An angry tear broke through. "The old Becks would have understood." With one final look, he turned on his heel and crossed the rooftop, yanking open the heavy metal door and disappearing.

Becks sucked in a breath, not completely understanding what just happened. He wanted to go after Nicky, to tell him he was the best person Becks knew—even back in high school when their two-year age gap meant more than it did now.

But before he could stand, the door opened again and Sofie appeared. "Beckett, it's time to get ready for the next show."

He followed her inside to where his band waited. They were his family in a way his high school friends had once been—including Nicky. He'd do anything for them. But a part of him wondered if the only way to help Nicky was to stay away and let him deal with this on his own like he seemed to want.

Yet, Becks had always been a meddler. Why did that have to change now?

Becks loved playing at festivals because he got to be around so many country stars he'd grown up idolizing. They saw him as one of them. The girl currently dancing across the stage was someone Becks knew but also didn't know. There was a lot of that going around in the music business.

Nari stepped up to Becks' side and leaned in. "What's wrong?"

He sighed. Once upon a time, he'd have lied to her and told her he was as good as always, but she could read him better than anyone else. "I don't know."

She slipped her hand into his. Harrison and Quinn stood in front of them, both bouncing with nervous energy as they always did before a show. Harry was a drummer like no other. Talent oozed from his fingertips, but his quiet personality and smart-guy looks stood in contrast to his profession.

Quinn, on the other hand, played into the rock star image. Long hair, tied away from his face, tattoos stretching up his arms. He looked as if he belonged in a grunge band rather than backing up the all-American good boy country singer Beckett Anderson.

Nari squeezed his hand, drawing his attention back to her. "I can't remember seeing you this tense before a show."

He wouldn't admit it, but the upcoming performance barely registered in his mind as he replayed his fight with Nicky. Becks always had a need to please people, to make them like him. He rarely got into arguments even with his difficult sister. It was all part of the face he showed the world. No cracks except the one parting his lips into a smile.

But he wasn't smiling anymore. "Why didn't you tell me Nicky was still dating Kenny?"

Nari pushed pink-highlighted dark hair out of her face and peered up at him. "Umm… I guess I didn't think about it. Avery told me you weren't keeping in contact with anyone back home except your family."

She wasn't wrong. He'd moved on from his life in Twin Rivers, yet thinking of Nicky hiding who he was for some guy twisted his gut. He'd always been protective of the kid, but Nicky wasn't a kid anymore.

Becks closed his eyes for a moment, soaking in the soothing voice of Etta Morelli. When he opened them, Nari's gaze met his.

"I wasn't," he admitted. "I've been too busy to try to stay in touch." What had he always told Avery and Nari? High school was only a tiny blip of their lives and there was no use holding on to it.

Yet, they managed to still keep up with their old friends. They lived in Nashville but traveled home regularly. Becks hadn't been home before two days ago.

"Is he still with Kenny?" He thought back to Nicky's words. Something happened to make Nicky think his boyfriend was an asshole.

"No."

Becks released the breath he'd been holding. Then Nari continued, dousing Becks' relief in cold hard reality.

"Kenny broke up with him last night to date a girl. We all knew he was bisexual, but I don't think Nicky actually thought he'd choose a girl over him, or anyone over him, really. I hate it. Nicky is hurting. I've never seen him quite like this. And Kenny… I wish he'd just go die a slow, painful death."

A laugh burst free of Becks. "What have you done with Nari Won Song?"

She smirked. "It's Nicky, Becks. He's the best of us all. I'll do anything to protect him even if that means castrating that son of a bitch, Kenny."

Becks almost choked on his next laugh. He liked to think Nashville hadn't changed him, but Nari couldn't say the same. Gone was the nerdy, shy girl who wouldn't curse to save her life. In her place stood a woman who'd rip some poor guy's balls off if he hurt someone she loved.

No, not some poor guy… Kenny. And he couldn't say he hated the idea.

Etta played the last notes of her final song. As soon as the cheering crowd quieted, she spoke into the microphone. "Who wants to hear Beckett Anderson?"

"That's your cue." Sofie showed up out of nowhere, urging the band up the steps and onto the stage.

Becks gripped the neck of his guitar as the blinding lights struck him in the face. Once his eyes adjusted, he could make out faces among the crowd who'd come out in the early evening. The sun sat low in the sky, ready to make its descent. Before then, Becks would finish playing and be able to head back to Nashville, to his home.

He didn't notice what he said into the microphone or how he introduced himself. The crowd already knew him. Before long, he lost himself in a guitar solo, his fingers plucking the strings.

Nari's voice entered the song first before Becks joined her. They'd been playing together for so long they knew exactly what each other would do, which notes would make it into the atmosphere. Harrison and Quinn joined them less than two years ago after the label signed them and decided they needed a full band.

It worked. No one tried to outdo each other, and they all understood one thing. Beckett was the star.

Sweat dripped from his short hair, rolling down his cheeks. His sopping shirt clung to his chest as the summer heat soaked into his skin. When finally, he couldn't take it anymore, he lifted his shirt over his head and threw it out at the crowd.

A roar wound through them. This was what they wanted. Beckett had to give them everything of himself, holding back only the darkest parts no one wanted to see. They wanted a country star? He'd write chart toppers. A sex symbol? He'd smile seductively while standing in front of them half naked. A role model? A musician? A good boy?

They were all masks he wore, and he didn't regret them. He'd chosen this life, dreamed of it even. As long as they never asked him to give them Becks, the man he truly was with all the doubt and worry and love, he'd be okay.

Movement near the front of the crowd caught his eye. Becks kept singing, but he stepped to the edge of the stage and peered toward them. He'd recognize Kenny anywhere. The big hockey player had a face that just screamed "punch me." Beside him stood a petite girl with curly brown hair.

But that wasn't who caught his attention. Nicky faced them, his hands in his pockets. He rocked back on his heels as Kenny's mouth moved a mile a minute, his face growing redder with each word.

Becks couldn't remember ever seeing Nicky look so lost, so vulnerable.

"Maybe he's the best I can do."

Were Nicky's words really Kenny's? Was that douche the reason Nicky thought so little of himself?

Becks didn't realize he'd missed his guitar entrance, but he didn't skip a single word of the song. Soon, they dove into the next.

"I'll do anything to protect him."

Nari's earlier words might as well have come from Becks. Even after being away from Nicky for two years, he had the same desire to make him smile he'd had before. And right now... Nicky looked more like he wanted to cry.

Becks stumbled over a word in the song, forgetting the lyrics, as he watched Kenny step closer to Nicky. Nicky shrank in on himself.

"Becks, where are you going?"

He only faintly heard Sofie calling to him from the side of his stage. There was no time to think. Nari and the guys continued to play with Nari singing Becks' parts as Becks jumped off the front of the stage, landing in the grass. He pulled his guitar off over his head and put it on the stage before edging his way past the barriers separating the crowd from the low platform.

Fans screamed as he neared, scrambling to touch him, hoping they could get a piece of him. He shouldered his way through, making it to Kenny and Nicky. They didn't notice him at first.

"I don't want you, Nicky." Kenny's words would haunt Becks for a long time, but not as long as the crestfallen look on Nicky's face would. Something inside Nicky shattered right before Becks' eyes and it gutted him. Becks had to be the one to put him back together again.

Nicky lifted his tearstained face, probably noticing how the concert had changed. He glanced around at the people squeezing in on them, holding their phones up to capture the drama about to unfold. Finally, he saw Becks, but not before Kenny.

"Dude, Avery already threatened me. I don't need Nicky's other brother getting into our business."

Becks' chest heaved as the words he could never take back rolled off his tongue. "I'm not Nicky's brother."

Without another thought, he yanked Nicky to him. Nicky let out a surprised grunt, his eyes wide with fear.

"Don't be afraid of me, Nick-Nick. Never me." He wrapped a hand around the back of Nicky's neck, pulling his face closer.

Awareness struck Becks as he kissed Nicky, the kid he'd protected in high school, the one he'd always been drawn to. There was nothing kid-like about him now. For a moment, Nicky stood frozen, and Becks wrapped an arm around his back.

"It's just me, Nicky," he whispered against his lips.

Nicky's answering sigh traveled through Becks, lighting every nerve ending on fire, and he finally kissed him back, taking everything Becks gave.

Becks didn't understand it—why he'd abandoned his concert to save Nicky from the humiliation of seeing his ex with a new person. Maybe it was just protectiveness, maybe it was something else entirely.

But as he kissed Nicky, there was no weirdness.

When the crowd's cheers broke through, Becks pulled back, taking in Nicky's bewildered stare.

Nicky shook his head as if to clear it. "Kenny's gone."

Those two words were like a bucket of ice crashing over Becks' heated skin as he remembered why they were there. Becks wasn't gay. Nicky wasn't in Nashville. The kiss was only meant as a stab at another man.

Becks brushed a hand through his sweaty brown hair. Nicky glanced down at Becks' bare chest, and red crept along his skin from his neck to his ears.

Taking a step back, Becks finally mustered up the courage to look at the damage he'd done. No music played as his three band mates stared at him from the stage. Off to the side of the stage, Avery stood rubbing the back of his neck and watching them carefully. How could Becks face Avery after kissing his brother?

And the crowd? Those wonderful people who allowed Becks to keep making music? They surrounded him, their phones out as they snapped photos and took video.

"Becks." Nicky's voice was hoarse. "Umm…you should…"

"Yeah." Becks gave Nicky one final glance as a man from security appeared to help him back to the stage.

Becks stepped up to the microphone as if nothing had happened. "So, how bout them Reds?"

Laughter rang out with a few catcalls and yelled derogatory terms. Becks could never unhear what some of his onetime fans now called him. But Nicky had lived with this for years—even from his own father at one time.

What right did Becks have to be bothered and hurt?

As he started in on the last song of the evening, he watched Nicky's retreating back, taking in his hunched shoulders.

Becks only ever wanted to help Nicky, to be there for him. But what if he'd only made the world a lot more confusing for him than it already was?

Nicky:

Nicky pulled into his regular parking space behind the Main, turning the ignition off on the crappy car he used to share with Avery. Nari bought his brother a new car for his last birthday, and Nicky enjoyed teasing him about his sugar mama.

A loud thud against the driver's side window made him jump a mile in his seat.

"What are you even doing here right now?" Wylder gave him a look that said he had lost his mind.

"Jeez, Wylds, you scared the crap out of me." Nicky opened his door. "I'm going to work like a normal person." A normal person who wasn't still reeling from the fake kiss that was better than any real kiss he'd had in his life. Images of a shirtless Becks had haunted his dreams. What amounted to a PR stunt for Becks had come out of nowhere and ripped Nicky apart.

"Why haven't you answered your phone? We've been trying to call you all morning."

"I turned my phone off after Avery and Nari called me a million times last night." Nicky tried to get out of his car, but Wylder shoved him back in.

"Then you haven't seen it?" Wylder pulled her dreadlocks over her shoulder. "You are not working today. Get in the passenger seat, I'm driving us out of here."

"What? Why?" Nicky tried to protest as Wylder shoved him to the other side of the car.

"Trust me, damn it. We need to get out of here, now."

"Fine." Nicky scooted over to the passenger seat and handed her the keys. "Where are we going?"

"Anywhere but here." Wylder gunned the engine and raced out of the parking lot. Nicky got a glimpse of the front of the Main when she turned to head toward Riverpass, the next town over.

"What's going on?" Nicky stared at the street full of news vans. "Did something happen to the Callahans?"

"No, you idiot. Something happened to you." She shoved her phone at him. "Watch that."

Nicky's hands shook when he saw the paused video on her screen. His tear-stained face stared back at him. "I don't want to see this."

"Well, the rest of the country music world has seen it, and they've lost their damn minds over it. The hashtag SexyBecksy is even trending because of it. It's a big deal."

Nicky pressed play and watched the whole thing play out again. The part where Kenny smashed what was left of his heart right before Becks jumped off the stage and took Nicky in his arms. It was like watching it happen to someone else. The fire in Becks' eyes caught him by surprise. Even watching it now, Nicky brushed his fingertips over his lips. He'd never been kissed like that. He watched his own stiff reaction followed by the moment he'd lost his mind and kissed Becks back. It was probably the hottest moment of his entire life, and it was staged. SexyBecksy... He couldn't argue with that.

But watching the video, he also saw the heartbroken look on Kenny's face and felt a momentary stab of satisfaction before he remembered he was watching this on YouTube. It had over fifty thousand hits in less than twenty-four hours. He scrolled through the comments, wincing at some of the negative vitriol fired at Becks. Even some for Kenny, the Ohio senator's son. But most of the fans were screaming for more. They loved the romantic and spontaneous moment and were dying to know who Nicky was.

Nicky thrust a nervous hand through his hair. "So, all of that back there was about me?" His voice rasped like sandpaper in his throat.

"You are the it boy of the hour, my friend. My idiot brother's fans are dying to know everything about you."

"Why?"

"They think there's some kind of desperate love story there." She turned to glance at him. "Is there?" She raised a brow at him in question.

"With Becks? No." That wasn't entirely true. Nicky had a mad crush on him in high school, but that was ages ago, and it was only ever one-sided. "We've always been friends. I have no idea why he did this. It has to be some kind of PR stunt. You know he isn't even gay."

"Becks wouldn't do that to you just for the attention." Wylder shook her head.

"He pulled you on stage and hammed it up for the audience."

"That wasn't about the PR—not entirely. He wanted to remind me how much I love music. After everything that went down with the *Powerplay girls* last year, I haven't played much. He wanted to show me I've still got it. That music will always be part of me."

"But it still made him look like the adorable big brother in front of the audience."

"He is my adorable big brother, Nicky. I don't know what he was thinking, but that kiss was spontaneous. I think he shocked himself as much as everyone else."

"I need this job, Mrs. Callahan," Nicky said in a rush. "Vanderbilt is expensive, and I'm counting on working all summer to save up for school expenses." His boss had called him into the Main for a meeting, and he was afraid she was going to let him go. "I'm so sorry about all the media attention. I promise, if it happens again, I'll take care of it."

"Oh, honey, I'm not firing you," Mrs. Callahan said. "I just wanted to make sure you're okay." She pulled him into a warm hug. "You have a job here for as long as you need it. Brian has worked with the local authorities to keep the press out of the diner so you can work in peace."

"Thank you, Mrs. C, I'm a little overwhelmed from all the online attention, but I think it's slowing down. They'll forget about me soon."

"Well, they can't get to you in here, so get to work, young man."

"Yes ma'am, thank you." Nicky left the kitchen to stock the dessert case and make fresh coffee before the early dinner rush. After the Callahans' daughter Peyton left for college, he'd taken over her shifts and was grateful for the work. Once upon a time, the St. Germaines had more money than they knew what to do with, but Nicky's alcoholic father, an NFL Hall of Famer, had lost most of the family's money to gambling debts. But after a stint in rehab, Greyson St. Germaine was much better now, and they'd learned to live within their means. Like his brother, Nicky received a scholarship to Vanderbilt University, but his was only a partial academic scholarship. Nicky still needed to cover his basic expenses. To save money, Nicky was moving into the apartment Avery shared with Nari, and neither of them would let him pay rent.

But Nicky was having second thoughts about moving in with them. Becks lived right across the hall. How was he supposed to handle living so close to him? He could get over the kiss, but it would be a lot easier if Becks wasn't a big part of his life like he used to be. Nicky didn't ever want to go down that road again, loving someone who wasn't available. Kenny was bi but so far in the closet he couldn't see the light under the door, and Becks was straight. What Nicky needed was some time to be single and a new start at Vanderbilt where he might eventually meet a guy who wouldn't leave him for a woman.

"Penny for your thoughts?" A familiar voice brought Nicky out of his reverie.

"Funny guy." Nicky slid into the booth across from Julian Callahan.

"I thought it was fairly clever." Julian didn't even pretend to hide his smirk. "They just sound like the perfect asshole couple don't they? Penny and Kenny. You can do better, little man."

"I'm taller and bigger than you and everyone else who still calls me 'little man.'" Nicky felt the tension ease from his shoulders as he laughed with Julian.

"You had the most ridiculous growth spurt I've ever seen, but you'll always be 'little man' to us."

"How's Addison?" Nicky leaned back against the booth. Once upon a time, Julian's girlfriend had been one of Nicky's least favorite people, but she'd changed for the better when she'd started dating Julian. Nicky still missed her and the rest of their group of friends, including Nicky's brother.

"Crazy busy. She's taking summer courses at Defiance University again this year. She wants to finish her undergrad in three years so she can get started on her MFA."

"Before you know it, she'll be your official editor."

"I think she's trying to race me." Julian rolled his eyes. "My money's on her finishing both degrees before I finish this book."

"But your first two books were so good this one will be just as brilliant."

"I think all of them suck, so maybe it's just me." Julian slammed his computer shut. "Seriously, how are you doing?" He leaned forward. "The attention has to be killing you."

"I never knew I was so interesting." Nicky tried to laugh. "But they're everywhere I go. It'll blow over eventually." He shrugged. "Better get back to work." He started to slip out of the booth.

"Not so fast, you little liar. You're a private person, Nicky. Having your personal drama splashed across the internet is no small thing."

"No. It sucks, actually. I'm embarrassed and confused enough as it is. I don't need the added drama on top of what turned out to be a very public breakup with Kenny. That's the last thing he needs too."

"Screw him. Who cares if he got dragged into the limelight along with you. The guy's a total jerk for stringing you along for the last two years."

"Well, up until the last few weeks, we were actually happy. But this mess with the media, his parents are going to kill him." Nicky sighed, reaching for Julian's hand. "I appreciate your concern, but I'm fine. I'm headed to Vanderbilt in a few months, so I'm just going to focus on that and getting a fresh start there in the fall."

"Uh-oh, Nicky." Julian pulled his hand back, nodding toward the bank of windows on the opposite wall. "No, don't look."

"Too late." Nicky's heart thundered in his chest at the sight of so many cameras pressed up against the windows. Brian Callahan was outside, trying to get them to leave the premises, but that didn't stop them from congregating in the parking lot. Lights flashed and reporters beat on the windows to get Nicky's attention.

"They're going to break the freaking windows." All the blood rushed from Nicky's face.

"Look at me, little man." Julian pulled his attention away from the sea of faces watching him like he was a rare fish in an aquarium. "You're going to get up and run to the back room like you're going to make a break for the back door. Most of them will race around to the parking lot. When you get to the kitchen, wait for my signal."

"For what?" Nicky wiped the sweat off his brow. The idea of facing all those cameras and making some kind of statement made him nauseous.

"When I tell you to run, you're going to come back into the dining room and out the side door."

"Out there with them?" Nicky's eyebrows shot up. "Are you crazy."

"Is Wylder working at the hardware store today?"

"Yeah, but—"

"Text her to meet you at the front door."

"Okay." Nicky nodded, following Julian's plan.

"She'll let you in, and you two can go out the back together. Have her drive you to my house, and you can hang out there for a little while. They won't have a reason to come look for you there. Here's my house key. Have Wylder park in the back, and you can go in through the back door. Addie's at school, so you'll have some peace and quiet while this all blows over."

"Thanks, Julian. I better go." Nicky cast a worried look at the media frenzy building in the Callahans' parking lot. He was hurting their business. The place was empty because no one in Twin Rivers wanted to deal with that shitstorm. "I need to lead them away from the restaurant. Your parents don't deserve this."

"Don't worry about it, Nicky. We're all behind you. I'll take your car and lead them on a merry chase." Julian grinned. "We'll call it research for my next book."

"Okay, Wylds is ready." Nicky tucked his phone into his pocket and darted out of the booth and into the kitchen. He waited behind the swinging door for Julian's signal. It didn't take long before Julian waved him back out of the kitchen.

"Go, Nicky."

Nicky crouched low and ran from his hiding spot in the kitchen. The side door of the dining room led to the alley between the buildings, but Anderson's Hardware store was just across the street. As Nicky charged out of the alley, he saw Wylder waiting for him across the two-lane road.

"Hurry," she called to him. Grateful the afternoon traffic down Main Street was light, Nicky darted across the street and through the front door of the hardware store. Wylder slammed the lock in place and flipped the sign to closed.

"Thanks." Nicky leaned over to catch his breath.

"Let's go out the back before they realize what just happened." Wylder craned her neck to see Julian occupying the media as he made a show of climbing into Nicky's car.

"This is insane." Nicky shook his head. "I'm a nobody." He followed Wylder to the parking lot out back. He slid into her back seat to hide.

"Unfortunately"—Wylder threw the car into reverse—"my idiot brother has turned you into the super star of the week."

"This is insane," Nicky repeated, scooting down to the floor. He didn't know how else to describe it.

"Sorry, Nick. They're onto us. There's a blanket back there, put it over your head."

With his face pressed into the carpet, Nicky tossed the blanket over his head.

"Nicky!" voices demanded his attention. Fists hammered at the windows. "Are you cheating on Beckett? What's his name, Nicky? Why aren't you with Beckett?"

Nicky squeezed his eyes shut to keep the tears from coming. He wouldn't give them the satisfaction. If this was what it was like to be with Beckett Anderson, Nicky didn't want any part of it.

Becks:

Becks' bed shifted, jostling him awake, but he didn't open his eyes. It moved again as someone's foot connected to the frame.

"Beckett Anderson."

He groaned, knowing his cousin was only here for one reason—to make him leave his apartment for the first time in a week.

"Go away, Sky," he groaned.

"No." Skylar was the most stubborn woman Becks had ever met. He hadn't even known he had a cousin until she found him online during his last year of high school. They struck up a relationship until she convinced him to move to Nashville. Becks and Nari even lived with her for their first year in the city.

Now, though? Now, she was just a pain in his butt.

She threw herself down on the bed beside him, shaking him until he finally lifted his head to stare at her with bloodshot eyes. He'd barely slept over the last week as he watched video after video of his career crashing to the ground.

He'd kissed Nicky in front of everyone, and now the whole world had seen it.

"Why are you hiding?" Sky asked, leaning back against a pillow. "Are you ashamed everyone thinks you're gay now and that kiss was some massive closet burning?"

"What?" He met her gaze. "Why would I care if people think I'm gay? I'm not—for the record. Thanks for asking. But even if I was, I wouldn't be ashamed."

"Then why have you ignored all calls from your PR team? Sofie says she tried coming over, but you wouldn't let her in. Even Nari and Avery haven't been able to reach you."

Sometimes, it sucked having the person Becks was closest to working for the label that owned him. "I just... I don't want them to tell me what I already know."

"And what is it you think you know?"

He sighed and pushed himself up so he was sitting. "Country music isn't exactly a place for people who are different." Some people described it as a "straight white guy with a guitar" industry, and Becks fit their image...until now.

"First of all, that's stupid. Secondly...you're stupid for having the stupid thoughts."

He couldn't help the smile parting his lips. "So, basically, it's all stupid?"

"Shut up." She shoved his shoulder.

Becks loved being around Sky. She reminded him so much of Wylder. He shot from the bed. Wylder. "Shit."

"What?"

"I meant to transfer the money for Wylder's new school. It's due tomorrow."

Sliding her phone out of her pocket, she unlocked it and tapped a message on the screen. "You have an assistant for a reason, Becks. Sofie will take care of it." She leveled him with a gaze. "That girl's in love with you. You know that, right?"

"I didn't ask her to fall for me." He crossed his arms over his chest. Sofie had been there for him when he was lonely in a new city, and it just kind of continued. But when he kissed her, he'd never felt half the energy as that kiss with...

Scrubbing a hand over his face, he forced himself to push it from his mind. He'd only been helping Nicky out.

But he should have thought of it beforehand, of the repercussions. He saw videos online of press finding Nicky in various places in Twin Rivers. Becks hadn't only hurt his own career; he'd thrown Nicky to the wolves.

Sky scooted to the edge of the bed. "We never ask people to fall, Becks. Sometimes, we want the very people we'd never considered before."

There was a hidden meaning in her words, but Becks was too tired to decipher the Skylar code. She ran a hand over her short blond hair. The top was parted, and bangs hung into her eyes, but she'd buzzed the sides of her head. It fit her.

She stood and looked down on him. "You can't avoid this forever, SexyBecksy." Her dimple winked as she grinned at the new name his fans had for him. "You need to face your team. For what it's worth, I don't think your career is over. Maybe country music isn't ready for everything you are, Beckett Anderson, but we can give you to them all the same."

She stopped at the door. "Take a shower. You stink. I'll have Sofie send you a car in one hour. You're a grown man. Act like it."

As soon as she was gone, Becks sank back onto the bed. *"Sometimes, we want the very people we'd never considered before."*

He grabbed his iPad off the nightstand and scrolled through the various videos clogging the YouTube channels. The captions caught his eye.

Country Love Story.

No one needs to see this.
I wish someone would kiss me like that.
SexyBecksy is right.

And on and on they went. Some called Becks words he'd never expected to hear directed at him. He focused on Nicky's tearstained face. Becks had wanted to take all his pain and humiliation away. That was what friends did, wasn't it?

He set the iPad aside. Sky was right. He couldn't hide from this anymore.

After taking a shower, Becks pulled on a pair of dark wash jeans with a light-blue polo. He ran a comb through his hair as he wiped condensation from the mirror so he could see his face.

The man who hid from the world wasn't Beckett Anderson. Becks leaned forward, gripping the sink with both hands. "You're a good-looking dude," he told himself. "And you'll probably keep your looks long after Avery is a balding man with a belly. So, man up. This world needs you to make it more interesting. You can do this. You can face them. Why? Like I said, you're damn sexy."

Chuckling sounded from the hall outside his bathroom, and Becks met Avery's eyes in the mirror. He'd barely spoken to his best friend since kissing his brother and fleeing home to Nashville before the rest of the band.

"Shut up. You wish you looked this good." Becks turned, crossing his arms over his chest.

Avery's grin widened. "Do you give yourself that little pep talk every day?"

"No," Becks scoffed. He totally did.

"I don't believe you, but whatever you have to do to get up in the morning, man."

Becks pasted on a smile that held only fake joy behind it. "At least you can't say I'm lying to myself." He ran a hand down his chest, feeling his muscles underneath the soft shirt.

Avery lifted an eyebrow. "If you're trying to get me to call you SexyBecksy, you can forget about it."

"Avery, buddy, I don't need you to call me anything. The rest of the world does it enough." He bumped Avery's shoulder as he walked past him into the open living room. Becks didn't buy in to the star lifestyle, but his apartment was nice enough. The best thing about it was that Nari and Avery lived across the hall.

"It's good to see you upright." He rubbed the back of his neck—a nervous tick Avery had always had. "I, uh, stopped by a few times, but you were sleeping." Avery had a key to his place just like Sky. Maybe it was time to be more careful about who had access to his life. Then they'd stop sticking their noses in it.

Becks grabbed his shoes and sat on the white leather couch in the living room to pull them on. Avery perched on the arm of the couch, not meeting Becks' eyes. Their humor from moments before no longer existed as an unfamiliar awkwardness stretched between them.

Becks sighed. "Don't be weird."

"I'm not being weird," Avery mumbled.

"I never thought you'd be one to care if I was gay."

Avery snapped his eyes to Becks. "Dude, I don't care if you're gay. You kissed my brother." He shivered. "Do you see how epically weird that is?"

A laugh burst out of Becks. "That's a kiss Nicky won't soon forget."

"Ugh, stop. Please. This is Nicky. My little brother. I've spent the last week thinking through every interaction you had with him back in high school. I knew how much you cared about him—like he was your family—but this..."

Becks offered him a carefree smile as he clapped a hand on Avery's shoulder. "Relax, dude. I'm not even gay."

"You're not... What? But you..."

"I know what I did." He shrugged. "Nicky needed help."

"Help?"

Becks remembered the moment like it happened that very day. He'd seen Nicky with Kenny and felt a surge of protectiveness. "Kenny decided to throw his girlfriend in Nicky's face. I could see it from the stage. He looked so broken." And after their conversation earlier that day, Becks had wanted to show Kenny just how much better Nicky could do.

Avery looked at Becks as if he'd never seen him before. "And you thought jumping off a stage mid-concert to kiss Nicky in the middle of a crowd of fans would help him? What century do you think we're living in, Becks? Did you consider that my shy, quiet, private brother would become a source of fascination for the country? That paparazzi would suddenly invade Twin Rivers? Have you even talked to Nicky since it happened?"

Becks bent forward, putting his head in his hands. "This is such a mess."

"You've always gotten everything you've wanted, Becks. Your life has been a damn fairy tale with few repercussions for anything you've ever done. But this… You have a brain in that thick skull of yours for a reason. Maybe, it's time to stop relying on your looks and voice. Your mind will get you further than either of those things."

Becks lifted his eyes to his best friend, marveling at how much he'd changed from the cocky football player. "Since when did you become such an expert on anything?"

Avery chuckled. "While you've been stripping your clothes off for adoring fans, I've been sitting in classrooms learning about sports psychology. It's not really that different from what you do."

One corner of Becks' mouth tipped up. "I only take my shirt off when I can't stand the sweat anymore."

"Whatever you tell yourself, man." He stood. "Come on. The car the label sent for you is downstairs. Nari wanted me to get you. She's a bit more pissed at you than I was. Nicky is my brother, but the two of them have always been closer."

"Is she going to use her Korean kill factor on me?" Becks' eyes widened in mock horror. That was what Nari called her fiercest glare. But when she used it, it only made her cuter rather than scary.

"Nah, she knows you're immune. She'll get back at you some other way."

"Great," he groaned. Nari had a habit of telling embarrassing stories of their band days in high school. Harrison and Quinn were good at pulling them out of her.

Becks left Avery in the hall between their apartments and found Nari already in the car out front. The driver gave him a nod as he slid in.

He tried to start speaking, but Nari put up a hand. "I'm glad you showed, Beckett." She only called him that when she was mad. "I don't need you to explain anything. Nicky told me why you kissed him. I hate that you did that to my best friend."

"I thought I was your best friend," he interrupted.

She leveled him with a glare as she pushed her thick-rimmed glasses up her nose. "Don't even start. Nicky is supposed to be moving here to Nashville in one month. He'll be living with me and Avery while he starts at Vanderbilt. I don't want his life to become a circus. He doesn't deserve that."

"I know. I screwed up."

"Well, at least you seem to be taking this seriously." She had a point. Becks usually made light of any situation.

"Do you want to talk about the meeting?" They were on their way to what could be the end of their recording contract. Beckett Anderson and the band had a few chart-busting songs, but their full album drop failed to live up to their high expectations. The band hadn't been sent on tour following the release, instead playing random music festivals and gigs.

Despite becoming a household name in a couple short years, Becks didn't consider himself a success just yet.

And his kiss with Nicky wouldn't help matters, not in country music.

After a few moments of silence, Nari slid her hand into Becks'. She could never stay mad at him for long. "It's going to be okay."

Becks leaned his head back against the headrest and rolled his head to look at her. "Is it?"

She pursed her lips. "The Beckett Anderson I know never doubts himself. He'd walk into this meeting and tell them how they'd handle this situation. He wouldn't look like he was marching to his death."

"Sorry to disappoint, darlin', that Beckett isn't here today."

Nari didn't get a chance to respond as they pulled up outside the label's offices. Inside those walls, the PR team waited to drop the lever, severing any hope Becks had.

"It's going to be okay," Nari repeated.

"How do you know that?"

"I just do."

Becks wrapped an arm around her and sucked in a deep breath. She'd always believed in him. It was why she followed him to Nashville instead of going to college like her parents wanted. He didn't know if he could have made it on his own. Over the last two years, they'd struggled and fought for everything they accomplished.

She was right. They would make it okay. Releasing her, he reached for the door. "Let's do this."

Pasting a smile on his face, Becks stepped into the sun, shielding his eyes as he waited for Nari to join him. Together, they walked inside. He slid his sunglasses into his hair and winked at the secretary.

"Beckett." The older lady stood, flustered. "They're waiting for you."

"Thanks, darlin'." He strode across the modern-styled lobby to where a wall of glass separated the conference rooms. Inside the far one, Sky talked in low tones with Quinn and Harrison. April and Kyle, the Beckett Anderson PR team sat at the long table, matching hard expressions on their faces.

Nari joined the rest of the band as Sofie stepped into the room. "Excuse me, I'm just going to steal Beckett for a moment before we begin." Not waiting for their responses, she grabbed Becks' arm and pulled him through the door, shoving it shut behind her with her foot.

Whirling around to face him, she crossed her arms over her chest. "I get it now."

It took a moment for her words to register. "Get what exactly?"

"Beckett, you and I have been doing whatever it is we're doing for over a year, but in all that time, you never let me get close. Now, I know why. You're in love with someone else."

A million other excuses rolled through his mind. He never let most people in. He'd been lonely. Sofie was his assistant and a relationship would be frowned upon. But none of that rolled off his stupid tongue. Instead, he leaned back against the wall, propping his foot behind him.

"I… Yes. I'm in love with someone else." Man, he was a coward.

"A guy."

Wait, what? "No… I mean… What?" He assumed she meant he was seeing someone else in Nashville. She couldn't mean—

"Nicky."

"I'm not in love with Nicky," he scoffed. Did she realize how ridiculous she sounded? She, of all people, should know how much he loved women.

"Beckett…that kiss was hot. I honestly don't know if I've seen fire like that. The way he looked at you afterward… I'd kill for someone to look at me like that. And it won't be you. I know that now, and it's okay. I hope you'll still allow me to stay on because I believe in you and want to be there when you reach the highest levels of success." Tears sprang to her eyes.

Becks didn't argue with her about Nicky any longer. That wasn't what their moment was about. He wished he felt something for Sofie. She was sweet and kind and everything he should want. Pushing off the wall, he reached for her and pulled her into a hug. "Don't cry, Sof. Of course, we still want you. You're a part of this band too."

She sniffed and looked up at him. "Thanks. Now, the real reason I brought you out here."

His brow scrunched. "This wasn't about us?"

She poked his stomach and pushed him away. "Not everything in the world has to do with Beckett Anderson." It was said with affection. "Your mother..."

A sigh broke past his lips. The woman was not his mother. She'd abandoned both him and Wylder when they were kids, only showing up to pry money out of their father for her drug habit. And then Becks' first single hit the radio, and there she was with her hand out. He'd only seen her once, and the number she had was Sofie's. It was better to distance himself.

"She's been in contact, hasn't she?"

Sofie nodded, sympathy entering her green eyes. "This time, she sounded worse than normal. I only talked to her for a few minutes. She begged me to get you to call her."

"Just send her a check like we usually do. That'll keep her away. I don't want my sister to go through more drama with her. The money keeps her from speaking to the media. Wylder doesn't need our dirty laundry front and center."

Wasn't that what he'd done to Nicky? Put him front and center? He really was an ass, wasn't he?

She typed a note into her phone before lifting her eyes to him once more. "I'm sorry that—"

He cut her off and jerked a thumb toward the door. "We should get in there."

She smiled in acceptance and opened the door for him. The band had taken seats at the table, and every eye turned to him as he waited to hear just how badly he'd screwed up.

"You want me to do what?" Becks jumped from his chair and leaned forward with his hands planted on the table. "You can't be serious."

"Beckett." April pinned him with a glare. "Sit your butt down."

Chastised, he slid back into his chair. "Yes, ma'am." Something about the tall woman had always intimidated him. She was the label's head public relations specialist and currently looked at him as if questioning whether he was worth the trouble.

Nari shot him a grin. "Ma'am," she said under her breath, her entire body shaking as if trying not to laugh.

"Shut up," he whispered back.

"Make me."

He suppressed his grin. He could get back at Nari for the dig, and she knew it. He'd write a song with a curse word and make her sing it—which she hated—or, gasp, he'd make her do a solo. Yeah, the last one held merit.

April, seeming to miss the exchange, slid a folder across the table. "Open it."

Becks didn't have to be told twice. He stared down at a spreadsheet he didn't understand. He'd never claimed to be the smartest guy in the room. He understood music, guitar chords, harmonies—not whatever this was.

And April knew that. As Becks' ever steady confidence started to waver, she finally spoke. "This is why we want you to consider speaking to the media about your relationship."

His relationship. He sent Nari a panicked look, but her body shook with laughter. No sympathy there.

April leaned across the table and pointed to numbers on the spreadsheet. "In the week since your kiss went viral, album sales have skyrocketed. This here shows the improvement in iTunes downloads over previous weeks." The number was more than triple. "And here..." She pointed to another line. "This is how many times your songs have been streamed on services such as Spotify. As you can see, Beckett..." She paused dramatically as she liked to do. "You have become one of our top performing artists."

It took a few moments for those words to sink in. He rubbed his jaw, hating the stubble. He should have shaved. How was he supposed to digest this information with an unshaven face? It was a stupid thought, but it played through his mind over and over. "So...you're not dropping me?"

"Beckett." Kyle eyed him like he was crazy. "Why would we drop you when you've become a viral sensation? No, this isn't the end for you but rather the beginning. It seems the world wants your love story. What made a man interrupt his own concert to kiss another man?"

"But none of it was real. Guys, I'm not gay. I was only helping a friend." None of them seemed surprised by this which must have meant Nari already told them the truth. And yet, they still wanted him to play the gay country singer.

April folded her hands on the table. "Reality doesn't matter, Beckett. The world wants a fairy tale, fiction. If we feed it to them right, there is no limit to your power in this industry."

A shudder raced through Becks, and he rested his elbows on the table, hanging his head. "I thought it was over."

A hand landed on his shoulder. Sofie. "They believe in you too, Beckett."

He looked at each face around the table. Only Nari seemed unsure of what they were asking of him. Unsure or disapproving, he didn't know.

"So." He sighed. "What do you want from me exactly?"

April smiled as if she'd already won. "This boy." She glanced at her notes. "Nicky. You say he's a friend. We'd like you to convince him to enter into a relationship with you. In front of the cameras, he will be your boyfriend. While the media and your fans are going crazy over this, I want you working on your next album. Include some Nicky-inspired songs. You'll start in the recording studio next week with the songs you already have finished. There's a tour beginning in August. Etta Morelli is headlining, and we've managed to get you an opening spot."

Quinn and Harrison let out excited whoops. Nari's hard expression softened into a smile. Even she could get past her disappointment in Becks to be excited about a tour. It was a sign the label truly was putting them out there.

Kyle picked up where April left off. "Beckett, I'm not sure you quite understand how much you need this. After how big the story has gotten, if you come out as straight, your fans will feel lied to."

"But...this is a lie. What if the truth comes out?" Becks wanted to laugh at the fact he'd have to "come out" as straight, but he couldn't muster up the sound. So many questions entered his head. What if the world found out he was a fraud? Was he doing the wrong thing? What if Nicky said no?

And the biggest: What if Nicky hated him? Of all the questions he didn't have an answer to, that was the one he couldn't live with.

Kyle pursed his lips. "The truth doesn't leave this room except for Nicky. That's how we lock this down. We have the go ahead from label execs, but the fewer people who know the better."

"And if I say no?"

"Then I'm afraid the label cannot support an artist who lied to an entire concert full of people."

But they were asking him to lie now. What Kyle meant was he had no choice in this. The label held every single card, and he'd bet his last penny.

He closed his eyes, hating himself for the next words that came out of his mouth. "Okay. If Nicky agrees...you have your gay country star."

April and Kyle wore matching grins as they exited the room moments later. Harrison and Quinn talked excitedly about the tour. Nari left without waiting for him, her phone pressed to her ear. Despite what Kyle said, he knew she'd tell Avery the minute she could.

Becks' best friend would know he planned to use said friends' brother as a prop in his career. The same driver he'd ridden with to the meeting took Becks back to his apartment. He went inside, throwing his keys on a table by the door and toeing off his shoes. Retrieving his iPad from the bedroom, he flopped onto the couch.

The video was still pulled up, and he hit play, watching the way Nicky reacted to the kiss. It was impossible to take his eyes away. How was he supposed to put that sweet man through the publicity gambit?

He closed his eyes, surprised when Nicky's face was the first thing he saw. Brown hair that flopped into his eyes. A firm jaw and soft lips. He'd do anything for the kid. No, not kid, not anymore. Nicky was all grown up, and it hadn't escaped Becks' notice.

Maybe, thinking of him as a kid was a way to stave off the unfamiliar feelings rolling through him.

Opening his eyes, he pulled up the notes app on his iPad and stared at the lyrics to a new song he'd started days ago. Even before they told him to write a song about Nicky for a new album, he'd started one.

It was titled "That Girl" because he hadn't been able to bring himself to call a song "That Boy." Deleting the title, he typed in "That Boy."

After writing a few more lines, he found himself scrolling through airline tickets. If Nicky was still the same boy Becks knew two years ago, he wouldn't agree to any of this.

So, Becks had to go home. He needed to give Nicky a reason to say yes.

Nicky:

"After you take the trash out, you can leave for the evening." Brian Callahan patted Nicky on the back. "The night shift will pick up the last of your tables."

"Thanks, Mr. C."

"You doing all right?" Brian craned his neck to search the parking lot for lurking reporters.

"Yeah, I think they've finally realized I'm not going to talk to them, so they've just resorted to making up stuff about me so they have something to say."

"Well, this town has your back, Nicky. Everyone knows you're a good kid, and the media is just poking their nose into your private business."

"Thanks, Mr. C. Have a good night." Nicky grabbed the trash bags and headed out to the dumpsters in the alley.

As he shoved the bags into the dumpster, Nicky thought he heard someone whisper his name. Fear lanced through him at the thought of facing a reporter in a dark alley all by himself. Nicky fumbled with the door back into the restaurant, but it was locked after eight o'clock.

"Psst, Nick-Nick." A familiar voice came from the other side of the dumpster. "I need to talk to you."

Nicky rolled his eyes and stomped down the alley. "If I wanted to talk to you, I would have answered my phone." Nicky kept walking toward the rear parking lot. "Go back to Nashville, Beckett."

"Wait," Becks called after him, jogging to catch up.

Nicky turned to face him and resisted the urge to roll his eyes again. "I can't talk to you when you look like that." Becks glanced down at his skinny jeans and T-shirt.

"What's with the bleach blond man-bun and Jackie O. sunglasses? It's dark."

"I'm in disguise," Becks whisper-shouted.

"You look ridiculous."

"I'm sorry about the media shitstorm." Becks shrugged his wide shoulders with his hands stuffed in his pockets. He had the "aw, shucks" guilty five-year-old look down pat. But it wasn't going to work this time.

"You're sorry?" Nicky took a step back. "What the hell was that, Becks?"

"My attempt at an apology?"

"Are you serious right now?" Nicky paced a few steps down the alley and back. "Are you this big of a ditz?"

"Hey now. You know I'm trying to apologize here. No need to be mean." Becks poked out his bottom lip.

"Then tell me what the hell were you thinking when you stopped in the middle of your concert to kiss me like that? Please, I'm all ears, man, because I'd really like to know what could possibly have gone through your head that night. Do the smoke and lights make you hallucinate? They have doctors for that kind of thing."

"I don't know, Nicky." Becks tried to shove a hand through his hair but dislodged his absurd blond wig and tossed it on the ground instead.

"You owe me something better than 'I don't know.'" Nicky folded his arms across his chest.

"You're right." Becks sighed and leaned against the brick wall. "I saw you in the crowd, and you were upset. That douche-nugget, Kenny, was yelling at you, and that girl stuck on his arm like a barnacle just looked so damned smug. I heard your voice in my head saying he's the best you could do, and I just lost it."

Nicky gave a miserable laugh, scratching the back of his head. "I would have been less surprised if you'd charged into the audience and just hit him. I don't understand how you went from protective big brother to...to...that?"

"I don't know, Nicky, but I've made a mess of everything, and I really need your help."

"You want my help?" Nicky stared at his clueless friend, astounded he had the nerve to come here asking for help after he'd turned Nicky's life into a train wreck.

"The media ran away with the story, and my PR people say I have to ride it out." Becks shuffled his feet against the crumbling asphalt.

"And that includes me, how?"

"I have two choices, Nicky. Behind door number one is my dream. A new album and a real tour opening for Etta Morelli. It's the fast track to the top of the charts. But behind door number two is nothing but a one-way ticket back to Twin Rivers. Nick-Nick, you're about to decide what door my future holds."

"Bullshit, Beckett Anderson. You are not pulling that emotional blackmail crap on me. I won't fall for it. You made this mess, and you need to clean it up."

"I'm trying. That's why I'm here."

"Spit it out, Becks. What do you want from me?"

"I, ah...I need to be your boyfriend for a little while. Just until this all blows over."

"My boyfriend?" Nicky wanted to laugh or cry, but he wasn't sure which. "You do realize I'm a guy, right?" Nicky threw his hands up in frustration. "You like women. Lots of them—like all of them."

"My fans want our love story, Nicky. If I don't give it to them, I'm done. So what do you say, Nicholas, can I wine and dine and dump you?" Becks flashed his winning smile, the one that always got him everything he wanted.

Nicky's back went stiff with anger as the temptation to strangle Becks overwhelmed him. *I could stash him in the dumpster. No one would ever know it was me—and if they did, they couldn't possibly blame me.* "You are a colossal asshole, you know that?" Nicky took a step toward him, his fists clenched. "You never take anything seriously. You just do whatever the hell you want, and you never give another thought to the people you hurt!" Nicky's voice echoed against the brick walls. "You've turned my life into a circus of hiding in the back seat of your sister's car to avoid strangers demanding to know the intimate details of my love life. I can barely make it through a shift at my job—a job I really need—without someone trying to take a picture of me. You thrive in the spotlight, but I hate being the center of attention. This is all a big joke to you, but this is my life, and I don't need any of this."

"I know, Nicky. God, I know they've been horrible to you, and I'm so sorry."

"What about Kenny? Did you even think about him?"

"He's a tool, and you're too good for him. Besides, didn't you break up?"

"Yeah, we broke up. But we were together for two years. You don't stop caring about someone you once loved just like that. He's not ready to come out, Becks. His father is an Ohio senator. A conservative, very Republican senator who does not want a gay son. Do you have any idea how this has affected him? He was in that video too. The media has hounded him just as much as me—and not the entertainment media. His face has been all over CNN and Fox News. Did you think about that when you swept in with the PR stunt from hell? It might have launched your career into the stratosphere, but you've stepped on a lot of people to get there. Was it worth it?" Nicky's chest tightened, and his nostrils flared as his breath came in short, rapid gasps. He was so angry, he just wanted to give one really good throat punch to see how well Beckett Anderson would sing then.

"I'm sorry, Nicky. It wasn't a PR stunt. I didn't plan it, it just happened."

"How does a straight man suddenly decide to make out with another guy on the fly—in front of the whole Goddamn world? You want me to help you with this mess you've made, then give me an honest answer right freaking now. Why did you kiss me?"

"I told you." Becks' shoulders slumped. "Kenny was breaking your heart right there in front of me, and all I could think about was how much better you could do than him."

"And better is what? You? We're back at the part where I'm not sure you realize I'm a guy."

"I don't know, Nicky. I guess I don't have an answer."

"Then you need to figure it out, Becks, because until you can give me an honest answer, you're going to need to find someone else to be your fake boyfriend. It's not going to be me."

"I, ah…I need to be your boyfriend for a little while." Nicky closed his eyes, forcing himself to relax and think about anything other than Beckett Anderson. This was his last summer before college. He wanted to spend it working at the Main, hanging out with his friends, and on his off days, at home by the pool with a good book and some peace and quiet.

Nicky was a quiet guy. Not shy, but he liked his alone time. He preferred spending time with his few close friends over noisy nights out among strangers. He didn't do small talk either. He could talk all day about issues that mattered with someone who had something interesting to say, but he'd rather be alone than among strangers.

The last two weeks had pushed him to his limits, and he needed to recharge in his own environment.

"Hey, get out of here!" Nicky's father roared, turning the hose away from his black flower garden—his pride and joy—to the photographers lurking in the trees. "Stay away from my son."

"Is that Grayson St. Germaine?" The voices came from above. Nicky slid his sunglasses down to see the photographer in the tree right above him.

"Seriously?" Nicky winced at the camera flashes.

"Nicky, you didn't tell us your dad's an NFL Hall of Famer."

"He's not telling you anything."

Nicky choked back a laugh as his dad hosed the two photographers down until they were drenched and running for the street.

"Nice one, Pop."

"Damn vultures," Grayson grumbled. "Worse than when I was drafted. But I asked for it, you didn't do anything to deserve this. And you can kiss whoever you damn well want to."

"Thanks, Pop." Three years ago, his father would have been drunk by ten a.m. and yelling at his disappointment of a son—not gardening and protecting Nicky like a papa bear. Rehab had brought his father back to him, and he was grateful for it.

"Well, look at what the cat dragged in," Grayson said.

"Hey, Pop," Avery said. "Finals were tough this year, but I had some time off this week."

Nicky glanced behind him to see his brother coming in through the back gate.

"You wouldn't know anything about the half drowned photographers that just ran past me, would you?" Avery eyed the garden hose their father held like a weapon.

"Trespassers," Grayson grumbled.

Avery tilted his head back and laughed. "Pop's turned into the 'get off my lawn' guy." He settled down on the lounge chair next to Nicky beside the pool.

"I'll just let you two catch up. I have some black sunflowers to plant." Grayson marched back across the yard to his ever-growing flower garden.

"That garden is damned creepy." Avery shuddered.

"Why are you here, Avery?" Nicky sighed.

"I wanted to check on my little brother. Is that a bad thing?"

"As long as you aren't here to talk me into being Becks' fake boyfriend, then we're good." Nicky slid his sunglasses back on.

"I'm staying out of that," Avery said.

"But?"

"But, I'm worried about Becks."

"He'll land on his feet. I'm sure he'll talk his way out of this mess and manage to get his album and his tour too."

"I don't know, Nicky. I've never seen him like this. I'm worried—have been for a while. Becks hasn't been himself lately—even before whatever that was with the...thing."

"The kiss?"

"Yeah, that."

"He seemed like the same old Becks when he was here." Nicky shrugged.

"Let's face it, Becks' head has to be a scary place on his best day, but he's been down lately. He doesn't always show it. But Nari and I know him better than anyone else, and something isn't right."

"And what am I supposed to do about it?" Nicky crossed his arms over his chest.

"Be his friend, like you've always been. Try to understand that he might be going through something he doesn't understand yet."

"Are you saying he's no longer God's gift to women? Now he's gay and doesn't know it?" Nicky rolled his eyes.

"No, but I would think you would be among the first to understand everything isn't always black and white. He's had two crazy, stressful years. I can imagine it's not always easy to be Beckett Anderson."

"Okay, now what are you trying to say?"

"Becks loves you, Nicky. He loves all of his friends, and he's never been the type to get hung up on labels and rules. He saw you were hurting and wanted to fix it. I think it's as simple as that. And now his career is on the line."

"Ugh, you weren't supposed to talk me into this." Nicky threw his towel at his brother. "You've taken too many psych classes."

"All I'm saying is he could use a friend right now."

"You know if it was anything else, I'd have his back in a heartbeat. I just don't think I can do this fake boyfriend thing with all the cameras and attention."

"Believe me, I understand, little man. We would all understand if you decide you can't help him. Just be his friend. That's all he really needs."

Nicky paced across his bedroom, a towel draped loosely around his hips.

"I do not want to do this, damn it." He ran a hand through his damp hair. After a few laps in the pool and one very long, hot shower, Nicky still wanted to choke Beckett Anderson with his bare hands.

Just the thought of pandering to the reporters and photographers he'd spent the last two weeks dodging turned his stomach. "And I'm a terrible actor. No one will ever believe we're actually together." He threw his arms up in the air and rested them on the back of his neck. "How did my life become this insane circus?"

"Nicky, you asked for the truth." Becks barged into his bedroom without knocking.

Nicky jumped at the sound of his voice. "What the hell is wrong with you?" Nicky lunged for his towel as it fell to the floor. "Dammit, don't you know how to knock?" Nicky grabbed a pillow off his bed to cover himself.

"S-sorry." Becks stared at him, stumbling back toward the door. "I-I'll come back when you're dressed."

Nicky's heart raced, and he knew his face was bright red. He scrambled to his closet and threw on some jeans and a t-shirt. "You can come in now." Nicky cringed at the way his words came out all husky. *Get it together man. You've both been in a locker room before.*

"Right. Sorry about that." Becks dropped his gaze to his feet in a very un-Becks kind of way.

"You were saying something about the truth."

"Yeah." Becks rubbed the back of his neck. "I think I need to sit. Can I sit?" He sank down onto the desk chair across the room.

"Sure, make yourself at home." Nicky leaned against his dresser, his arms folded across his chest.

"So, yeah. I can't really explain why I kissed you. That's the simple truth, I don't know what came over me, other than what I said before. I wanted Kenny to know you could do so much better. I wanted to make him hurt the way he hurt you. It didn't mean anything. I'm comfortable enough in my sexuality to say it was no big deal. You know I love all kinds of people. I love women—especially pretty blond ones, but I love Avery too. And you … and Julian—hell I tried to date Addie all through high school.

"My label is going to dump my ass if I have to come out as straight. They are prepared to react with a statement that it was a

PR stunt of my own making that they never approved. No one in Nashville will touch me after that."

"Becks, I—"

Becks held up a hand. "Just let me get this out." He rubbed a hand over his sweaty brow. "Jesus, it's hot in here," he muttered, taking a deep breath. "I need your help, but I understand if the spotlight is more than you can handle. I just need to know we're still friends. I have a lot of people in my life, Nicky, but I don't have that many friends, and I don't want to lose you over this."

"You're a son of a bitch." Nicky shook his head.

"I'm not blowing smoke, Nicky, I swear—"

Nicky held his hand up. "It's my turn to talk."

"Okay." Becks actually shut up for once in his life.

"I love you too, you big idiot. I'll help you." Nicky sighed, hoping he wouldn't live to regret this.

"You'll be my boyfriend?" Becks' face split into a wide grin.

"Yes, but can you please break my heart as soon as possible so I can go back to my nice quiet life? I'd really like the whole world to forget my name before I start at Vanderbilt this fall."

"I swear you will not regret it." Becks shot across the room to pull him into a hug. He whirled Nicky around and dipped him, a stupid grin on his face. "It will be a whirlwind June romance, and then it will die a quick death, I promise." Becks pulled Nicky back up and glanced down at him, his lips just inches away. Nicky licked his lips, thinking about how soft and hungry those full lips were against his.

This was a very bad idea.

Becks:

"Sometimes, you just know." Becks leaned back in the leather chair they'd seated him in for the interview. He flashed one of his brilliant smiles at the camera and reached out beside him to graze a fingertip down Nicky's arm.

Nicky sat with a rigid posture, his jaw set with tension. He'd barely said two words. Becks could hardly look at him without guilt gnawing at his insides. It was his fault Nicky was in this position, uncomfortable and nervous.

But Becks didn't let his smile drop. He couldn't.

"Nicky." Calvin Harding leaned forward against his desk, his ironed suit pressing against the wood. "How long have you known Beckett was in love with you? He says it's been a long time coming, but we haven't gotten your side of the story."

Nicky swallowed heavily as his wide eyes shifted to the morning show host. Becks tried to grip his hand in support, but Nicky moved it out of his reach. "Um…I didn't."

Becks forced a laugh. "What he means, Calvin, is that I tried to tell him, but he didn't believe me. You see, I'm not one to hold my feelings back."

Calvin smiled at that, accepting it easily. The good-time country singer was known for his open nature. They'd never believe an ounce of dishonesty in him. That was one of the reasons the country found it so easy to become entranced in his whirlwind romance with the non-famous Nicky.

"You have a song called 'About a Boy.' You sing it as if you're speaking of a girl who couldn't have the boy she loved."

Becks interrupted him. "I can't go telling you the story behind all my songs. How would I remain so mysterious?"

The audience laughed at the joke. He was seen as anything but mysterious.

Calvin looked to the audience. "That's all we have time for today, folks." His eyes shifted to Becks and Nicky. "Thank you both for coming."

The red light on the camera flickered off, and Nicky let out an audible exhale.

Calvin shook his head. "It gets easier, kid." He grabbed the papers from the top of his desk. "Good luck, boys." With a nod, he walked toward the side of the stage where the producer awaited him.

Becks turned to the still-seated Nicky. "Nick-Nick." His voice softened. "You okay?"

This was only interview number one. If Nicky couldn't handle the simple morning shows, how was he going to get through this? When Nicky lifted his dark gaze to Becks, all Becks wanted to do was take the uncertainty from his eyes.

Running his fingers under Nicky's jaw, he tilted his head back so their eyes locked. "Are you okay, Nicky?"

Nicky pushed his hand away. "No." He stood, forcing Becks back. "This will work a lot better if you stop touching me all the time." With a shake of his head, he left Becks standing there and joined Avery at the side of the stage.

How were they supposed to act like boyfriends if they didn't touch? Becks curled his fingers into a fist. He'd imagined Nicky arriving in Nashville and making everything okay with his sweetness. But where had that guy gone?

Skylar appeared at Becks' side, offering him a bottle of water. "You did great out there." The label sent her to babysit. She'd officially become the point runner on the Beckett and Nicky romance tour. "Nicky, on the other hand...we need to give that boy some interview lessons."

"It was only his first one, Sky." Becks had always felt the need to protect Nicky, but this went deeper than that.

She crossed her arms. "This morning."

"What?"

"His first one this morning. You two are set to meet with a reporter from the *Country Chronicle* this afternoon. Tomorrow, you'll have a radio interview in the morning and a late show appearance that's being filmed in the afternoon. And that's really only the beginning."

Becks' jaw worked. He had no words for what the label was putting Nicky through. "Why all this attention?"

She leaned in, dropping her voice. "Because you're a sensation, cousin. This is wonderful for you. Don't let the opportunity slip away. PR is how careers are made."

"I need to talk to Nicky."

"He already left with Avery."

Becks cursed. "Of course, he did."

"Avery asked me for some time alone with his brother. I told him I'd send a car to pick Nicky up for the meeting later. As for you..." She looked down at the schedule on her phone. "You're due for a session with the writers."

"I write my own songs, Sky."

"Sorry, Becks. You write what the label wants you to write. No one is saying they can't be your words, but it won't hurt to have some of our best songwriters look at them to at least see how they can be improved upon."

He sighed. Welcome to his new life. He gestured to the door where his driver waited. "Lead the way."

Tired was the new normal for Becks. He walked into the café they'd chosen for the meeting with his driver following him. Ryan tended to stay out of Becks' way, so he didn't mind it when the label assigned him.

Stepping up to the counter, Becks pretended not to notice the wide-eyed stare of the barista. She fiddled with the ends of her auburn hair. "You're... Are you Beckett Anderson?"

He wiped all tiredness from his face and smiled. Meeting fans was the best part of his job, and he loved their support. He was never sure anymore if they loved his music or had just seen the video of him stopping the concert to kiss Nicky.

"I am. It's nice to meet you."

Her cheeks reddened. "My sister is never going to believe this. Can I get a picture?"

"Of course."

She pulled out her phone, and he leaned across the counter for her to take a selfie. "Thank you so much. Your song 'Can't Stop Dreaming of You' is basically my life right now. I listen to it every day."

His smile turned genuine at the mention of his music. That was the real star. He didn't care if anyone knew him, but the songs he'd poured his soul into deserved the recognition.

"What can I get you?" she asked.

He considered the menu hanging overhead for a moment. "Sugar. I need sugar. Something so sweet it'll rot my teeth out."

That was the kind of day he was having. The label's writers didn't get the new songs he'd written at all. It was frustrating not to be understood. Being told to change his lyrics was like being told he needed to change himself.

The barista considered him for a moment. "What about a strawberry frappe with mountains of whipped cream?"

"That sounds perfect." He'd always loved girly-sounding drinks. Sue him. Drinks shouldn't have genders anyway, so if anyone made fun of them, he'd smash a guitar over their heads. Okay, not really. He was just in a really bad mood.

He pulled out his credit card. "I also need a coffee, black, and a vanilla latte with one of those fun designs on the top." He didn't know how he remembered so much about Nicky from being around him two years ago.

After paying for the drinks, Becks dropped the coffee off with Ryan, who'd taken a seat by the window, then made his way to the only person in the place who looked like a reporter.

A pretty middle-aged woman with smooth, dark skin and braided black hair said, "Beckett Anderson." She gestured to the chair across the table. "It's a pleasure to meet you. I'm Latisha Martin. I'm beyond happy I get to do this interview. Is your boyfriend joining us?"

Becks glanced toward the door. Nicky was late. Maybe he'd changed his mind about everything after the morning show.

"I honestly don't know."

She shrugged off his answer. "Well, while we wait, why don't you tell me what's next for you."

He smiled, knowing he could talk about his music all day. "We've been in the studio a lot working on our second album."

She jotted a few notes down. "Will we get to see you on tour any time soon?"

He unleashed his patented sneaky grin. "Well, Latisha, that is not something I can divulge quite yet."

"Not even to a friend?"

He laughed. "Nice try. You'll find out soon enough. I will promise you, though, it'll be spectacular."

"Well, we wouldn't expect anything less from the man who jumped off his own stage for a kiss."

He lifted one shoulder. "What can I say? Nicky has that effect on me." A throat behind him cleared, and Becks turned to find a rosy-cheeked Nicky, loving how just about anything could make him blush.

Nicky sat in the final empty chair. Becks slid the latte in front of him, and Nicky gave him a confused look.

Becks leaned in to whisper in his ear. "I remembered."

Shifting away from Becks, Nicky looked to Latisha. "Hi," he squeaked.

She smiled. "Let's get started, shall we? Tell me how you two met."

Nicky rubbed his jaw. "I don't really remember the exact point we met."

"It was raining," Becks cut in. "Just coming down in sheets. It was spring. I was a high school sophomore, and my football coach sent me to the St. Germaine house. Nicky's brother, Avery, had been in an accident months before where his best friend died. He'd stopped showing up for school, and Coach was worried. I stood on the doorstep, waiting for someone to answer. I probably looked like a drowned rat by the time Nicky appeared."

He sent Nicky a smile as he remembered that day. He'd instantly liked the kid; something about him just drew him in. Maybe it was the complete honesty in his eyes, or the loneliness that accompanied it.

"What did Nicky do?" Latisha leaned in.

"He told me Avery wasn't in any shape to see me but that I should come back because he could just tell Avery needed me in his life." For years after the accident, Avery treated Nicky horribly. Yet, Nicky never stopped caring about him. "Nicky was the first person to think I could make a difference in anyone's life. He believed in me."

Latisha wiped a tear from the corner of her eye. "That's beautiful."

"I don't remember that day," Nicky whispered.

Hearing the words cut Becks, but he only shook his head. "It's okay. I didn't just become friends with Avery after that. I became friends with you. No one had ever needed me like you two did."

"But you two didn't date in high school, correct?" Latisha eyed them both.

Nicky shook his head. "I wasn't really important to him back then."

Those words would haunt Becks long after this interview. "Nick-Nick, of course, you were."

"Then why?"

"Why what?"

Nicky lowered his voice and spoke as if he forgot the reporter was even there. "You cut me out. For two years. After you graduated, you left Twin Rivers in your past, and it kind of felt like that's where you left me too."

Both boys turned at the scratching sound of Latisha writing on her notepad. That would have to be a conversation for another time, not when everything they said could end up printed in a magazine.

"You cut me out." He had. Without realizing it, he'd abandoned Nicky. He wanted more than anything to take his hand, but part of him knew that wouldn't be well received.

Latisha, as if sensing the discomfort, changed topics. "Beckett, your rise to country fame has been rather fast. What has that been like for you?"

Becks pushed thoughts of Nicky's pain from his mind, putting his Beckett face back on, calm, collected, and happy. He leaned back in his chair and sipped his Frappuccino. "Well, I had a bit of an advantage when I came to Nashville. My cousin has connections. Within months of my move, I had a record deal with my friend Nari. The label found us two more band members, and Quinn and Harrison have become like family. That's what really matters to me. Playing music with people I care about."

"In your first band, *Anonymous*, your sister was your drummer, is that right?"

He smiled at the mention of Wylder. "She's the best drummer I've ever known. No offense to Harrison. I'm a bit biased, but she's damn good."

"What does she think of your fame?"

Nicky released a laugh. "Wylder kind of just makes fun of him for it. She's made a sport out of it, actually."

Becks shared a private smile with Nicky. For once, it felt like they were on the same team. "I love my sister more than anything. I'm assuming you've seen the video of her singing?"

Latisha nodded. "She has a bright future ahead of her."

Becks shrugged, knowing Wylder would laugh in this woman's face. She couldn't care less about fame. They spoke more about Becks' career to that point. Latisha even asked Nicky a few questions about what he thought of everything Beckett had accomplished.

Nicky seemed to relax as the interview went on, and Becks even caught a hint of pride in his eyes when he spoke of the music. Becks reached over, testing Nicky's temperament by taking his hand. For once, Nicky didn't pull away.

Becks went further, intertwining their fingers, smiling when Nicky squeezed his hand.

Latisha finished her questioning and packed up her things before wishing them well. When she was gone, Nicky stared down as his hand, still holding Becks'.

"Nick-Nick." Becks met his gaze. "I need to know we're in this together. I know it's asking a lot of you and you aren't happy about your life being turned inside out, but this is new territory for me too. If you're going to be angry with me for the next month, I don't know if I can keep this up. It's killing me that you feel that way. Nic—"

"Stop," Nicky cut him off. "Stop talking. My turn, Becks. I was angry. For a long time, I wondered why someone I thought was my friend cut me out of his life. Two years. It hurt when I realized you were never my friend, only Avery's."

"I didn't—"

"I said stop talking."

Becks clamped his lips shut.

"Those two years have nothing to do with this. I promised I was in this, and I am. I'm sorry I've been a jerk, but do you realize how nervous this makes me? The cameras and reporters and general lack of privacy terrifies me." When Becks didn't respond, he sighed. "You can talk now."

"What can I do to help make it better?"

"Just give me space when I need it." He slipped his hand free. "And seriously, I know you're this touchy-feely dude, but stop holding my hand. I-I can't handle that."

Becks pushed out a breath. "Okay."

Nicky offered him a smile, so rare since he'd come to Nashville. Becks wanted to bottle it up and keep it with him always. He'd always felt that way around Nicky. Maybe that was why he'd been drawn to him since that first day he'd stood on his porch in the rain.

Around Nicky, he never felt like he had to be anyone else. He didn't have to hide who he was, and it was a feeling so unfamiliar it scared him.

It wasn't until right then Becks realized the answer to the most important question Nicky had asked. Why hadn't he spoke to him for two years?

Because Nicky St. Germaine was the only person in this world Beckett Anderson feared.

Nerves tumbled in Becks' stomach like they were practicing for the Olympics. He brushed a hand through his light brown hair, suddenly hating the way it looked messy no matter how long he fussed with it. It had always been what girls loved about it. Why? He didn't know at the moment.

Staring into the long mirror, he realized he had no clue what a straight dude wore on a fake gay date. No, not gay date. Just a fake date. He had to make himself stop thinking of everything as straight or gay. It wasn't fair to Nicky for him to treat this as anything other than normal.

But a normal date didn't make Becks' hands shake.

For a normal date, he didn't change his clothes five thousand times.

A knock on his door made him jump. Before he could walk toward it, his saviors strolled in. Sky and Sofie took one look at him in his slacks with no shirt and shared a laugh.

"You're kind of hopeless, cousin." Sky shook her head, her grin widening.

Sofie scanned Becks from head to toe as she pursed her lips in concentration. "Don't wear those pants."

"What?" Becks looked between the girls. "These are the fifth ones I've tried on."

"You're hopeless." Sofie put a hand on his bare shoulder. Once, he'd wanted to kiss her every time she touched him. But that feeling was gone, and he wasn't quite sure why. Now, she was just Sofie, his assistant and friend.

Skyler strolled into his walk-in closet. "Black?" she called back.

Becks was about to ask her what she meant when he realized the question wasn't for him.

Sofie joined her. "Yes, definitely. And green. That'll bring out his eyes."

When they emerged, Sky handed him a pair of black skinny jeans and a light-green button-down shirt. "Cowboy hat?" she asked.

"I'm not wearing a cowboy hat," Becks said at the same time Sofie said, "Of course. He's a country star."

Sofie turned to Becks. "You're not dressing for Nicky. You're dressing for the cameras."

"No hat."

She sighed. "Fine. Get dressed." She crossed her arms.

"Uh...are you guys going to leave?"

"No."

Sky turned her back on him, but Sofie watched as he stripped out of his pants, pulling on the black jeans as quickly as he could. They were so tight he had to jump to get them on, making Sofie giggle as she bit her fist.

Once he was dressed, Sky considered him. "The hair. Something needs to happen with the hair."

They forced him into the bathroom where they gelled his hair, twisting it this way and that until it no longer looked like he'd just gotten out of bed. Sofie opened her bag, pulling various makeup brushes out.

"No." Becks backed away. "I'm not wearing makeup."

"Beckett, this is the most important date of your life. Trust me. I'll make you camera ready."

The most important date of his life? As if he wasn't nervous enough already. He'd spent the last two days with Nicky doing various radio, TV, and blog interviews. Yet tonight, it would just be the two of them for the first time in a long time. Sure, the paparazzi would be following them, but they wouldn't be close enough to hear anything that was said.

Sofie and Sky brushed powder over his cheeks, but he stopped them before they put eyeliner on him. They both sighed but relented. Looking at his phone, Becks cursed. He was supposed to pick Nicky up twenty minutes ago.

Kissing both women on the cheeks, he headed to the door. "Good luck," they called after him. Out in the hall between Becks' apartment and Avery's, he took a deep breath, reveling in the brief moment of silence.

Closing his eyes for a moment, he lifted his hand to knock. As he waited, he realized it was probably the first time he'd knocked on this door. He had a key and usually just walked in. But he wanted to do this date right—even if it wasn't real. Nicky deserved that.

Second-guessing his outfit, Becks ran a hand down the buttons of his shirt. He should have worn a suit, right?

When the door swung open, he was relieved to be face to face with Nari rather than either of the other two options. She looked him up and down, a smile coming to her lips. "You look handsome, Becks."

"Thanks, Narisaurus." He clasped his hands together to keep them from shaking.

Nari didn't miss much when it came to him. They knew each other too well for that. "You're nervous."

"What? No."

Her grin widened. "It's cute. I like that you're nervous. Just…be careful with Nicky, okay?"

"Of course, Nars. We'll just be hanging out like old times."

"In these old times you speak of, you didn't have to pretend anything, Becks." She stepped back, and he followed her inside.

Avery appeared from one of the bedrooms, grimacing as he looked at Becks. "Dude…I don't know what to do here. Do I play the big brother and threaten you, or do I play the best friend and tell you to have fun?"

Nari gripped his hand. "Remember it's not real, Avery."

"Yeah, but my best friend is still showing up at my place to take my brother on a date."

Becks didn't get a chance to respond because Nicky rounded the corner, stopping when he spotted Becks. His eyes widened. "Uh, hi."

"Hey, Nick-Nick." Becks met his gaze, unable to look away.

Nicky cleared his throat. "You, um, ready to go?"

"Yeah. We have reservations."

They left Avery and Nari staring after them as they walked in silence through the halls. A car waited at the curb out front, and Becks opened the door for Nicky to slide in the back.

Nicky's lips twitched. "Becks Anderson is a gentleman?"

The statement snapped the tension between them, and Becks laughed. "As if you had any doubt."

They talked the entire car ride about nothing and everything, never lacking for what to say. The restaurant wasn't far, but when the car pulled up, they didn't get out.

Becks turned in his seat to face Nicky. "Carmichaels is where people go when they want to be seen in this town. The label pulled some strings to get us a table on such short notice. You can bet there'll be paps as soon as we open these doors. You ready for that?"

Nicky stared at him as if he were his lifeline. He reached forward, brushing something off the collar of Becks' shirt. "Beckett Anderson." His voice lowered as he tried to suppress a laugh. "Are you wearing makeup?"

Becks meant to push his hand away but gripped it instead, holding it to his chest. "You can tell me if you're not ready for this, Nick. I know I've been asking a lot of you, but I never want to push you further than you're prepared to go."

Nicky's fingers dug into Becks' shirt. "I can do this." He said the words as if trying to convince himself. "We only have a few weeks until we're free of this fake relationship. I won't back out now."

His words were like a million tiny ice cubes shoveled into Becks' shirt, cooling his heated skin. The time limit on this should have been a comfort to Becks, but he enjoyed having Nicky at his side. Most of the time, he was alone in his career. Yes, he had a band, but they weren't the headliners. They didn't understand. Right now, Nicky shared the spotlight with him, taking some of the burden away.

But it was more than that. With his friend by his side, Becks felt like he could do this. His dreams were attainable.

"Only a few more weeks." Becks dropped Nicky's hand. "We can do this." As soon as he opened the door, flashes went off. Pulling Nicky from the car, he rushed into the restaurant. The hostess recognized them and seated them immediately.

Carmichaels did a good job of keeping paps outside, but they stayed by the windows and waited at the doors.

"Your life is crazy, Becks." Nicky shook his head as he lifted the menu.

He wasn't wrong. "Yeah, but if it means I get to make music for the rest of my life, I'll deal with the chaos."

"Can I confess something?"

"Being that you're my boyfriend, I expect you to."

Nicky laughed. "I'm kind of a Beckett Anderson junkie."

"You listen to my music?"

"All of it. I know the words to every song."

Becks leaned forward. "Which one is your favorite?"

Nicky hesitated. "'Small Town.' When you sing about leaving people behind, I always wondered if I was one of those people. The line 'I still think about how it was' hit me hard the first time I'd heard it. I missed you, and it was the first inkling I had that maybe you missed me too. It was stupid though because you left a lot of people. I know it wasn't about me."

"It wasn't." Becks hated the way Nicky deflated. "But I missed you like crazy. You know I love you, Nick, right? Always. No matter what happens, I could never just forget about you."

Nicky shrugged as if he didn't believe him. Becks scooted his chair around the table so they sat side by side. "Nicky, look at me."

When Nicky met his eyes, the look he gave him reminded him of the boy he'd first met who'd been an open book.

A shadow fell over the table, and Becks looked up to find a tall man holding a camera. Somehow, one of the paparazzi got into the restaurant. "Beckett Anderson," he began. "What do you say to the rumors that your entire relationship is a PR stunt?" He held his camera up, catching the stunned look on Becks' and Nicky's faces.

Becks recovered first. "I'd say I love my boyfriend." He turned to Nicky, trying to communicate his next actions with his eyes.

Nicky sucked in a breath with a nod. Their first kiss wasn't planned. Becks rushed through it, just wanting to wipe the sadness from Nicky's face. He hadn't taken the time to consider what it meant. This time was different.

He leaned forward, capturing Nicky's lips with his own, exploring the shape and feel of them. It wasn't like kissing Sofie. She'd give him full control, softening under his touch. Kissing Nicky was a battle of wills, both boys wanting to take everything they could from the other.

Nicky wrapped a hand around the back of Becks' neck. Gone was the stunned boy Becks kissed at the concert. This was a man who took what he wanted.

And for the first time, Becks felt what Nicky wanted was him. He pulled back, letting Nicky rest their foreheads together. Both breathed heavily.

The photographer was gone, having been escorted from the restaurant.

"Nicky," Becks whispered. "What..." He couldn't finish the question. He knew what that was supposed to be. The pictures of them kissing would be all over the internet by morning. Fans would flip for them.

Yet, now, the paparazzi was gone, and all Becks wanted to do was try that again. Nicky scooted his chair away and released a long breath. "Ever thought of doing movies, Becks?" He shook his head with a sarcastic laugh. "You sure sold that."

Sold it? Yeah, he guessed that was what he'd done. Acted. Pretended.

"Can we just go?"

"You want to leave?" The restaurant or Nashville? He didn't ask because he feared the answer.

"I'm tired, Becks. We've been doing this PR shit for days. I'm not even hungry."

Becks didn't understand how their evening changed so quickly. Before the kiss, Nicky seemed fine with everything. "PR shit. You mean my job?"

"Yes. Your job. Not mine. I didn't sign up for being accosted in restaurants or having to kiss you for the cameras."

He made it sound like that was the worst thing in the world. "No, but you did agree to help me."

"Only because you were so pathetic," he whisper-shouted.

"Pathetic?"

"Hiding from reporters in Twin Rivers. Coming to my room to beg me to be your little prop. You're so hell-bent on achieving your dreams you'll do anything, no matter how degrading."

"Degrading." He stood to leave. "Right."

Nicky followed him, not speaking again until they were seated back in the car, neither having eaten. "You're not even gay, Becks. Do you know how sad it is to pretend you are? Not to mention offensive."

"You know why I couldn't tell the truth."

"Because you jumped off that stage to kiss me thinking I needed a savior." He punched the seat in front of him. "I'm not fifteen years old anymore. I can take care of myself. I didn't ask you to kiss me in front of the whole world."

Becks rubbed the back of his neck. Nicky's anger hung like a shroud around them. "Nick-Nick—"

"No, don't call me that. That's what my friend Becks calls me. Right now, you're not him. You're Beckett Anderson, just trying to get ahead in his career."

"I'm the same person."

"You kissed me! Again!"

Becks dropped his voice so low he wasn't sure at first if Nicky heard him. "And you kissed me back."

Silence hung between them for a long moment. Nicky kept his eyes on something out the darkened window as the car pulled up in front of Becks' apartment building. The driver opened Nicky's door.

Nicky hesitated. "The difference between you and me, Becks, is that for you that kiss was a way to make other people happy."

"And for you?"

"For me, it was real." He exited the car and didn't wait for Becks as he entered the building.

Becks leaned back against the seat. His driver stuck his head in. "Are you getting out, sir?"

"No. Please take me to Skylar's place." She was the person Becks had become closest to in the last two years, and she was also honest to a fault.

If anyone could tell him what to do to fix this, it was her.

He just hoped it wasn't broken beyond repair.

"For me, it was real."

Those words played on a loop through his mind. Nicky had been wrong though. When Becks kissed him, he hadn't been thinking about anyone else. Even the paparazzi faded to the back of his mind until all he saw in front of him was the boy he'd always been drawn to in different ways.

He'd kissed him because, in that moment, he'd wanted to. That was all there was to it.

Becks rubbed his eyes. "Shit."

Nicky:

Nicky sank down low in his seat at the diner just around the corner from his brother's apartment building. An apartment he refused to return to. He couldn't face Becks—at least not any time soon. Not after nearly confessing his true feelings.

How did I get myself into this mess? But he hadn't. Becks dragged him into it.

"For me, it was real." He wished he could take those words back. He didn't need Becks feeling sorry for him. And he really didn't need all the staring. Even now, people took a second look at him, trying to place how they knew him.

"I gotta get out of this town." Nicky pulled his phone from his pocket, ignoring the texts from his brother and one from Becks.

Nicky: Can you grab my things and meet me at the diner on the corner? I just need to go home.

Nari: What happened? Did Becks … Never mind, I'm on my way.

"Can I get you anything else, honey?" the waitress asked. She couldn't have been much older than Nicky.

"Just coffee, thanks," Nicky muttered.

"I know you." She frowned, refilling his mug. "You're dating Beckett Anderson, right? You're Nicky?"

"Nah, I just look like him, I guess." Nicky refused to meet her gaze.

"You know he comes in here all the time." She set her coffee carafe on the table, like she didn't plan to move for a while. "He lives somewhere around here, but a lot of country stars do. I've met some of the greatest singers in this town working here."

"That's cool." Nicky fumbled with an empty creamer pack.

"You sure you're not Nicky St. Germaine?

"No, he just looks like him," Nari said, sliding into the booth across from him and dropping his suitcase under the table. "He has one of those faces."

"You're Nari Won Song," the waitress said with reverence.

"Nope, I guess I have one of those faces too." Nari flipped over her coffee mug and filled it herself. "I've got a hundred-dollar tip in my pocket if you'll leave us alone and keep anyone else from bothering my friend." Nari poured several creamers into her coffee until it looked more like milk.

"You got it, Miss." The waitress winked. "No problem." She trotted back to the kitchen, leaving them sitting in silence.

"What happened?" Nari finally said.

"He kissed me again, can you believe that?" Nicky absently stirred his coffee.

"Okay." Nari leaned back against the vinyl booth. "Um… Isn't that kind of what you signed up for? You two are supposed to be dating for the media attention, so that probably means a kiss here and there."

"No, he really kissed me, Nari. Just like the first time. I can't separate that reality from the fiction of this stupid relationship. Not when he makes everything around us disappear, making me think the only thing that matters is me. He's a damn good actor." Nicky snorted a laugh.

"He cares about you, Nicky."

"He's always cared about me. Cared about his best friend's kid brother. This is different territory. I don't know how to do this kind of pretending."

"I know there's something going on with Becks and his feelings for you. I don't pretend to know what goes through that boy's head. But I don't think he understands what box to put you in, Nicky."

"Box?"

"We are creatures of habit. We sort the people in our lives into these categories—family, friend, lover, enemy, and every other label you can think of. For Becks, I think he had you in the friend box with Avery and me, but it's like he took you out of that box because you didn't fit there, but now, he doesn't know where to put you, and he's confused."

"Are you saying you think he's suddenly gay? After years of dating every pretty girl that comes his way, he's now into guys?"

"No, I don't think he's gay, Nicky. But I also don't think everything in life has a simple answer. Let the guy have some time to figure you out."

"How do you do it?" Nicky glanced outside where a few paps lingered just waiting for him to come out. Or maybe they were there for Nari.

"What, the cameras?" She sighed. "That's been the hardest part about all of this. I love what I do. I love being on stage with Becks, playing our music and hearing him sing the lyrics we wrote together. I wouldn't trade it for anything in the world. But sometimes, I wish I was Hannah Montana."

"You're such a dork, Nars." Nicky laughed.

"I'm serious." She shoved his hand playfully. "Sometimes, I wish people would forget who I am once I leave the stage."

"You're a private person, like me," Nicky said. "How do you get used to being in the Beckett Anderson spotlight?"

"I try to stay in his shadow, to be honest."

"But you seem so comfortable with your fame now."

"I see it as the price I pay so I get to do the thing I love most. It wasn't always easy. In the early days, I didn't think I was going to make it, but Becks helped me through it. To him, standing in front of a camera at a moment's notice isn't a big deal, but he learned really quickly that was a surefire way for Nari Won Song to make a giant fool of herself. Now we have a deal. Any spur-of-the-moment stuff he handles, and I've learned to adapt to the planned interviews and public speaking engagements. If I have time to prepare myself for it, I can get through it. And these days, it doesn't bother me so much anymore."

"You put a camera in his face, and he becomes a version of himself I don't know if I really like," Nicky said. "The way he panders to the press, it's humiliating.

"Well, give the guy some slack, Nicky, he's currently pretending to be something he's not. Yeah, he might be the one that landed us all in this mess, but he's the one trying to save his career…and mine."

"I know." Nicky's shoulders slumped. "I thought I could help. But I don't think I can do this anymore. It's too much."

"You two need to have a talk about boundaries. What you're willing to do or not do on camera. I know Becks—probably better than anyone. He will bend over backwards to make you comfortable. He's been a lifesaver for me. I would never have survived this industry without him. He just needs to be reminded that not everyone is a natural-born star like he is. And if you decide you can't do this, he will understand."

"I have to get out of this town, Nari." Nicky stood up, grabbing his suitcase and his car keys. "I need a break so I can think because, right now, I'm reconsidering my college choice."

The pictures and videos were worse this time. Nicky's lovesick face was plastered all over the internet, and videos of their most recent kiss haunted Nicky's every waking minute. Because the kiss was hot. Every bit as hot as the first kiss they'd shared. Watching it now, he could see the instant where it seemed Becks forgot about the camera recording their intimate moment. Either Nari was right and Becks had some confusing feelings for Nicky or Beckett Anderson was in the wrong business because his performance deserved an Oscar.

"Hey, Nicky." Wylder hopped onto the barstool at the Main where Nicky was busy cleaning the coffee machines.

"Here for your lunch order?" He darted a look back at the kitchen to see if her food was up yet. She'd just called in the daily order from the hardware store across the street. "It's not ready yet."

"Yeah, I just needed a break." She leaned her head against her arm propped up on the counter.

"You look tired. Late party?" He hoped she wasn't getting back into that again. Her days with the *Powerplay* all-girls band had gotten her into a lot of trouble.

"No, that's not really my scene anymore." She sighed, picking at a napkin hanging out of the dispenser in front of her.

"Why so…gloom and doom today?"

"It's nothing."

"It's clearly not nothing." Nicky leaned against the counter, setting his work aside for the moment. "Come on, Wylder, it's me. I'm your best friend, so if you can't talk to me, it must be pretty awful keeping it to yourself."

"I just… I don't need this getting back to Becks."

"Since I'm not speaking to he-who-must-not-be-named, your secret is safe with me. Spill it, Wylds. You know it'll make you feel better."

"Fine." Wylder took a deep breath. "So, um…for the last year, I've been looking for my mother. My drug-addict, sorry-excuse-for-a-mom, birth mother."

"Wow, okay." Nicky reached for her hand. He hadn't realized this was going to be such a serious conversation. "And how's that coming?" He nudged her to keep talking.

"I found her." She turned her anxious eyes on him, pleading for help.

"Have you seen her? Where is she?"

"I've lived my whole life thinking she was somewhere far away, living her life without me. But this whole time she's only been an hour away. She lives in Cincinnati. And she's clean now. And now that I've found her, I'm too chicken shit to go see her."

"Do you want to see her?" Nicky squeezed her hand.

"Yes. No, I don't know. I thought I did when I started looking for her."

"What were you looking to find in your mother, Wylder?" Nicky asked carefully.

"Dad always told me I'm the best part of both of my parents. That I'm just like her in all the right ways but that I have enough of him in me to balance her crazy. I guess I wanted to meet the good part of her. But I'm scared I'll just find the bad stuff. And maybe she doesn't want to see me."

"Honestly, if you want to see your mother, you have every right to. She's your mother, of course she wants to see you. If she didn't, she wouldn't live so close."

"I'm scared, Nicky." She turned her wide, dark eyes on him. "I don't know what I'll do if she rejects me."

"At least you'll know and can stop wondering."

"Good point. All the wondering is making me insane."

"And I'll go with you if you want a buffer."

"Would you?" She visibly relaxed.

"Of course, Wylds. Whenever you're ready, we'll go find her, and I'll be there for you every step of the way."

"Thanks, Nicky." She slid off her stool and came around behind the counter to hug him. "You're the best."

"When do you want to go?" He glanced down at her, not wanting to push her into anything she wasn't ready for.

"Tomorrow? Before I lose my nerve?"

"Perfect timing. I'm off tomorrow with nothing to do."

"You know, I wish my brother would get his head out of his butt and see what's right in front of him. You're so good for him, Nicky."

Becks:

Beads pressed into Beckett's face as he shifted against the uncomfortable beaded pillow he'd passed out on. A groan sounded. Was that him?

Someone hammered nails into his head, causing a pulsing pain. Or maybe that was just his hangover.

"Wake up, Beckett." Sky's voice was too loud.

Pressing a hand over each ear, he squeezed his eyes shut.

"Oh, for God's sake." She wrapped long fingers around his ankle and pulled with a surprising amount of strength.

Becks held tight to the pillow as his body slid to the floor. "Go away, Sky." He cracked one eye open. "How are you upright?"

She'd had just as much to drink, if not more, as he had the night before.

Hands on hips, she stared down at him. "Because I'm not a lightweight who gets drunk on three beers."

"I don't get drunk on three beers," he grumbled.

"Could have fooled me, dinkus." Anyone who saw Becks and Sky together would assume they'd known each other their entire lives. They were more like siblings than cousins, yet they'd only known each other for three years.

A year before moving to Nashville, this crazy girl messaged Becks online, claiming to be related to him as the daughter of his deadbeat mom's sister. It wasn't until Becks asked his father about having an aunt out there that he'd learned the truth.

When his mom chose drugs over her own kids, his dad cut Becks and Wylder off from anything having to do with her. But now, here he was in Nashville passing out on his cousin's couch. He owed her more than he could ever repay. Without Sky, he wouldn't have had a hope of a career in country music.

"I'm going to be sick." He picked himself off the floor and ran to the bathroom, making it just before the contents of his stomach emptied into the toilet.

After cleaning himself up, he emerged feeling much better. In the kitchen, Sky handed him some kind of concoction she'd made that looked no better than the grossness that had just spewed out of him. "I'm not drinking that."

"Don't be a baby. This is my hangover cure." She shoved the glass at him. "Take it."

With a sigh, he accepted the drink, gagging as he sniffed it.

"Hold your nose while you drink it."

He did as she said, but it didn't help. The foul liquid slithered down his throat, and he breathed deeply to keep from hurling again. Once he'd finished it, he bent over the sink, shoveling water into his mouth with his hands.

"What are you? An animal?" Sky hid a laugh behind her hand.

Becks only eyed her suspiciously as she looked anywhere but at him. "That wasn't a hangover drink, was it?"

Her eyes widened in innocence. "Well…no." She laughed. "I kind of just wanted to see if you'd drink it."

"You're an asshole." He took a hand towel from the counter and snapped it at her.

She shrieked. "You are feeling better though, right?"

She had a point. He'd forgotten his hangover. But he hadn't forgotten the night that led to his drinking. Sky had been surprised when he showed up on her doorstep only an hour after the date started. She'd never been one to turn him away when he needed her though or one to ask questions before he was ready.

He caught her staring at him and sighed. "If I'm going to spill my guts, are you at least going to make me breakfast?"

She shook her head. "You're helpless, dude. My toaster is on the counter. Bagels are in the fridge. Have at it."

He eyed the appliance of death. "I'll just eat the bagel cold." He opened the fridge, pretending like he didn't see her smirk. Yes, Beckett Anderson, rising star, burned even toast.

He paid a meal service to deliver things with explicit instructions that took very little preparation, and even those sat mostly unused in his freezer in favor of either takeout or stealth attacks on whatever Nari and Avery were eating.

"How are you still alive?" Sky smiled, patting his cheek. "This face won't get you everywhere in life."

He shrugged, taking a bite of his cold bagel and pretending it tasted just as good as a toasted one slathered in cream cheese.

Hiking herself up to sit on the counter, Sky waited for him to speak.

"I think I messed up."

She gave him a "no shit" look. "What did you do to the poor guy?"

"I mean this entire thing was a mistake. Sky, I'm lying to my fans. Do you know how sleazy that makes me feel? Who does this?"

"I don't think you had much of a choice. The label made that pretty clear. Your fans would have blasted you for that kiss if we didn't play this right."

"There's always a choice, Sky. Always. Nicky deserves better than this."

"Ah, so this is about you feeling sorry for the kid."

"He isn't a kid." Becks threw his half-eaten bagel in the trash, turning his back on his cousin.

"No, I guess he's not. At least, not with a body like that."

Becks' face turned red as he whirled to face her. "Don't talk about him like that."

A smile slid across her face. "Ah...I see." She jumped off the counter.

"See what?"

"You care about him."

"Of course, I care about him. He's Nicky."

"No, I mean you care about him."

Becks' eyes widened at her insinuation. "That's ridiculous."

She strolled into the living room where her laptop sat on the coffee table. Lifting it up, she perched it on one hand while typing with the other before spinning it so the screen faced Becks.

A picture loaded, one he hadn't wanted to see. The kiss. It had already hit the gossip blogs. Nicky looked like he'd been caught by surprise, but Becks' eyes were closed, his face calm.

"You kissed him." Sky set the computer down. "Again."

"Like I said, I screwed up."

"It's only a screwup depending on what happens next." She sat on the arm of the couch and looked up at him. "Okay, cuz, I love you more than I thought I would when I first reached out three years ago. You're kind of my only family now other than my mom. But can I be honest for a moment?"

"When are you ever not?"

"You're an idiot."

"Gee, thanks. You always say the nicest things."

She laughed at that. "Come on, dude, you're the most unobservant person I've ever known. You were with Sofie for over a year, and you never even took her out to dinner."

"It wasn't like that with us." His defenses rose.

"It was for her. But Sofie, being who she is, forgave you for your blindness because you may be a fool, but you're just about the most lovable fool I've ever known."

"I feel like there may have been a compliment in there, but..." He spread his hands wide.

"What did Nicky do after you kissed him?"

Becks scratched his cheek. "He got pretty angry with me."

She nodded as if there was some big secret in those words he should be seeing. "For God's sake, Beckett, the kid has feelings for you."

Becks stumbled back. "No way. It's Nicky." They'd known each other for years. Becks would have noticed. Right? "Sky, none of this is real. We're just pretending. He's Avery's brother."

"And I'm guessing you've always treated him like Avery's brother instead of his own person."

Becks thought back on the accusations Nicky had flung at him. He hadn't spoken to him after leaving Twin Rivers. But surely, Nicky knew he cared about him just as much as he did Avery. Maybe more.

Lord, maybe more.

"I need to go, Sky."

"Brush your teeth," she called after him. "Your breath smells like vomit."

By the time Becks made it back to his apartment building, rain pounded into the pavement and his just-out-of-bed hair had turned into drowned-rat hair.

The glass doors swung shut behind him, and he stepped in front of the row of elevators. The center one slid open, revealing a tired-looking Nari.

Disappointment shone in her eyes when she looked at him. "If you're looking for Nicky, he left."

"He left?" He said the words as if he couldn't comprehend their meaning.

She sighed. "Yeah, last night. It's too much for him, Becks. You know Nicky. He's not meant for the spotlight."

"I need to find him."

"No." She took his hand, imploring him with her eyes. "Please, Becks. For my sake and for Nicky's, promise me you'll leave him alone. At least for now. Give him space. He's moving to Nashville soon. You'll get your chance to make it up to him and show him you can be a good friend. He doesn't really see that right now."

Blowing out a heavy breath, Becks rubbed his eyes. "You're right. You always are."

She smiled. "Go get some dry clothes on, and hurry. I'm going across the street for coffee, but we're due at the studio soon." She glanced at her watch. "We have to lay down the new single. Maybe if the music is good enough, the label won't care your fake boyfriend is gone."

He moved to step around her into the elevator.

"Oh, and Becks?"

"Yeah?"

"We've been asked to perform at a political rally at the Central City Hotel next week."

Becks shrugged. He'd perform wherever the label told him to perform. He didn't understand much about politics, but to him, it was always about the music. "We'll be ready."

The elevator doors shut, cutting them off from each other. When he exited on his floor, he found Avery striding toward him, fury in his eyes.

Becks swallowed his anger. He didn't get to be mad about Nicky when it was his fault.

Avery pushed him into the wall, his eyes blazing. "What did you do?"

"Avery..." Becks tried to push him off, but Avery had always been stronger than him.

"My brother left pretty damn fast. I know it was your fault. What did you do to him?"

"Nothing."

Avery yanked him off the wall. When he released him, Becks stumbled back, rubbing his neck.

"I knew this wasn't going to end well." Avery slammed his fist into the wall. "Why him, Becks? If you needed some PR stunt, why couldn't you choose someone else?"

"Because he's Nicky." That was the only explanation he had. Nicky was special, always had been. Becks thought he'd kissed him at the concert because Nicky needed him. But what if Becks was the one who needed Nicky?

"Exactly." Avery deflated as all the anger left him. "He's Nicky. Fragile."

Nicky's words came back to him. He didn't need someone to save him. "He's not fragile, Avery. You and I always treated him like he was, but I'm starting to think he's the strongest of us all." He'd had the strength to walk away from their arrangement. Something Becks wasn't sure he had.

Avery ran a hand through his hair. "Do you realize what this entire ploy has done to him? He's had to pretend to be dating the guy he's crushed on for years, the one he always knew he couldn't have. You're straight, Becks."

Becks was beginning to think it was a lot more complicated than that, but his mind caught on one word. "Nicky was crushing on me? Even back in high school?" The thought spread warmth through him.

"More than crushing. I think you were the first guy he ever had real feelings for. I'll be so dead if he knows I ever told you this." He paused. "Why are you smiling like that?"

Becks hadn't realized a massive grin stretched across his face. Nicky had feelings for him when they were younger. His smile fell as he realized those were no doubt gone.

"Look." Avery rubbed the back of his neck. "I'm sorry I got mad at you. You're my best friend. But I'll never stop looking out for Nicky."

"I won't either. He's my family too."

"Then stop messing with him. He doesn't need his feelings for you to return."

Before he could respond, Nari appeared at the end of the hall juggling two coffee cups. "Didn't I tell you to hurry, Becks. Go change already, you look like a drowned rat."

He nodded, unlocking his apartment before slipping in and changing as quickly as he could.

When he stepped back into the hall, Avery had Nari pressed against the wall as he kissed her. The Becks thing to do would have been to make gagging noises or interrupt in some other obnoxious way. But as he looked at them, he realized, for the first time, he wanted what they had.

He'd spent years dating multiple women, finding a connection with none. It never bothered him until that moment.

Nari broke away from Avery with a sheepish expression. She tried and failed to hide her smile as she looked back over her shoulder at Avery. He sent her a wink.

Nari looped her arm through Becks', giving him a look that said she knew every thought tumbling through his mind.

But if she did, she'd probably never look at him the same way again.

Because when Becks pictured kissing someone in the halls of their building, it was Nicky he saw.

Nicky:

"Are you sure about this, Wylder? You look a little green." Nicky studied his friend out of the corner of his eye. Parking a few streets over from their destination, he took her hand to get her attention.

"What-I'm-fine," she said in a rush.

"No, you aren't, and that's okay. You want to go home? Try again another day?"

"Oh, hell no. I'm not doing this twice." She took a deep breath. "I just… I don't know what to say."

"Did you call her?"

"No, um, I was afraid she'd hang up on me. I really just wanted a chance to see her. So I have a clear memory of what she looks like. If she doesn't want to talk to me, that's okay."

"Then let's do this." Nicky pulled out of his parking spot and followed the GPS directions for the last few turns to the tiny house where Wylder's mom lived. "At any point when you want to go, you just say the word and we're out."

Wylder's hand shot out and grabbed his, clutching so hard her nails pressed into his palm. "Thank you for being here." Her voice seemed so small. Not at all the pillar of strength she normally was.

"I'm always here for you, Wylds." He squeezed her hand back, waiting for her to choose when she was ready to get out of the car.

"What if she's not here?"

"Then we'll come back later."

Wylder nodded, brushing her long blond dreadlocks over her shoulder. "She's probably at work. We'll just check real quick and then maybe go get some lunch or coffee or something," she babbled, reaching for the door handle.

When she stepped out, Nicky rushed around to the passenger door to her side. Her dark eyes grew wide and terrified for just a moment before she took another deep breath and crossed the gravel drive to the front porch. Nicky followed, so proud of her for doing this on her own. She didn't need him, but he was happy to be here for her. She'd been there for him a thousand times before.

Catching a glimpse of herself in the polished window panes of the front door, Wylder brushed a hand over her dreadlocks. "I should have cut these a long time ago."

"No way, you're not Wylder without your dreads. She's not going to judge you. She's going to love you, and she's going to be so proud of you."

"And what if she's not?"

"Then you haven't missed a damn thing not having her as a mother."

"Right." Wylder nodded. "And I have the most amazing mom I could ask for at home. I just want to know where I come from." She stood taller, reaching to knock on the door.

"Just a minute," someone called from inside. "Be right there."

Wylder turned determined eyes toward Nicky. "Here goes nothing," she whispered just as the door opened.

"Sorry, I was just making some tea." Sadie Anderson opened the door, holding a steaming mug in one hand. The second she laid eyes on her daughter, the mug slipped from her hands and crashed to the floor. "Wylder?" Her eyes misted. "It can't be." Her hands fluttered nervously to her throat. "In my head, you're still five years old. But look at you." Tears spilled down her cheeks. "All grown up and so beautiful."

"Hi…Sadie…Mom," Wylder said, struggling to contain her emotions. "You're just as pretty as I remember."

"You remember me?" Sadie scrambled to pick up the pieces of the broken mug.

"Some." Wylder nodded. "I remembered you had blond hair just like mine."

"Well, I was never cool enough to pull off dreads, but you look amazing. Would you…" She took a step back, shoving the broken mug onto a side table. "Would you like to come inside?" She laughed nervously.

"Yes, thank you. Sorry, this is my friend Nicky." Wylder grasped his hand as she followed her mother inside.

"Nice to meet you, Nicky." Sadie smiled. "Let's go sit out on the back porch. It's nice out there. Can I get you some tea? Or water?" She led them through to the kitchen at the back of the Craftsman house. It was old, and the décor simple, but it was beautiful.

"Tea would be nice, thank you," Nicky said, and Wylder nodded. He wasn't a fan of hot tea, but he was here for moral support, so he'd drink whatever was offered.

"How is everyone?" Sadie asked, her hands shaking as she poured hot water over Earl Grey tea bags. "Your brother? Dad and stepmom are all okay, right?"

"Everyone's good." Wylder fumbled with the honey her mom offered.

"Good, good." She nodded, passing Nicky his tea before she turned toward the screened-in porch. "Come have a seat and tell me all about yourself. How is school? Last your father told me, you were in a band with Becks. But that's been a while."

"Yeah, that was a couple of years ago." Wylder sat on the wicker loveseat with her mom. Nicky made himself at home in the armchair right next to her. "Before Becks left for Nashville."

"Right, right." Sadie nodded.

Wylder fell silent for a moment, her fingers tapping furiously against her tea cup.

"Wylder was in an all-girls band for the last two years," Nicky prompted, trying to keep them talking.

"Yeah, that was fun for a while. But I got into some trouble with the older girls, so Dad made me quit. I'm not playing much music these days."

"I heard you sing with Becks at one of his recent concerts," Sadie said.

"You were there?" Wylder's eyes widened.

"No, darlin', couldn't afford the tickets, but I saw the video online. You have a beautiful voice. You kids got your music talent from me, but Lord knows, you and Becks have more talent in your little pinkie toes than I ever did. But I always loved to sing and play the piano."

"I play drums mostly." Wylder relaxed some, flashing a hint of a smile at Nicky.

Nicky cringed as his phone chirped in his pocket. "Sorry about that. Sadie, would you mind if I take a closer look at your garden?" Nicky gestured to the backyard. "You have such beautiful flowers. I'd love to see them and give you two some time to talk."

"Of course, Nicky, thank you." Sadie stood to open the screen door for him.

"I'll be right here if you need me," Nicky said.

"I'm good, thanks, Nicky." Wylder looked relieved so he knew she'd be okay for a few minutes at least.

Nicky walked along the stone pathway across the backyard full of flowers in bloom. It was like a little oasis in the middle of the city, but the whole garden looked new. Like maybe Sadie had developed a passion for gardening recently, along with her sobriety.

With a sigh, Nicky sat down on a concrete bench, slipping his phone from his pocket. The text message he'd been expecting but didn't want to see stared him in the face.

Becks: Are you okay?

He didn't know how to answer that question nor any of the others that would surely follow if he replied. "Am I okay?" He had no idea. Nicky ignored the text, about to return his phone to his pocket when it chirped again.

"Damn it, Becks, I don't want to talk," he muttered at his phone. It was the same text but from his brother this time.

Avery: Are you okay?"

Nicky: Depends. Are you asking for Becks?

Avery: No. I'm your big brother, it's my job to make sure you're okay. And ouch, man. I'm not getting between you two, and if I'm helping anyone, it's going to be you."

Nicky: Thanks Ave. I'm fine.

Avery: You're not going to bail on me are you?

Nicky: Bail?

Avery: You're still coming to Nashville in August, right? I was looking forward to showing my little bro around the Vanderbilt campus.

Nicky: I'll be there. I just don't know if I can live across the hall from Becks. Not after all this drama. At least not right away.

Avery: I understand, little man. I just want you to know I've got your back. But if you want to live in the dorms first semester, I get it.
Nicky: It might be easier all around if I just move into the dorms permanently.
Avery: Easier for who?
Nicky: You and Nari need your space.
Avery: Dude, do you even know how often they aren't here? I was looking forward to having a roommate when they travel. Someone not into the country music scene if you know what I mean.
Nicky: Their world is intense.
Avery: It gets easier.
Nicky: Let's just see how things look before school starts.
Avery: Call me if you need me.

Nicky's shoulders slumped. A few weeks ago, he had the next four years of his life planned, and he was excited about them. Excited about living in the heart of Nashville with his brother and two of his best friends. How had one fake kiss changed all of that?

Nicky heard laughter coming from the porch behind him. Over the last hour, he'd heard Sadie and Wylder run the gamut through tears and some anger too. Now, mother and daughter were laughing, a safe bet he could return to the conversation.

"Becks was such a precocious child. I really don't know how he made it to adulthood in one piece." Sadie chuckled.

"Well, some things never change," Nicky said. "He's still a precocious child." Nicky closed the screen door behind him. His smile came easy at the thought of Becks as a little kid. Becks the adult was just not his favorite person at the moment.

"Oh, he can't be that bad," Sadie said, her eyes shining bright with happiness.

"No, Nicky's right," Wylder said. "Becks still needs regular adult supervision, but Sky is usually on Becks duty these days."

"I'm glad to hear you two are getting to know your cousin. It makes me happy to know my sister and her daughter are looking out for you both."

"You don't talk to Aunt Angela regularly?" Wylder frowned.

"No, darlin', I burned a lot of bridges with my addiction. I love my sister and my niece, but I put them through hell."

"Well, I'm here to talk about happier things." Wylder's smile lit her eyes in a way Nicky hadn't seen in a long time, making him think maybe he hadn't been there for her as much as he should.

"We've talked all about school and music and crushes," Sadie said.

"Crushes?" Nicky darted a glance at Wylder. "What crushes? I don't know anything about crushes. Who're we talking about?"

Wylder hit him with the needlepoint pillow she'd clutched in her lap. "Nothing you need to know about."

"Come on, Wylds. I'm your best friend. You gotta give me something."

"These lips are sealed. But since we're talking about crushes, how's my brother today? I saw you angry texting out there."

"I was texting my brother, thank you very much. You know I'm not talking to you-know-who."

"Trouble in paradise?" Sadie asked. "From what I've seen online, you two are steaming up the camera lenses all over Nashville."

Of course, she recognized Nicky because she was Beckett Anderson's estranged mom. She probably knew every sordid detail of Becks' life from the tabloids and gossip sites.

"Um... We just don't see eye to eye on PDA issues." Nicky's cheeks warmed. He couldn't tell anyone—not even Becks' mom—that the relationship was fake.

"But he's happy?" She looked expectantly at Nicky.

"Of course," Nicky lied.

"He's always been so angry with me. I've missed so much of your lives because of my addiction. Tell me about Becks, please?" She cast hopeful eyes at both of them.

"Well, he hasn't changed much since infancy." Wylder rolled her eyes. "He's always been the protective older brother. When I was little, he never treated me like the pesky little sister I probably was. He always made time for me. He played with me when I was a kid, taught me to love music, and encouraged me to play drums to annoy Dad." She laughed at the memory. "And when he was in high school and wanted to start a band with his friends, he didn't think it was weird to have his fifteen-year-old little sister on drums when the rest of *Anonymous* were seniors."

"That's because he adores his little sister. He'll tell anyone who will listen that you're the best drummer since John Bonham, whoever that is."

"Led Zeppelin, really? Oh my God, how are we friends?" Wylder dropped her head into her hands. "He's only the greatest drummer of all time—and my brother is totally wrong by the way, I'm no Bonham."

"I'm so glad you've had Becks looking out for you," Sadie said.

"Sometimes, he's like having another mom." Wylder laughed. "I remember when I was little, like maybe eight or nine and I decided to walk to Defiance Falls all by myself. I wanted to see if there was a cave behind the falls like the rumors say."

"Oh my, I hope someone stopped you. That waterfall is dangerous!" Sadie grasped Wylder's hand.

"I left Becks a note saying I was going exploring, and if I didn't come back I'd found a portal to a lost world and not to come looking for me."

"Which, of course, Becks did exactly that, right?" Nicky laughed. "He couldn't have been more than twelve himself."

"That didn't stop him from stealing Dad's car," Wylder continued. "He came flying across the park—completely ignoring the roads. He was out of the driver's seat, clucking and squawking at me like a momma hen, before I could even get near the falls. He grabbed my hand and dragged me back to the car." Wylder wiped her eyes, laughing at the memory.

"He shoved me into the back seat and wouldn't even let me talk." She rolled her eyes. "And then he couldn't figure out how to back the car up in the mud, so we had to walk all the way into town to get Dad to come help. Becks was more mad at me than Dad was. He thought it was funny. Becks argued with him all afternoon, insisting I needed to be grounded for life."

"You gotta love Becks." Nicky shook his head, staring at a point over Sadie's shoulder, lost in his thoughts. "He can be so ridiculous, funny as hell, and irritating all at the same time, but he'd protect his sister with his life and give you the shirt off his back and the last dollar in his pocket. And if he didn't have anything to give you, he'd write you a song."

"I'd give anything to see that side of him." Sadie smiled. "I've only ever seen the angry Becks."

"Angry Becks is a hard one to deal with." Nicky's hands fidgeted in his lap. "But he loves so fiercely, and I know he doesn't forgive easily. That's probably really hard for you, Sadie, but Becks is a good man. One of the best I've ever known. In many ways, he's a lot like his dad, but they tend to butt heads sometimes. I can't help but think he gets a great deal of himself from his mom. You should be proud of the man he's become."

"Oh, I am." Sadie's eyes filled with tears. "Even if he never forgives me or speaks to me again, I'm damn proud of my boy. And I'm so glad he has someone in his life who sees him clearly and loves him for exactly who he is. We should all be so lucky."

Nicky forced a smile. *Is Sadie right? Am I in love with Becks?* He wasn't ready to admit that to himself or anyone else. He'd only ever crushed on Becks, knowing it was safe because it would never be reciprocated. Nicky did not want to go down that road again with an unavailable guy. Not with someone who wasn't secure in their sexuality. But a nagging thought echoed in his mind. *Since when has Becks ever not been secure in anything he says or does?*

Sadie turned to Wylder. "I'm so proud of my beautiful baby girl, too. You kids are the best things I've ever done with my life. I just hope it's not too late for me and Becks to find some peace with each other."

"He'll come around, Mom," Wylder said. "I'll bring him with me next time I visit."

"Nicky, you'll come back too, I hope?" Sadie said. "It would be wonderful to see you and Becks together."

"I'd love to." Nicky said the words she wanted to hear. But he just couldn't see a future where he got to be with Becks in the way he wanted. And he wasn't prepared to pretend anymore. Pretending he loved Becks would only end in another broken heart, and Nicky didn't think his heart could survive losing Becks like that.

Becks:

Beckett Anderson wasn't a beggar. He didn't need to be. People came to him. They texted him without prompting, constantly worried they'd fall out of the rising star's circle.

There were few people Becks trusted, but he'd started to realize even they didn't know him. Not really.

Nari and Avery lounged on the white leather sofa in his living room, flipping through channels and bickering like the old married couple they were.

Leaning against the kitchen counter, Becks ignored them and stared at his phone. Texts popped up on his screen. Sky, Sofie, and plebes from the label. They all wanted something from him. Sofie fielded all requests from reporters as well as a lot of his personal business. Only a select few had this number.

One of them now being Nicky. All because of Becks' stupid text.

Becks: Are you okay?

What kind of question was that? Of course, he wasn't okay. He'd been used to make the country world happy, to give them a love story that didn't exist.

But hadn't Becks been used as well? It wasn't like he'd had much choice. Maybe if he'd known the whole scenario would rip Nicky from his life, he would have refused no matter the consequences.

"None of this matters." He tore the phone from the counter and threw it across the room. It hit the wall and landed on the floor with a definitive thud. "Damn iPhone. Can't even give me the satisfaction of breaking something."

Avery got off the couch and walked over to the phone. He turned it over when he picked it up. "If it makes you feel better, the screen is cracked." He held it up as proof.

Becks nodded. "It does. It really does." He rested his elbows on the counter and hunched over, burying his face in his hands.

Nari and Avery were silent for a long moment before a hand landed on Becks' shoulder. "Dude." Avery's grip tightened. "You okay?"

A harsh laugh escaped Becks' throat. That was the same question Nicky hadn't responded to. Before he could answer, there was a pounding on his front door.

Nari jumped up to answer it, letting out a squeal as she did. "Wylder!" She threw her arms around the younger girl.

Great. Just what Becks needed. His sister was here to meddle as she was so fond of doing. Wylder didn't smile as she scanned the room. Her eyes locked on Becks.

Pushing away from the counter, he faced her. "Hey, Wylds." He tried to wipe all strain from his face, becoming the happy Becks she'd known all her life. She crossed the room and surprised him by pulling him into a hug.

"Hey." He breathed into her hair. "I missed you too." Pushing her back to arm's length, he took in the dark circles under her eyes and the crease between her brows. "What are you doing in Nashville? Did something happen? Are Mom and Dad okay?"

At the mention of their dad and stepmom, she stepped away from him, pulling at the ends of her dreads. "Have you heard from Mom recently?"

"Yeah, she calls me every week."

Wylder shifted her eyes away. "Not Mom. *Mom*."

It hit him. She didn't mean the stepmom who raised them but the woman who'd given birth to them before choosing drugs over her own children.

"That's our cue to leave." Nari pulled Avery toward the door. "Becks, don't forget, the anti-hate rally tonight. Soundcheck is at three, but we can do that without you. Spend time with Wylder. Just get there by six." She turned to Wylder. "It's good to see you."

Wylder offered her a strained smile. "I'll make sure he's there."

"I don't need a keeper," Becks grumbled.

Both women shot him a look he knew only too well. The "shut up, Becks" look.

"Avery and I will take the car the label sends then." She fixed Becks with a stare. "Please, don't be late. This rally is kind of a big deal."

Avery only sent him a sympathetic smile as Nari led him out.

"You want something to drink?" Becks tried to busy himself in the kitchen to avoid having to answer Wylder's question. "Or something to eat? I could make us lunch."

Wylder set her purse on the counter. "If you make us lunch, you'll be late to your rally because we'll both be dead."

"Hardy, har, har." He slid an arm around her neck. "I have missed you."

She peered up at him with wide eyes he knew weren't so innocent. His sister had a knack for trouble. It was why he'd had to agree to be the poster boy for Defiance Academy just to get her in after she failed her junior year at Twin Rivers and ended up getting expelled.

"Now, I know you didn't come just to see my beautiful face. You asked about our mother." He refused to call the woman Mom.

"Has she contacted you?"

He couldn't lie to his sister even though it would be so much easier. "I haven't talked to her, but she's been trying to get in touch with me through Sky."

She nodded as if she'd already known that and went to sit on the couch. "So, while I've been searching for her for the past year, you could have just talked to her any time?"

He knew the tone in her voice. Wylder didn't have a temper. She didn't explode. Instead, her anger simmered until it corroded everything inside her.

He dropped onto the couch beside her. "What do you mean you've been looking for her? A year, Wylds? Really?"

She let her head fall back and stared at the ceiling. "Who else was going to do it? Please, tell me. She sure as hell wasn't going to come back to us on her own."

"Why does she need to be found?"

Wylder snapped her eyes to his. "I don't know. Maybe because she's our mother. She used to come see us. A lot."

"How do you know that?"

"Dad admitted it. He forced her to leave and paid her to never come back."

The same thing Becks had done. He didn't know whether to applaud his mother for knowing how to play her ex-husband and son or to feel sorry for her that the people who should care wanted her gone enough to pay for it.

"You did it too, didn't you?" She turned, pulling her legs up under her. "You paid her."

He shrugged. "What else was I supposed to do?"

"Um, I don't know. Try to help her? Convince her to come see us? Basically anything except telling her to stay gone."

He reached for his sister's hand, but she tore it away. "Wylds, the last time she talked to my assistant, she was out of her mind high."

That seemed to deflate her anger. "I've spent so long searching for her, terrified what I might find. I missed too many classes to make up—"

"That's why you couldn't pass junior year? You were wasting time on that … addict?"

She nodded and went on. "But I've found her now." She pushed out a breath. "And she's sober. She's been sober for a while."

Those words hit Becks with the force of a truck. His mother was sober. Could he believe it? "How do you know?"

"I went to see her. She's living in a little house in Cincinnati."

Becks stood, turning away from his sister as his mind worked furiously. He had few memories associated with his mother—none of them good. There was the time she'd taken him and Wylder with her to the park. They'd thought it was to play, but she'd only been meeting her dealer. She shot up right there in front of them and passed out on a bench.

One of the hardware store customers found Becks wandering down the street holding his sister's hand and took them home.

Becks was six. Their dad had been searching for them for hours after an ambulance took their mother to the hospital. It was the last straw for him. He sent their mother to rehab, telling her not to return until she was sober.

Every time she'd come back, the cloud of drugs veiled her eyes.

But Wylder was too young to remember that. She didn't know that kind of fear.

"Why are you here, Wylder?" He'd asked the question before, but he didn't believe she'd driven all this way just to tell him she'd found their mother.

"She wants to see you."

He paced the length of the room and turned. "Are you serious?" He laughed humorlessly. "She wants to see me? Right."

"She said the words herself."

"Probably wants to see my money. Don't fool yourself, sis. That woman cares nothing for her children."

"What happened to you, Becks?" Her voice took on a sad note. "Has Nashville really changed you this much? You sound... cold. The brother I knew in Twin Rivers never went an hour without smiling. He made everyone feel like they mattered. You were the kindest among us."

"I was an idiot." It was true. No one would have ever called him smart. They loved his music and his pretty face. He could charm anyone. And he'd used that to get ahead in this business.

But what did it get him? Fans he had to lie to? A label who forced him into terrible situations? A mother who was no mother?

And feelings he didn't want.

"Is this about Nicky?" The question was so sudden he hadn't been expecting it.

"No," he scoffed. "It's about me." That wasn't a lie exactly. In part, everything was about Nicky lately. But more than that, it had to do with Becks figuring out who he was and who he wanted to be.

"I want you to see Mom." Wylder approached him. "But I understand if you can't. I just needed to tell you she's ready for us." Slipping her arms around his waist, she peered up at him. "As for the other thing, you realize I love you no matter what, right?"

He held back the tears threatening to break free and wrapped his arms around her. "I wasn't exactly telling the truth. It's a little about Nicky."

"I know."

Mom is sober.

Those words bounced around Becks' brain as he ducked into an alcove outside the hotel. People were lined up down the block, waiting for the doors to open. The anti-hate rally was an annual event in Nashville, drawing performers and speakers from across the world. Becks hadn't looked at the list of this year's speakers, but he'd been asked to perform last minute—probably due to his current status of gay icon of country music.

And he was nothing but a fraud.

Mom is sober.

What would it be like to see her again? Did she watch her son lie to the entire world and believe the words he said?

Would she be disappointed?

He hated that he cared.

Becks knew one person who'd be mad. Nari. Because he was half an hour late. Wylder dropped him off out front before driving toward the parking garage. If he'd been with his driver, they'd have known where the back entrance was.

Instead, he stood among a sea of people who'd probably go bonkers if they recognized him. Pulling his hat down lower on his head, Becks slid the hood of his black jacket up over it. He wore oversized glasses Nicky would have made fun of him for. Darting around the corner, he tried to keep to the shadows.

If his mind had been in a better place, he'd have laughed at himself. Instead, it was just sad.

At the entrance, men in black suits guarded the doors. He needed to slip past them without being seen. If they recognized him, the crowd would demand the smiling good boy of country he wasn't ready to give them.

"Excuse me," he mumbled when he bumped into a looming man.

The man only stared him down. Becks backed away, ducking behind one of the pillars lining the walkway. He pressed himself up against it, breathing heavily. This stealth stuff was not for him.

He was about to move again, when the crackle of a radio alerted him to a guard's presence. "Have you found him?"

"Not yet," the nearby guard responded.

Becks stood impossibly still and closed his eyes, waiting for them to pass. They probably didn't even know who he was. If he revealed himself now, it would only cause pandemonium.

The breath rushed out of him when a large body slammed into his side, knocing him to the ground. Others moved in, surrounding him.

"Stay down," the guard on top of him yelled.

"What did I do?" Becks wheezed. "Can't. Breathe."

The man let up but only a little. "You're coming with us." He searched Becks' body with his hands, probably looking for weapons.

"Hey," Becks yelped. "Getting a little personal there."

The guards ignored him as they hauled him to his feet. The eyes of the crowd followed them in curiosity rather than the adoration Becks was used to.

"If you wanted a date, big guy, all you had to do was ask." Becks stumbled as they pushed him toward the hotel entrance. "Sorry, I don't get hotel rooms with people I just met." A woman stood inside the doors, her black hair tied into a bun. "Unless it's her."

"Shut up." The guard shoved him forward. Outside, people tried to peer into windows to watch what was happening in the quiet lobby. Black-clad men and women flooded the room with their presence. Becks couldn't remember this many guards at any event he'd ever performed at.

And why would they care about him?

They led him around the reception desk, pushing him into an office. Another guard led a similarly frazzled man from the room.

"Explain yourself." Two imposing men faced him, their arms crossed.

"Me? You're the ones who just abducted me." He ripped the hat from his head and the sunglasses from his face. "I was just trying to go unseen."

"Young man, you were skulking in the shadows looking like some kind of troublemaker."

"Troublemaker? Me? I didn't want my fans to go nuts seeing me."

"Fans," big man number one scoffed. "Right."

"You don't recognize me?"

They both shook their heads.

"I do," a third voice came from the doorway where a young man gripped the frame in excitement. "Beckett Anderson." His mouth opened and closed like a fish.

"Ash." One of the men sighed. "You shouldn't be in here."

The young man eyed both guards. "I can be anywhere I'd like. I was looking for my sister."

"She was by the entrance."

The woman Becks saw on his way in? He could see the resemblance now. Caramel-colored skin and curly black hair. Streaks of blond ran through Ash's natural hair.

Ash rushed into the room. "I can't believe I get to meet you, Beckett. When I heard you'd been added to the program, I just... Okay, I may have squealed a bit. I'm your biggest fan." He sucked in air like he'd just run a marathon.

Becks didn't know how to take this man, but he did know he was his way out. "Well, biggest fan, can you call off the dogs? I'm late to meet my band."

"Yeah, yeah. They won't bother you anymore. I'm sorry for the inconvenience." He held out his hand. "Asher Brooks. It would be my pleasure to escort you to the dressing rooms." The kid spoke like he was a thousand years old.

"Wait, Asher Brooks as in President Brooks?"

Asher nodded. "Guilty. First kid at your service."

"So..." He pointed to the guards. "These are—"

"Secret service. Don't worry, though, I call them dogs all the time." He stuck out his lip as he grinned at his men. "You're good dogs though."

They shot him indulgent scowls.

"Come on." Asher led Becks back out into the lobby. "The rally is in the grand ballroom. There are dressing rooms toward the back." He pushed through a doorway, seemingly oblivious to the secret service agents on their tail.

How did Becks get here, walking side by side with the president's son?

The ballroom stretched out before them with grand gilded columns and a balcony wrapping around the upper levels. TV cameras had been set up on the balcony to broadcast the rally. Becks swallowed heavily.

He'd lied to so many people, but this was different. Here, he was supposed to stand up on stage to fight for people who were supposedly just like him. And yet… Were they?

"I didn't lie when I said I was your biggest fan." Asher grinned sideways.

Becks tried to recall everything he'd read about the kid. Seventeen. Gay. Artist. That was all he knew.

Asher continued. "You're paving the way for so many people. What you're doing is brave. I know how cliché that sounds and I hate it when people say that about me. But, I can't tell you how much it means to me and countless others, to see someone like us on stage." He stopped at a closed door. "We don't have long before the rally starts, so I'll leave you here. But I'm going to find you after." He shot Becks one final smile before walking away.

The door opened, revealing a frazzled Nari. "Oh, thank heavens." Grabbing Becks' arm, she yanked him inside. "We don't have much time, thanks to you. Strip."

He did as she said. Quinn and Harrison only watched in amusement as Nari got Becks ready for their performance. They'd been asked to sing two songs. One of them was called "Just Like Me." It celebrated being different and embracing who you were.

Something Becks had yet to do.

By the time the rally started and they were called to the stage, Becks was ready to jump out of his skin. He'd never been so nervous about any performance. For weeks, he'd played this role of gay singer in love with his old friend.

But now, he was supposed to stand in front of his fans, facing them as he lied.

Each part of his life collided as he stepped up to the microphone.

"Mom is sober."

"It's about Nicky."

"You're paving the way for so many people."

He closed his eyes, letting all his feelings pool in the fingertips currently plucking the strings of his guitar.

He liked to think he didn't care what his mother thought of him. But maybe she'd be proud.

Nicky would come back to him. He'd let Becks figure out just what it was between them. He wasn't the kind to write someone off.

And yes, he was paving the way.

Because Beckett Anderson stood on the stage at an anti-hate rally finally ready to see who he was.

He leaned in to the mic. "Hello, Nashville."

They cheered. Some chanted his name and held up rainbow flags. He smiled at the sight. "I'm Beckett Anderson. Now that I'm here, this party can start. I love you guys." He flashed them a brilliant smile.

Harrison counted out beats on the drums before the rest of them joined in, playing Becks' newest song, "Just Like Me."

Becks sang like everything in his life was dependent on that one song. The crowd picked up the chorus and sang it along with him.

As soon as the band finished their second song, the stage manager rushed them off to prepare for the next act.

Becks found Asher waiting at the side of the stage.

"That was amazing." Asher wiped a tear from his eye. "That song."

Becks grabbed Asher's arm, but dropped it when a secret service agent moved in. "Come with me."

Asher nodded, giving his secret service a signal to let them know he was okay. Becks entered the dressing room and shut the door as soon as Asher was through.

"Look, kid," he started. "I can't be your role model."

Asher's smile dropped. "I never said you were my role model. I said you were blazing a trail, and you are."

Becks sighed. He didn't know why the honest, open face of Asher Brooks hit him so hard. He'd been lying to people for a while now, but being face to face with someone taking hope from his lies made it impossible to keep going.

Asher's eyes softened in sympathy. "Did you and Nicky break up?"

It was a personal question from a complete stranger, yet it constricted something inside him. "No."

"I know you don't know me, and I know people don't think they can approach me because of who I am...but you look like someone who has been broken."

"It wasn't real!" The words burst out of Becks. He sank onto the red velvet couch along the wall and buried his head in his hands. "None of it was real."

Asher shifted between his feet. "I...um..." The eloquent teen was at a loss for words.

Way to go, Becks, he thought. *Ruining kids.*

After a long moment, Asher dropped down beside him. "I won't begin to try to understand what that means..."

"I'm not gay." There, he'd said it. He was out of the closet, a straight man. Right?

Asher pinched his lips together. "Okay."

Becks sighed. "I asked him to pretend. After I kissed him at the music festival, I couldn't very well tell the world I hadn't meant it. They were already writing our love story."

"Why not?"

"What?"

"Why couldn't you tell the world?"

Becks shrugged. "My career, man. I'd have been torched."

"I gotta admit. I kind of feel like you just told me Santa isn't real." His shoulders slumped.

The door to the dressing room burst open and Nari rushed in, the excitement from the performance still on her face. Her eyes widened when she saw who Becks was with.

Asher recovered quickly. "Nari Won Song." He stuttered over her name. "You...you're..." He blew out a breath, his cheeks going red. "Kind of amazing."

A slow smile spread across her face. "Thank you. I'm going to go find Sofie. Quinn and Harrison are hanging backstage and could probably use something to drink." She backed out of the room.

Asher whistled. "She's so talented. I can't believe I'm sitting here with Beckett Anderson right now. Or that I just met Nari Won Song."

Star struck teens weren't anything new to Becks, but this wasn't just any teen. "Don't you spend your life meeting important people? I wouldn't think we'd be anything special to you."

"How do you define important, Beckett?"

Becks shrugged and perched on the arm of the couch. "People who do amazing things, things that matter."

"And you don't think the music matters?"

"It does to me. But it won't put food in mouths or save lives."

Asher jumped off the couch and walked forward, his back to Becks. He rested his hands on his head. "I came out to my family when I was thirteen. It was both the hardest and easiest thing I'd ever done. One on hand, I've never been so sure of anything in my life." He turned. "Do you know how powerful that is? To understand exactly who you are and to choose not to be ashamed of it? But there will always be people telling me who I am is wrong. My parents fight for equality for all people, but that's what it is. A fight."

He lowered his arms, crossing them over his chest as he stared down at Becks.

How did Becks get here? Two years ago, he came to Nashville as a single face among the hordes of people with dreams of music careers. Now, he sat in front of the president's son, shrinking under his young gaze.

Asher continued. "The first time I heard one of your songs, it was being played by a secret service agent who used to think he did a good job hiding his disgust of me. I went back to the residence and listened to more. You weren't considered some gay icon yet, but still, I felt this connection to your words. You spoke to me. The day I saw the video of you kissing Nicky, I knew a wall had been broken. The story blew up, and suddenly, the chants of those protesting my rights were drowned out by a love story I could finally identify with. And that secret service agent? He started rooting for you too. The looks he sent my way changed. He no longer hated me for what I was because of your actions."

Becks couldn't look at him as the words sank in. He clasped his hands together and fixed his gaze on the rough calluses of his fingers. His hands, their talent with a guitar, brought him to this point.

Asher crouched down in front of Becks, forcing him to meet his eyes. "You want to know how I define important? When a single man with a guitar can change the hearts of those around him. That's important. When a love story can give people hope and open their eyes to the many facets of love. That's important. You're telling me none of it was real, but that doesn't change the fact that you inspired people."

A tear slipped down Becks face. "I inspired everyone except the one person I wanted to help."

Asher sat back on his heels. "We're complete strangers, Beckett, but I'm going to go out on a limb and assume that one person is Nicky."

Becks sighed. How did everything end up so messy? Was Asher right? Becks had been focusing so much on the lie he'd been blind to everything else.

"It's never okay to lie, Asher."

"No." He shook his head. "But you can't change what you did. Besides…how much of it was a lie and how much was truth? I won't pretend to know what exactly happened or why Nicky isn't here with you when the entire world thinks you're still dating, but—"

"I hurt him."

Cocking his head to the side, Asher smiled as if a big secret had just been revealed. "You hurt him? I thought everything was fake."

Becks only shrugged, unable to find the words to describe something he didn't understand.

"You claim to have lied to everyone about dating Nicky, but have you ever thought the only people you were lying to were Nicky and yourself?"

"I never lied to Nicky." The words held none of the strength he wished he had to defend himself.

"Really? Have you told him you miss him?"

"You don't know me, kid. It wasn't like that with him."

"You're right. I don't know you. But I spend my life watching people, always on the peripheral, never truly involved. That's what it means to call the White House home. I know what love looks like."

"I don't love Nicky. I'm not even gay."

Asher pushed himself to his feet with a sigh. "Is everything really that rigid for you?" He shook his head. "You don't have to be gay to fall for another man. We've all seen the pictures of you with women on your arms. Maybe, you're bisexual. Hell, maybe you're pan."

"I don't even know what that means." It was like Asher spoke some other language, one that scared Becks.

"Pansexual. It means you fall in love with a person regardless of their gender."

"I can't be in love with Nicky." His voice lowered to a whisper, only meant for himself. "I can't."

"Why not?"

Becks lifted his eyes to Asher's. The question seemed so simple, yet the answer was just out of reach.

"I… He's Nicky. My friend. The kid I always looked out for. I don't want to even consider what my life would look like without him." His throat constricted. "If I'm in love with him, if I'm…pan…I could lose him. I could lose them all." If it ever came down to a choice, he knew Avery would choose his brother, taking Nari with him.

Asher's gaze softened. "It kind of looks like you've lost him already."

He was right. The words sank into Becks, and he hunched over, curling in on himself. Had he lost Nicky? Would he never get to talk to him again as they used to in high school? Joking around and having fun.

He'd do anything to be able to kiss him again.

He rubbed a hand over his face. Everything made so much sense now. How could he let Nicky leave like he had?

Becks shot to his feet, forcing Asher to jump back to avoid a collision. "I have to go."

"Thought so."

A knock sounded on the door moments before Sofie stepped inside. Her mouth rounded. "Oh, Asher Brooks. They're looking for you. It's almost time for your speech."

Asher fixed Becks with a stare. "Important people make a difference. It doesn't matter how small." He left, joining the secret service agents waiting outside the door.

"Sof." Becks pulled her into a hug. "I need to leave."

She pulled back to study his face. He didn't know what she saw, but it brought a smile to her lips. "I'll have Harrison handle the media interviews after the speeches are done. You're going to Twin Rivers, aren't you?"

He nodded, unable to contain his grin even as guilt twisted inside him for how he'd treated Sofie.

She cupped his cheek. "Nicky is an idiot if he doesn't want you."

"Thanks, Sof." He pecked her cheek before leaving her watching after him.

Nari, Avery, and Wylder stood near the side of the stage watching Asher's speech as Becks joined them. He leaned in close to his sister.

"I need a favor."

She turned to face him, one eyebrow raised. "Go on."

"I want to get to Twin Rivers. Tonight."

"My car had some issues on the way here. It's probably okay for city driving, but I wanted to get it checked out before taking it on the highway again."

Another idea struck him. He watched the rest of Asher's speech, wondering if the kid was as inspired by his romance as he claimed.

"I'm sorry." Wylder touched his arm.

Would he help him?

Asher strolled from the stage with all the confidence someone his age shouldn't possess. His smile faltered when he noticed Becks. "Shouldn't you be gone already?"

"I need your help."

A grin slid across his face. "You mean I get to be part of the Beckett-Nicky love story?"

"It's not a love story."

"What love story?" Avery asked, looking from Becks to Asher. "What's going on?"

"It's nothing." Nari grabbed her boyfriend's hand. "Becks is just in love with your brother."

Becks didn't have time to consider how she'd known before Avery choked on his own tongue. "Excuse me?"

Ignoring Avery, Asher spoke into his phone before sliding it back into his pocket. "Follow me."

"Wait." Wylder called. "What about my car?"

Asher thought for a moment before turning to holler over his shoulder. "Jim!" A large, dark-skinned man ran over. "Can you take Miss Anderson's car to get it looked at tonight?" He turned to Wylder. "Give him your keys. Jim is my mom's favorite agent."

Jim's cheeks flushed at that. "Yes, sir."

Asher took Wylder's keys and passed them to the agent. "He'll get your car fixed and drive it back to Twin Rivers in the next day. I'll just tell Mom he's on a mission for me." He winked. "Thanks, Jim."

Wylder shrugged. "You crash it, you buy it." She tugged on Asher's arm and they started walking again.

Becks and Nari wasted no time trailing after him. Avery ran to catch up. "Can someone please explain what's going on?"

Asher shot him a grin. "I don't think we've met. I'm Asher Brooks, the son of the president of the United States. Currently, we're headed to the airport to board my plane."

"What about the rally?" Nari asked.

"My part is done. The congressman up next will handle the rest."

"I can't believe we're going to ride on Air Force One." Avery wrapped an arm around Nari.

Nari laughed. "It's only called that when the president is on board." She directed her next question to Asher. "What's it called with you?"

Asher shrugged. "The Love Machine?"

Nari descended into a fit of giggles, gasping for breath. "Because of Becks?"

Becks barely heard their banter as he focused on each step that brought him closer to the moment that could change his life.

"How about Flight of Love?" Asher asked as the secret service agents surrounded them near the hotel entrance.

Outside, the night closed in around them.

Becks sucked in air like he'd never breathe again. His lungs expanded painfully as nerves overtook his body. What was he even doing?

He hadn't realized he'd stopped moving until a hand landed on his back. "It's okay." Asher gave him a sympathetic smile. "He's going to forgive you for anything you did. He loves you."

"How do you know that?"

"Because this is a love story. And I refuse to follow one that doesn't have a happy ending."

Becks grunted and started walking again. "Stop calling it a love story, kid."

Nicky:

"Didn't I see you this morning already?" Brian Callahan frowned at Nicky across the kitchen at the Main.

"Hey, Mr. C, let me help you." Nicky took one of the heavy crates of produce from his boss. "I picked up another shift, trying to make up for lost time during the media frenzy." Nicky was relieved it was finally dying down now. It seemed there were much more interesting topics to fill the gossip sites than Nicky's boring life in Twin Rivers—and that was exactly what he wanted. A nice, boring, drama-free summer before school started in the fall.

"You know you don't have to make up the time. As far as we're concerned, you're free to work as much or as little as you like, but don't forget to have fun too, son. This is your last summer before college. We want you to enjoy it. Go spend some time up at the river with your friends—or whatever it is you kids do to blow off steam."

"Thanks, Mr. C." Nicky forced a smile. With the exception of Wylder, who was pretty much grounded for the summer after the stunt she pulled with the graduation party—except when she managed to sneak out—Nicky didn't really have friends in Twin Rivers. His friends all lived in Nashville. Well, his brother lived in Nashville with his friends and girlfriend. Nicky was certain he'd always be friends with Nari, but he wasn't sure his friendship with Becks would survive. The only thing Nicky really had to do anymore was work.

How sad is that? Nicky shuffled out of the kitchen to check on his remaining tables. Summer afternoons at the Main were pretty slow, but Nicky really enjoyed his job.

Grabbing a slice of Key lime pie and Mrs. Callahan's newest chocolate peanut butter cake creation, he headed across the dining room to his favorite customers.

"Hey there, Nicky, I think we're ready for dessert," Mr. Jones said.

"I'm way ahead of you." Nicky smiled. "Mrs. Jones, your favorite Key lime pie." He placed the slice in front of her.

"And what you got there for me, boy?" Mr. Jones picked up his fork and tucked his napkin into his shirt collar.

"Mrs. Callahan's new chocolate peanut butter explosion layer cake. It's disgusting-amazing, you'll love it."

"All right, that's two of my favorite things. Good job, son."

Nicky left them to their desserts. He'd learned from Peyton Callahan that Mr. Jones liked to experiment with the dessert menu, never choosing the same thing twice, while Mrs. Jones stuck to her tried and true favorite.

After refilling drinks for the rest of his customers, Nicky turned toward the kitchen to work on some of his side tasks, but he stopped in his tracks when he saw a familiar form sitting at the counter. Kenny? *What's he doing here?* He looked worn out and tired.

Nicky took a deep breath and stepped behind the counter. "Hey, Kenny. What can I get for you?" He said it in such a rush he doubted if anyone understood him.

"Hi, Nicky." Kenny gave him a weary smile. "I'm bored, exhausted, and starving. How are you?"

"Bored and starving." Nicky managed a laugh, his tension easing slightly. "How's Penny?"

"Good." Kenny sighed. "But she's busy with her summer internship in Cincinnati, and I'm busy with hockey camp, so we don't see each other much."

"Everything okay with you two?" He didn't really want to hear the answer. Nicky busied himself pouring Kenny a tall glass of the sweet tea he liked.

"It's good." Kenny nodded. "Listen, I'm sorry I didn't handle our breakup very well." He cast his eyes down to the napkin in his hands. "I was a dick about it. I care about you, Nicky, but our lives are going in different directions. I thought it would be best to make a clean break, but I screwed that up. I've always liked Penny. You knew going into our relationship that I'm bi. She's just... She's easier."

"I get it, Kenny. I do," Nicky said, surprised by Kenny's candor. He was never one to put a label on his sexuality.

"I shouldn't have thrown her in your face like that."

"It was a dick move," Nicky agreed. "But you tend to do things like that when you feel cornered. Try not to do that with her. I want you to be happy, Kenny, but I'm afraid you're never going to find happiness until you learn to love yourself and not let your family dictate your decisions." It was the most honest thing he'd ever said to Kenny.

"Easier said than done." He brushed a tired hand over his face.

"How's hockey camp so far?" Nicky tossed a menu in front of him, steering the conversation on to easier things.

"Good, I guess. I'm exhausted and in the mood for a giant steak and a side of pork chops after a full day on the ice." He perused the menu the whole town knew by heart.

"Just good? I remember when you couldn't talk about anything else after you got accepted into the program. You were so excited." Nicky didn't like the way things ended for them, but he also didn't want to see Kenny so...depressed. Nicky scribbled an order onto his notepad and pinned it to the wheel behind him in the kitchen window.

"No, it's great, really." Kenny leaned forward, resting his elbows on the counter. "Getting to train under an NHL player with so much experience and with such a talented group of players, it's exactly what I need right now. Hockey has never been the problem. You know the ice is my escape."

"It's all you've ever wanted." Nicky knew how much Kenny needed his chance to get to the NHL. That was the only future he could see that didn't lead to Washington. The only future where he'd have the means to take care of himself so he didn't have to follow the career path his senator father had laid out for him. The NHL would either save Kenny's life or break him.

"So, why so glum? You have the opportunity of a lifetime at your fingertips. An opportunity that put you on cloud nine just a few months ago. What's the problem?"

"You, all right," Kenny snapped. "I miss you." He threw his hand up to stop Nicky from responding. "Not like that. I just miss our friendship. It turns out I don't have that many friends, and with Penny so preoccupied with her internship, and Mom and Dad in Washington for the summer. I'm—"

"Lonely?" Nicky supplied. "Yeah, I get that." Nicky crossed his arms over his chest and leaned against the back counter.

"Well, you have Beckett Anderson," Kenny muttered, and Nicky couldn't help feeling just a little too satisfied at the sound of jealousy in his tone.

"I guess I do," Nicky said, unable to tell Kenny it was all a farce. "But he's in Nashville, and I'm here." He shrugged. "And with Wylder grounded after the stunt she pulled at graduation, I find myself short on friends too, Ken. I miss that part of our relationship." In reality, Nicky would like nothing better than to salvage their friendship, but he wasn't sure that would ever be a possibility.

"I am happy for you, you know." Kenny fussed with the straw in his glass. "I hate the guy, but if he makes you happy, then I'm really glad you have someone who is so out and proud. You deserve that after all I've put you through."

"Thanks." Nicky dipped his head, surprised by such honesty. "But truth be told, I'm not sure I can really trust Becks' feelings."

"Sorry about that, I really am, but I don't think I'm quite there yet, Nicky. I can't talk about the guy you were cheating on me with. It's too soon."

Nicky's head snapped up. "Cheating? Ken, I wasn't cheating on you with Becks."

"So, he, what, just jumped off the stage to kiss you like that for no reason? I'm not stupid, Nicky, I know you've had a crush on him forever."

Nicky's face flushed red. Kenny was too close to the truth, and it killed him to maintain the lie, but he'd rather be a liar than a cheater. "He saw the way you were treating me, and the kiss was just meant to make you jealous. But it turned into more than that. I guess Becks has had feelings for me all this time too." Nicky felt like a jerk, but it was the best he could do. "That kiss started the whole thing, Ken. I didn't cheat on you. I swear. The kiss surprised me as much as anyone else."

Kenny nodded, but Nicky wasn't sure if he believed him. "Just don't let my bullshit issues keep you from a relationship that makes you happy. Becks isn't me, and anyone who sees you two together knows they're looking at the real thing."

"Order's up, Nick," the line cook called through the kitchen window.

"That's our dinner." Nicky pushed away from the counter, unable to look Kenny in the eye.

"I didn't order anything." Kenny frowned.

Nicky shrugged. "I know what you like."

Nicky found a seat toward the back of the hockey arena, not sure why he was even here. He watched Kenny on the ice with the other players. Even after two years of dating a hockey player, he knew next to nothing about the sport. Kenny never wanted Nicky to come to his games before, and he'd never pressed the issue.

But, after their conversation at the Main, Nicky realized they were both feeling down and short on friends. So, here he was, trying to be a friend to his ex.

The camp attendees had divided into two teams for a no-hit scrimmage. Nicky laughed at the thought. He might not have seen Kenny play much, but he did know the guy and could only imagine how aggressive he liked to get on the ice. No-hit would be hard for him.

Kenny stood in the center of the circle in the middle of the ice. Nicky wasn't really sure what they were doing. Kinda looked like there were preparing to dance. Both players bent over as a ref dropped the puck. They battled for it. Nicky thought Kenny won, but then the puck slid to his opponent.

Searching the recesses of his mind, Nicky tried to recall all the hockey terms Kenny had tried to teach him over the years. Deking? Was that what he was doing? There were cross-ice passes, and he thought Kenny drove down the center of the ice. Driving meant skating, right? Unless one of them came out on the zamboni-thingy. Then they'd actually be driving on the ice.

Nicky snorted to himself.

The scattering of onlookers around him gave him odd looks, but he was too focused on the ice to care.

The guys out there were fast. Nicky knew that much. He leaned forward in his seat, his eyes following Kenny as he twisted out of the way of a guy on the other team. By some magic, the puck stayed with him. He kicked it forward with his skate, almost like he was playing soccer instead of hockey. His stick moved so fast Nicky could barely follow it as Kenny snapped off a shot, beating the goaltender over his shoulder.

"That was so cool." Nicky didn't speak to anyone in particular. Why hadn't he watched hockey before? These guys weren't even the professionals yet; though one day they would be. Only the best got to go to a camp like this.

After a while, and a million line changes Nicky couldn't keep track of, the coach blew a whistle, and both teams skated to their benches.

Kenny took a water bottle and stood off to the side, holding himself apart from any of the discussions before walking toward the tunnel.

Nicky waved when he caught Kenny's eye as he left the ice, not sure if this was a good surprise or a bad one.

"Stupid idea, Nicky." He muttered at the blank look on Kenny's face. He waited until Kenny made his way up to Nicky's seat.

"Hey. Didn't expect to see you here." Kenny stood a safe distance away.

"Thought maybe we could do the friend thing." Nicky shrugged.

"You drove all the way here to watch us scrimmage?"

"I rode with Wylder to see her mom and just had her drop me off here." It was a lie. She was in Nashville, but if the night went as he'd planned, Kenny would never know about the fib. "So, I don't know. I thought we could hang out or something." Nicky felt ridiculous and totally out of his element. There was way too much sporty brouhaha happening in this arena.

Kenny laughed. "How much do you hate this?"

"It's actually kind of cool, but I'm a fish out of water here." Nicky smiled. "I'm also bored out of my mind just working at the Main every day. I could use a night out. As friends."

Kenny glanced down at his feet uncertainly before he finally nodded. "As friends."

Nicky followed Kenny from the movie theater, checking his messages as they walked down the busy sidewalk. He was having a good time with Kenny and wasn't ready to call it a night yet. And it seemed neither was Kenny.

"I'm starving."

"You had like three buckets of popcorn." Nicky laughed, always amazed by how much Kenny could eat. It was nice spending time together like this. It felt...normal. The whole evening reminded him that even before all their relationship stuff happened, they were friends. Nicky had missed that friendship.

"That was a snack. I'm ready for a meal. Let's go get some seafood. Or pasta? What are you in the mood for?"

"Wylder's waiting for me, so I've got to head back."

"I can give you a ride home." Kenny stopped at the crosswalk. "Or just tell her to meet us at the restaurant, and we'll all hang out."

"Really?" Kenny had never wanted to hang out much with Nicky's friends before. That was part of dating someone who wasn't out yet. But they weren't dating now.

"Of course. I've always liked her, she's hilarious. I just don't think she cares too much for me."

"Well, now that we're just friends, she likes you a whole lot more. But she's actually in Nashville right now." Nicky's face flushed red.

"You totally lied?" Kenny laughed.

"Yeah, I didn't want to tell you I drove to the arena on the off chance you'd want to hang out. Sounds pretty pathetic." Nicky shrugged sheepishly.

"Oh, hey, Thai food." Kenny gestured at the restaurant across the street. "You feel like Thai?"

"I could eat my weight in some Pad Thai right about now." Nicky breathed a sigh of relief.

"Perfect. I'm getting spicy basil rolls to tide me over till the real food is ready." Nicky and Kenny walked side by side across the street, laughing and enjoying each other's company in a way they never had as boyfriends. It felt right, just being friends. Their relationship had never been easy, and he often wondered if they'd just tried too damn hard to make it work.

"Hey, Nicky?" A camera flashed in his face. "Where's Beckett? Does he know you're cheating on him with the senator's son?" Another camera flashed, and someone stuck a microphone in his face.

"Kenny, what's it like as a gay teenager with ultra-conservative parents?"

"I'm not gay," Kenny insisted. "Nicky and I are just friends."

"So, your politics aren't in line with your father's?"

"Nicky, can you give us a comment on the rumors that say you have a fetish for famous straight boys?"

"Oh, come on!" Nicky laughed as he whirled around to face the swarming media circus. "If you knew me at all, you'd know how ridiculous that statement is. I'm not a fame seeker. I went to high school with Beckett Anderson, and I've known Kenny since we were kids. Twin Rivers is a small town, guys. I'm not news. I'm not a juicy source for gossip. I'm a regular gay kid out with my straight friend, Kenny. We're grabbing some Thai food, and then I'm going home...alone. How is that a headline for your gossip sites?" Nicky threw his hands up in disgust and tried to walk away.

"What's the status of your relationship with Beckett?"

"No comment!" He could feel his cheeks flushing red with anger.

"Did you know Beckett Anderson performed at a political rally today? He spent the day hanging out with Asher Brooks, and the two left the rally together under some strange circumstances. We hear the president's son has quite a crush on your man. How does it make you feel that Beckett might be moving on?"

Nicky felt an unreasonable stab of jealousy at the mention of Asher Brooks. He was a total hottie and a teen gay icon. Nicky had to remind himself that Becks wasn't gay and wouldn't be interested in Asher anyway. But his jealousy refused to listen to that logic.

"Just leave us alone, please." Nicky sighed.

"Doesn't look like there's an 'us' anymore," one of the reporters said.

Nicky turned to see Kenny's retreating figure as he walked around the corner, leaving Nicky to deal with the media all by himself. Nicky cursed the name, Beckett Anderson and his sexy soft lips that got him into this mess.

Becks:

"Beckett Anderson, you better still be in Nashville." Skyler's voice rang in Becks' ear through his speaker phone. He pulled it away from the side of his face to let her scream at him while he focused on the scenery rolling past the window.

Twin Rivers. Home. It felt like a lifetime had passed since he took in the small buildings of Main Street, when in reality he'd been there not long ago.

Why did life seem to have changed so much?

It kind of looks like you've lost him already.

Becks refused to let Asher's words be the truth. He leaned back in his seat, eyeing the secret service agents up front as if he didn't know how he'd gotten there. When they'd arrived in Twin Rivers, two cars met them, courtesy of Asher. Wylder glanced at him, her eyes sparkling as if it were all just some grand adventure to her.

"Becks, are you even listening to me?" He'd almost forgotten Sky was on the phone.

"Yes, cuz. What's up?" He was too tired to summon the energy to argue with her.

She lowered her voice. "You just left the rally without telling any of us."

"I told Sofie."

"Sofie is an assistant. When you abscond with the president's son, the least you can do is let the label know why you've kidnapped the most important teenager in this country."

Asher leaned over Becks. "He didn't kidnap me." He grinned. "I'm hunting love."

Wylder barked out a laugh.

Becks groaned. The kid sounded exactly like the Beckett Anderson of old—before his guts got all twisted up.

"I like that kid." Sky chuckled. "But it doesn't excuse you. He's the first son, Becks, and he just left a rally, ignoring all his press responsibilities after the speeches. And he left with you! The most prominent gay star in country music right now. Those reporters don't know you. They don't know everything was an act. What do you think they'll say about you running off with the underage Asher Brooks? Your PR team is having a fit. This doesn't look good."

Becks sighed. "Maybe I stopped caring about what looks good."

"And what's that supposed to mean?"

"Sky…I'm in Twin Rivers."

"Oh."

"Sof didn't tell you?"

"After she prepped Harrison for the interview you were supposed to give, she disappeared somewhere. I haven't been able to find her."

That made Becks smile. If Sofie was nowhere to be found, it was because she didn't want to have to tell them where Becks went. The label would alert the media and paparazzi would descend on him.

He needed to remember to give that girl a raise.

"I'm sorry I yelled at you." Her voice dropped.

"No, you're not."

She laughed. "Well, fine, I enjoy yelling at you. But, Becks, you're going to have a shit storm to clean up. So will Asher. He can't just go where he pleases, and neither can you."

"Will you hold off the guys at the label for a little while? Just give me a day."

She sighed. "Of course, I will. I take it you're there to see Nicky?"

"I don't understand it, Sky."

"Just…before you do this, be sure it's what you want."

Leaning his head against the window, he stared at the front stoop of his house as the car pulled into his driveway. The other car would take Nari and Avery to their families.

"I am, Sky. I've never been more sure about anything."

"That's good, cuz. Really friggin' good. I love you."

"Love you too." He hung up and slid the phone into his pocket before facing Wylder and Asher. "Look, I don't want to barge in on Nicky in the middle of the night. We don't have a lot of options here."

Asher grinned as he stared out the window. "A real house. I haven't stayed in one of these since I was little."

Wylder chuckled. "You live in a huge house. Remember? It's white."

"Yeah, but it's not like this. I was a kid when we moved in. There's staff everywhere. None of it is truly ours. But this…" He gestured to the small home Becks grew up in. "This is like real people shit here."

Danny turned around from the passenger seat. "We need to sweep the property."

Asher rolled his eyes. "It's Becks' house. I'm sure it's fine."

"Protocol. Just be glad your mother didn't send half the secret service to Twin Rivers when I called to tell her where we were."

At Becks' questioning look, Asher explained. "My mom used to be a lot worse. She wouldn't let me go anywhere without at least five agents. Now, she settles for two unless I go to big events. There had to have been at least a dozen on my service at the rally."

Danny got out of the car and motioned to the agent in the driver's seat. Together, they explored the yard, venturing around back. When they returned, Danny opened Asher's door.

Light flooded the porch as the front door opened and a disheveled man stood on the threshold.

"Dad." Wylder jumped from the car and rushed up the porch steps. For a moment, Becks wondered if Wylder had told their dad about her visit to their mom. By the way she hugged him, he guessed not. Wylder wasn't an affectionate person.

"Becks?" His dad stepped forward, pulling his robe tighter around him. "It's damn good to see you, boy, but do you have any idea what time it is?"

Wylder's phone screen flashed, the light setting her face aglow. "About midnight."

Becks approached his dad, relief flooding through him the closer he got. He hadn't realized how much he missed his family, especially when he spent most of his time confused. Lumbering up the steps, he wrapped his arms around his dad, his back shaking as tears came to his eyes.

Nothing made sense anymore, and all he wanted was for his dad to tell him everything was okay.

"Hey." His dad patted his back, not letting go of his son. "You're okay now. You're home."

His stepmom appeared in the doorway behind them, her brown hair loose around her shoulders and a kind smile breaking free on her face. "Beckett." When she said his name, Becks broke away from his dad and fell into her arms, releasing everything he'd kept inside. He didn't care that Wylder stood back with her jaw hanging open or that Asher watched silently.

He couldn't be the happy guy who never let anything affect him. Not anymore. Wylder knew where their mom was and even went to see her. Nicky wasn't speaking to him. He'd convinced the president's son to sneak away from Nashville with him to chase something Becks didn't even understand.

"You're going to be fine," his stepmom cooed.

"Becks never cries," Wylder whispered to Asher. "Ever."

But he barely heard her as his stepmom ushered them all inside.

"Um, Dad." Wylder kicked a toe against the ground. "So...this"—she jerked a thumb toward Asher—"is Asher Brooks."

Their dad's eyes widened as he took in the two large men in black and the smaller teen between them. "As in the president's son?"

Asher stepped forward and stuck a hand out. "In the flesh. I love your house, sir. Real people always fascinate me."

Becks wiped his face and glanced back at his bewildered dad shaking Asher's hand. "Asher seems to think he's fake or something."

"Like a robot?" His dad pursed his lips in thought. "Or some kind of clone? I guess you could be an alien in a really good disguise." His face remained passive as if he was completely serious.

Asher grinned. "I like you, Mr. Anderson."

"Come inside. You all must be exhausted. We'll get you settled, and in the morning you can tell me why you're here."

Becks loved his dad and stepmom. They didn't make a big deal over Asher's presence, maybe because they'd gotten used to having a famous son or maybe because they were just cool like that.

No matter what happened tomorrow with Nicky, being home was what he needed to feel more like himself again.

When Becks woke in his childhood bedroom, only a single thought flitted through his mind.

Coffee.

He needed coffee.

Because he was home in Twin Rivers. It was going to take a lot of the life-sustaining liquid to get him through the day.

Sounds came from the kitchen as he walked down the stairs. Pans clanged and forks hit plates. Rubbing his eyes, he entered the room.

Asher stood at the stove flipping pancakes while Becks' dad sat at the kitchen table with his newspaper spread before him.

"Dad," Becks groaned, making a beeline for the half-full coffee pot. "Tell me you're not making Asher Brooks cook you breakfast."

"He offered." His dad shrugged like it was no big deal.

Asher grinned, wiping his hands on the "Who's your daddy?" apron his father always wore.

"Real people stuff again?" Becks filled a mug and inhaled the scent.

Nodding, Asher flipped a pancake onto a plate and handed it to Becks. It had a smiley face on it made with food coloring. Becks gripped his shoulder. "You're a weird dude. But I like you."

He took his plate and slid into a chair next to his dad.

"Where are your secret agents?"

"Doing a morning property check."

"Of course, they are." Becks laughed. "Sleep well?"

They'd put Asher on the couch after he'd insisted he couldn't take Becks' room. His agents slept on air mattresses in the living room. Before he could answer though, the doorbell rang.

"Who would be here at this hour?" Becks' dad set his paper down.

Wylder bounced into the hall. "I called in reinforcements." She pulled open the front door, letting sunlight flood the house.

It wasn't until he heard a familiar voice that Becks stood.

"Where is he?" Julian Callahan called. "Beckett Anderson, get your scrawny ass out here."

Joining his sister at the door, Becks pouted. "My ass is not scrawny." Tilting his lips into a grin, he took in the sight of his old band mate turned romance novelist. He looked older with his dark hair tied back from his face and a short beard covering his cheeks.

Becks pulled him into a hug, thumping him on the back.

When Julian pulled away, he stepped past Becks into the house. "Been a while, man."

"Two years."

Julian whistled. "I can't believe it's been that long. So...you and Nicky, huh? Can't say I saw that one coming."

"You and me both." Becks' father leaned against the door frame leading into the kitchen, arms crossed over his chest. "Now that you're home, Beckett, and awake, we can have ourselves a little chat. Julian, you stay. I'm going to need some backup."

"Bacon!" Asher sang as he carried a plate around the kitchen, freezing mid-step. "Uh, what's going on?"

Becks sighed. "They're about to lecture me on my 'life choices.'" He knew it wouldn't be as bad as that sounded. His family wouldn't care that he was whatever it was he was. Not like that made any sense.

They filed into the living room as the front door opened again, and the two secret service agents barreled through, ushering quick hellos on their way to the kitchen. Julian turned on his heel, his mouth opening.

Wylder, ever so helpful, grinned. "Don't mind them, Julian. They're just here to make sure Becks' kidnapping of the president's son doesn't end up worse than it already is."

Asher set the plate of bacon on the coffee table. "Worse than the entire world thinking we're having some torrid affair?"

Becks collapsed onto the couch. "No one is stupid enough to think that. I mean, if I'm going to cheat on my boyfriend, it won't be with such a high-profile, not to mention underage, guy."

Wylder held out her phone. "Never underestimate the media's need for viewership." An article from one of Nashville's largest papers flashed across the screen with the headline "The Country Star and The First Son: The truth behind their relationship."

Great. Just what he needed. He handed his sister's phone back and leaned his head against the cushions.

Julian eyed him, all the fondness from moments before gone. "This is going to kill him. You know that, right?"

Becks sat up. "You've talked to Nicky?"

"He works at my family's diner, remember? I see him almost every day. I've been there when the paparazzi has chased him from his car or when he's struggled—which is basically every day since you kissed him at the music festival. You haven't seen what being with you has done to him, to his life. And you're willing to throw it all away?"

"I'm not throwing anything away."

"Really? Because Nicky hasn't been the same since he returned from Nashville. Wylder has seen it too."

Wylder nodded. "He's…not Nicky."

The thought of Nicky losing any part of himself sent a wave of grief through Becks. He didn't want that. When he'd started this entire thing, he'd never imagined it would take so much from both of them.

Julian sat beside him. "Look, I used to know you, Becks. It's been a while, but I like to believe people don't change that much. The guy I knew would have cut off his own foot before hurting Nicky. You've always cared about him. Now, I know why. But you can't just show up in town with a new guy. That's not cool. You're my bro, but Nicky deserves better."

Asher inched toward the door. "I, uh, think this is a family conversation."

Julian stood. "I said what I came to say." He looked down at Becks. "He's off today. Just in case you were wondering. He'll probably be at home since Avery is in town too." He followed Asher out, beckoning to Wylder to join them.

Becks looked up to find his stepmom in the doorway. She smiled at him, but she didn't come into the room. "I have to go open the hardware store for the Sunday afternoon rush." When her husband tried to rise to join her, she nodded toward Becks. "Stay. Spend some time with Becks. I can handle things on my own for a few hours." She offered Becks a smile. "Love you, kid."

"Love you too, Mom."

She placed a hand over her heart and turned on her heel to leave.

Silence stretched between Becks and his dad. Becks watched the door his stepmom had walked through as it shut behind her. "Did you know?" His voice was quiet. Suddenly he needed to know why his dad let it happen, why he allowed Wylder to search for their mom after everything she'd put them through.

His dad, seeming to understand what he was asking, leaned back in the chair, his shoulders dropping. "Not until after she went to see her."

"I can't talk about it with Wylder. I sort of yelled when she told me. She doesn't understand. She doesn't have the memories I do."

"People change, Beckett."

But Becks was with Julian on that subject. People didn't change that much. He still wasn't sure he could trust the woman who chose drugs over her own children time and again. "Do you trust it? Her sobriety?"

"Son, I'm not sure it matters if we trust it. Only that your sister does. You have a decision to make. You can take a risk on Sadie, hoping she doesn't hurt you again but acknowledging the possibility. Or, you can decide she's out of chances. But you can't get angry with your sister for making her own choices concerning her relationship with her mother."

"I know." A headache pounded at his temples. It was all too much. Nicky, his mother, and trying to keep his music career from ending before it even truly began. Every decision seemed to have consequences attached to it.

His father moved from the chair to sit beside him on the couch. "Do you want to tell me why you broke down last night? It was very un-Becks-like. Usually we have to pry any kind of emotion out of you. It's like you put on this face for the world—the happy guy who doesn't need smarts because he has the looks and the charm. You just forget we're your family. We know the real you."

A tear rolled down Becks' cheek, and he wiped it away. Another replaced it. His father was right. Emotional moments were rare for him; they always had been. And yet here he sat for the second day in a row with tears in his eyes. Lifting his face to his dad, he sucked in a breath. "Do you? Dad, what if you found out you didn't know me at all?"

His dad wrapped an arm around his shoulders. "Is this about dating the St. Germaine kid? Becks, I was only joking before. It's okay that you didn't tell us before telling the entire world. I don't get to decide how you reveal such a big thing about yourself. If you felt more comfortable with the way you did it, then that's all I want for you. You know we love you no matter what, right?"

Becks' shoulders shook as he rubbed his eyes. "It wasn't real, Dad. Nicky and I… We lied to everyone. I kissed him at first just to help him with his ex, and then it turned into this gigantic thing I completely lost control of. We've been pretending to date since then."

His dad leaned away from him, confusion contorting his features. "Why would you do that, kid?"

None of the reasons he'd had before seemed to matter anymore. He could have told the label no. The lies he told in interviews could have been truths. The kiss at the music festival…

If that hadn't happened, none of this would have been necessary. Hunching forward, Becks buried his face in his hands. "I don't know. I really don't know."

"Why are you in Twin Rivers then? Did you do something to Nicky? Is that what Julian meant? I'm just confused, Becks. You're telling me you weren't dating Nicky, that you aren't truly gay, but you showed up in the middle of the night with the president's son, of all people."

"The kid's just trying to help." Becks pushed himself from the couch and paced the length of the room before turning to walk back. "I…" He shook his head, unable to tell his dad how he felt, that it all started as some publicity stunt but now he needed to see Nicky as much as he needed his next breath.

"Ah." His dad stood to face him. "Can I answer your earlier question?"

"Which question?"

"You asked me what I'd do if I found out I didn't really know you at all. I know you're confused, Becks. But I'm not. You're my son. No matter who you fall in love with, you will always be the same person to me. It doesn't change who you are, not really."

"And who am I, dad? Because I don't know the answer to that."

"Look at me, kid." He met Becks' eye. "Beckett Anderson is the best man I know. He took care of this family even as a kid when his mother left. He has always protected his sister, his friends, and anyone else who needed it. I have spent the past twenty years amazed by your kindness." He tapped Becks' chin. "Your fans don't love you because of the handsome looks you inherited from me. They see someone to aspire to, someone to relate to."

"I screwed up, Dad."

"I know, kid. But it's not the first time, and it won't be the last. Do you remember what I used to say to you and your sister when you were kids?"

"The single most powerful thing is the truth."

His dad nodded. "Whatever your truths are, I think it's time you start telling them. Talk to Nicky."

The truth. He could do that. A smile brightened his face. "You're kinda good at this parenting stuff."

His dad laughed. "Well, you've always been good at the ornery kid stuff."

His father draped an arm over his shoulders. "Now, the son of the president of the United States has made us breakfast. It's probably a good idea if we go eat it. I don't fancy having the FBI tap my phones."

"Dad, Ash can't make that happen." He shook his head with a laugh. "Besides, what are you saying on the phone that would pique the FBI's interest?"

"Wouldn't you like to know?"

Truth. He could do this. Becks, Wylder, and Asher stood side by side by side on the sidewalk in front of the St. Germaine house, staring up at the modest home. Once upon a time, Nicky and Avery lived in a massive home—before their drunken father drained their bank accounts with his gambling problem. In the two years since, he'd been to rehab and managed to stay sober.

Becks couldn't help but think of his mom. Rehab changed the lives of every member in the St. Germaine family. They were healing from years of troubles. Maybe Sadie was capable of the same.

"Are we going in?" Asher asked. His secret service agents stood at a distance, giving him space. Becks couldn't help but wonder what Asher's parents thought of the first son traipsing around some small town when he was supposed to be home.

A honking horn jolted Becks from his reverie, and he turned to find Nari parking her mom's van along the street. As she got out of the car and walked toward them, he noticed she'd shed her usual rocker looks—ripped jeans, a tight shirt, and pink highlights—in favor of the leggings and oversized sweatshirt combo she would've worn in high school.

"What're we doing?" A smile flashed across her face.

"Becks is trying to work up the nerve to talk to Nicky," Wylder answered.

"And failing," Asher added.

"Well." Nari crossed her arms. "Standing out here won't help. Nicky left about half an hour ago. I'm just picking up Avery to go meet him at the river."

"The river." Of course. It was where their old group of friends seemed to spend too much time. Years ago, they'd lost a friend to the falls when a car carrying three boys went over. Avery was in the accident along with Julian's twin brother.

Since then, a lot had changed, and the river became something of an obsession.

Piling into the back of the black town car, Becks leaned his head against the window. He wasn't even sure what he wanted to say to Nicky, how he'd tell him about feelings he didn't quite understand.

The ride to the river was quiet, and by the time Danny opened the door to let them out, Becks' heart hammered in his chest. It wasn't supposed to be like this. He'd had a plan. He'd pretend to date Nicky and then go back to being his friend. The only future Becks couldn't fathom for them was not being in each other's lives at all.

The park spanned this section of the river all the way to the falls with expansive grassy hills. But Becks knew exactly where Nicky would be. The falls held terrible memories for the town, yet they were mesmerizing in their own way.

He didn't notice if Asher and Wylder followed him or if Avery and Nari arrived because, as he crested the hill, his steps faltered. Nicky lay on his back looking up at the cloudless blue sky. In his sleeveless shirt, he rested his toned arms behind his head.

But it was the person keeping him company that had Becks wanting to turn around. Kenny sat with his legs curled under him staring out at the tumbling falls. The thunderous water drowned out the beating of Becks' heart as he watched them.

Asher caught up, huffing out a breath. "Man, you gotta slow down. Holy shit." He froze, recognition sparking in his eyes when he spotted Kenny. Becks didn't have time to wonder about that because Nicky's head jerked up, his gaze crashing into Becks.

He couldn't do this. Not when Nicky looked so content with his ex. He'd moved on from the fakeness of what they were. It only served to remind Becks none of it was real. None of the kisses held meaning. The stolen looks were only fodder for the cameras.

Ignoring Asher beside him, Becks turned and marched back up the hill, ready to return to Nashville and try to forget these feelings.

A hand gripped his arm. He stopped moving but didn't turn.

"What are you doing here?" Nicky dropped his hand.

Becks didn't answer as he inhaled deeply, trying to calm the emotions swirling inside him.

"Beckett." A pleading note entered Nicky's voice. "Please. Answer me."

Without another thought, Becks whirled around, pulling Nicky into a bruising kiss. After a moment of hesitation, Nicky yanked Becks closer, returning every bit of fire. But it was over as quickly as it started. Nicky put a hand on Becks' chest, forcing him away.

"There aren't any cameras around." His chest heaved.

Becks ran a hand through his hair, shifting his eyes away. "I know."

"Then why would you do that? Are you trying to be cruel?"

"What? No. I'd never intentionally hurt you, Nick-Nick."

Nicky took a step back. "I don't know what you want from me."

"I don't know either. I'm so sorry, Nicky. God, you have no idea how sorry I am. This entire fake relationship was stupid."

Red crept up Nicky's cheeks, and he lowered his voice. "Tell me why you're here."

"I..."

"Spit it out, Becks."

"I think I need you."

"You need me?"

"In my life." He met his dark gaze again. "I know I'm screwing this up again, but I don't want us to be fake anymore."

Nicky took another step back and glanced over his shoulder to where Kenny watched them. "Do you have any idea how much I wanted to hear that?" He sighed. "I had this insane crush on you, Becks. You were my brother's straight best friend, but I didn't care. Every time you treated me like I was as much your friend as he was, it made me so happy."

"You have always been my friend just as much as Avery."

Nicky smiled, but there was something sad in the gesture. "I don't think that's good enough for me anymore. While you were gone in Nashville, I spent over two years dating a guy who chose women over me again and again. I let him and kept going back because I just wanted someone, anyone. But I'm not that guy anymore. I'm not desperate enough to settle for whatever scraps confused boys will give me. I deserve to be the only one someone wants."

"I want you." Becks stepped toward him, needing him to see.

"That's nice to say right now. But how about tomorrow? Or the day after that? One day, Becks, you'll wake up and decide I was just a phase. Kenny hurt me, but it was nothing compared to what you could do to me one day. If I don't protect myself from you, you'll shatter me." His breath shuddered on its way out. He kicked his toe against the ground. "I'm sorry." And he truly sounded it.

When Nicky turned to rejoin Kenny, Becks only watched him, wondering how all of this went so wrong. This was it. It was over. Avery and Nari offered him sympathetic pats before joining Nicky, and Becks had never felt more like he didn't belong.

Nicky wasn't his. He never would be.

Wylder slid an arm around his waist, turning him away from the river. "I'm sorry, Becks." Her words held no meaning, and they both knew it, but what else was she supposed to say?

Asher's lips tugged down, and he glanced at Kenny once more before turning away. "I can't believe someone like Nicky is friends with Kenny Montgomery."

"Friend of yours?" Wylder asked.

"He was once. Now he's just a jerk who does the bidding of his bigoted senator father."

They kept talking, but Becks didn't hear a word they said. He climbed into the car and closed his eyes, willing the tears to come. Unlike the night before or even this morning with his father, they stayed trapped.

His phone buzzed in his pocket, and he answered it without thinking. "Becks, when are you coming home?" Skylar sounded tired.

Becks knew the feeling. "Today, cuz." As he said it, he realized that was what he needed. Twin Rivers wasn't where he wanted to be. Not anymore. Nashville called to him. He refused to let this fake relationship affect his music career, and he didn't want to lie anymore.

It was time for him and Nicky to break up in the media.

He got off the phone with his cousin after she told him she'd gotten him on a commercial flight since he didn't have a car with him. Nari would fly back a day later to join the band in the studio.

Asher sighed. "I don't want to go back to Washington after this soap opera."

"The show's over, Ash." It hurt to say the words. "It's so over."

"I never imagined this love story wouldn't have a happy ending."

"I kept telling you not to call it a love story." Maybe those didn't exist.

After dropping Wylder at home and stopping to say goodbye to his parents at the hardware store, Becks had Danny drop him at the airport. He pulled a baseball cap down low on his head and stuffed his hands into his pockets.

By the time he sat in his first-class seat for the short flight home, exhaustion overwhelmed him with a world-weary tiredness that had nothing to do with a lack of sleep.

Nicky:

Nicky watched Becks walk away with Wylder, his shoulders hunched, looking like he wanted to let whatever weight he was carrying finally crush him.

"It's okay, Nicky." Avery draped his arm around his little brother. "I'm behind you a thousand percent in this, but I think you might have just broken his little Beckett heart."

"No, I didn't." Nicky shrugged away from his brother, turning back to see Kenny and Nari staring at him. "I'm just me. A nobody. He's Beckett Anderson, and whatever he's got going on in his head right now, it's just a phase. I will not be anyone's experiment. Ever again." Nicky walked away, heading in the opposite direction of Becks and his sister. He just needed to get away.

"Nicky," Kenny called, but Nicky walked faster. He didn't know where he was going, but he wasn't staying here. He needed a change. Needed to get out of Twin Rivers. And Nashville no longer held the bright future it once had.

Nicky surged through the cool water, relishing the silence beneath the pool's surface. The pictures from his night out with Kenny had hit the gossip sites in the last few days, and he was suddenly in the limelight again. They showed his picture with Kenny, laughing and smiling, right before they'd realized the media was on them. They just looked like two friends having a good time. Anyone could see that. But the stupid media had shown their picture next to one of Becks looking sad and alone just hours after his performance at the Nashville rally. The article called Nicky a heartless fame seeker and social climber hell-bent on ruining Kenny's reputation and breaking Becks' heart all in one fell swoop. Becks came out smelling like a rose while Nicky was labeled a Black Widow. Since then, he had fallen into a cycle of working and hanging out by the pool at home. At the rate he was going, by the end of the summer, he'd have a full bank account, a toned swimmer's body, and one hell of a tan with little else to show for his last free days before college.

Emerging from the depths of the pool, Nicky made his way up the steps, cool water streaming down his back. "What are you doing here?" Nicky frowned, wiping the water from his eyes.

"I don't really know." Kenny toed the tiled edge of the pool with his shoe. "I just wanted to see how you were doing."

"I'm fine." Nicky crossed the deck to the lounge chair to retrieve his towel. He didn't like the way Kenny was looking at him—like a man half-starved.

"The way the media is treating you isn't fair."

"No, it's not, but I've learned these things tend to blow over if you just give it time. I suppose your dad is giving you hell about the pictures?"

Kenny nodded with a sigh, taking a step toward Nicky. "It's so stupid. We weren't even doing anything. It's like I can't even be friends with a guy these days."

"Well, to be fair, your other guy friends probably aren't media magnets."

"I don't really have other guy friends. Or friends really."

"You have Penny."

"Yeah, Penny's the perfect girlfriend for the politician's son. Dad loves her. She's heading to Yale in the fall to major in political science. I'll see her in Washington…if I decide to spend more time there next year."

"I hear a 'but' coming," Nicky said.

"But, I don't want it—the life my parents want for me."

"Then why force yourself to be something you don't even want?" Nicky took a step toward him, concerned for what lay ahead for Kenny. He feared he'd never have a chance to be his own man; whether he was bi or straight didn't matter as much to Nicky anymore. Kenny deserved a chance to be the man he wanted to be.

"I don't know." Kenny shrugged. "I thought if we broke up I could spend the summer getting over you, and then you'd leave in the fall, and I could finally put you behind me, and everything would just be so much easier."

"And how's that plan working out for you?"

"It's not." Kenny's shoulders sagged. "I miss you. I miss our friendship too, but I miss us more. More than I thought I would." Kenny's hungry lips found his, taking Nicky by surprise. The familiar warmth stirred up so many emotions inside Nicky as Kenny's hands ran up his damp chest—but one thing he didn't feel surprised him even more. Desire. Whatever he'd once felt for Kenny was gone.

Nicky stepped away, breaking their kiss. "No." Nicky turned away from him, running a nervous hand through his wet hair. "You can't keep doing this to me, Kenny. It's not good for either of us. We are not good for each other. I see that now, and it's only a matter of time before you see it too. I will always be your friend. No matter what, you can count on that. But I've moved on."

"With Beckett Anderson." Kenny said his name like a curse.

"It's not going to work out for me and Becks. I really don't know where his head is, but...the heart wants what the heart wants. I care about him. Always have." It felt good to admit it out loud. Nicky couldn't ignore the declaration Becks had made at the river.

"I don't want us to be fake anymore. I want you." And God help him, he wanted Becks too, but the media frenzy that swarmed around him might make that impossible.

Nicky took Kenny's hands in his. "I mean it when I say I'm your friend. I want you to be happy, Kenny. I want to see you live your life on your own terms. If that ends up being with a woman or a man, it doesn't matter as long as you're happy with yourself."

"I'm sorry I'm such a mess." Kenny's eyes shone with tears. "I just don't think I know how to be just friends with you. At least not yet."

"We will figure it out. I promise, but right now, I need you to go."

"Nicky, would you mind running across the street to Andersons's Hardware to pick up a few things for me?" Mrs. Callahan asked. "You can take their lunch order over too and chat with Wylder for a bit."

"Sure thing, Mrs. C." Nicky took her list and some cash for the supplies and darted out the side door of the restaurant, eager for a chance to catch up with Wylder. He hadn't seen her much since she got back from Nashville. These days she spent most of her free time getting to know her mother.

Nicky didn't see them until it was too late. The swarm of paparazzi cut him off from his escape back inside the Main. The first few times this happened, he'd panicked. But now he was just pissed off.

"Hey, Nicky, what do you have to say for yourself?"

"Nicky, how could you break Beckett's heart like that?"

"What does Kenny have that Beckett doesn't?"

"Beckett's fans deserve an explanation."

"Get off my back," Nicky shot over his shoulder, trying to make it through the media frenzy to the other side of the street, but they blocked him.

"Give us a comment, Nicky." Microphones shoved into his face. "What's your relationship status?"

"My status is none of your business. That's the only comment you're getting from me today, so you might as well go home." Nicky shoved and elbowed his way through the cameras, but he wasn't getting anywhere. A horn blasted behind them. A very familiar horn from Wylder's car. It sounded like a train.

"She will run over you. I'd move if I were you." Nicky made a final shove as Wylder gunned the engine, rolling up on the sidewalk to prove her point.

"Knock it off, you vultures." Julian's voice carried through the crowd buzzing around for a piece of Nicky's soul. "You need to take this shitstorm across the street and let Nicky get back to work. Or we'll call the cops again and let them escort you out of town." Julian shoved and kicked his way to Nicky's side.

"Thanks, man." Nicky ran a hand through his sweaty hair, looking for a way out, but they were out for blood today, and it looked like he was trapped with Julian now.

"Move. Get out of my way, you bloodsucking turds." Nicky watched as Wylder elbowed her way through the media crowd. "Don't be a dick, and I won't stomp on your foot." She shoved through the last of the paparazzi with their cameras flashing.

"Let's get you out of here." She wrapped an arm around Nicky's waist. "Help me get him in the car."

With a shit-eating grin plastered to his face, Julian wrapped his arms around Nicky's waist and turned to the cameras. "We've got your title for your next headline right here. Check us out. We're a thrupple." He and Wylder made a show of kissing Nicky's cheeks as the camera flashes exploded.

The three of them made it through the throng of paparazzi to Wylder's car idling on the curb.

Wylder threw the passenger door open for Nicky. "Get in." She shoved his head down.

Nicky scrambled into the car as Julian climbed into the back seat. Wylder took off before he could get the door closed behind him. "What the hell was that about? And what did you just do, Julian? They won't treat that like a joke, man, you made it worse."

"You haven't seen it?" Julian asked.

"Seen what? How could they possibly have anything worth showing? I've been a hermit since the last photo."

"Check the sites." Wylder tossed him her phone and drove like a maniac out of town.

Nicky turned to watch the line of media vans following them. "I am not that interesting. Why don't they just give up?" He dialed the number for the Main and put it on speaker so he could search the gossip sites for whatever they were in a tizzy about now.

"Main Street Diner," an agitated Sophia Callahan answered.

"It's Nicky, I'm so sorry—"

"Oh, thank God. Are you okay, sweetheart? I saw them gang up on you and sent Julian out to help."

"Wylder rescued us."

"I was just heading in for my shift when I saw those jerks on him. Sorry, Mrs. C, I kidnapped your waiter." Wylder gripped the wheel tighter.

"It's okay, kids, just go somewhere they can't find you, and we'll handle the rest of Nicky's shift."

"I'm so sorry this keeps happening."

"Don't you worry about it, Nicky. We are all behind you."

"Thanks, Mrs. C." Nicky ended the call just as his eyes landed on the pictures. "How the hell did they get this?" Nicky felt violated that such a private moment was broadcast across the internet. That somehow his last moments with Kenny were so newsworthy someone hid in the trees behind his house and recorded the whole thing in a series of photos. Kenny's desperate kiss. The way his hands slid up Nicky's bare chest. The way Nicky held his hands, an intense look on his face. It all looked so clandestine and steamy when it was nothing of the sort.

Poor Kenny was back in the limelight with his sexuality once again called into question. It was disgusting and a huge invasion of his privacy.

"Oh no," Nicky whispered, tilting his head back against the headrest. "Has he seen this?"

"Kenny?" Wylder cast him a wary look.

"No. Has Becks seen this?" He felt sick. Like he'd been caught cheating on the one person he really wanted to be with.

"I don't know. Probably. The whole world has seen it by now."

Becks:

If there was one place that could make Becks forget all about the turmoil in his life, it was the studio. His band mates provided a wall of support between him and the outside world as they each did their parts to make the best music they could.

Becks shot Nari a grin as he leaned toward the microphone. Here, he felt like himself. Here, he belonged.

Nari, Harrison, and Quinn sat on the other side of the soundproof glass, and it made him feel like a caged animal at the zoo. But he didn't care. They'd each take their turns in the booth, laying down their parts of the song. This one only had vocals from Becks, but their instrumental parts drove the emotion.

He could hear it now. A heavy drumline taking the listener on a ride. Nari's piano would provide a sweet melody in contrast to the harshness of the drums, complemented by Quinn's bass. As soon as he'd started writing the song, Becks knew it would be a hit. He could feel it.

In the week since returning from Twin Rivers, he'd shut himself up in his house finishing the songs for their second album. Today was their second consecutive day in the studio, and he thought he'd be tired after a grueling day one where they didn't leave until one in the morning. But he didn't. Instead, adrenaline pumped through his veins.

Music, he could do. Music never let him down. It never abandoned him or left him standing like an idiot after confessing his feelings.

It loved him back.

He sang the last few words, lowering his voice into just above a whisper. Nari told him the tone was sexy, and he needed to play to that side of himself. SexyBecksy. That was what the fans wanted. It was what would save him once he revealed his supposed breakup with Nicky.

He'd put it off, telling himself he wasn't ready for everything to be over, but they were leaving to go on tour in two weeks at the beginning of August. He was running out of time.

The tour with Etta Morelli came at a perfect time. He'd done what the label asked of him, pretending to date Nicky. They wouldn't pull him from the tour now. It was exactly the distraction he needed.

The sound producer's voice came over the intercom. "I think that's the one, Beckett."

Becks breathed a relieved sigh. "Good. That's good." They could move on. There were two more songs they had to get right before leaving town.

"Come on into the booth."

He nodded and pushed the door open. His band lounged on leather couches, laughing about some nonsense. Sofie waited along the wall to hand him a towel.

"Thanks, Sof." He took it and wiped his sweaty face.

"You sounded fantastic." She smiled, and for a moment, he wished he could have fallen for his assistant. It would have been so easy. She'd never have left a freaking hole in his chest.

Pasting on his patented smirk, he bumped his shoulder into hers. "I was pretty good, wasn't I." When it came to music, he'd never had a problem with confidence.

"All right, all right." Nari stood, eyeing him behind her thick glasses. "Stop with the compliments, Sof. His head is already big enough."

"Ah, Narisaurus." He stepped in front of her and wrapped his arms around her tiny frame. "You know you love me."

"Ew." She swatted at his chest. "You're all sweaty." Managing to push him away, she laughed. "I don't know anyone who sweats as much as you in the recording booth."

"It was hot in there." Plus, he'd spent the last two hours trying to get the song right while his band mates relaxed out in the much cooler room. "Besides, I don't sweat. I glisten."

She snorted. "That was so bad."

"You're just jealous you don't glisten. Or is it that you want a hashtag like SexyBecksy?" Teasing Nari always made him smile. She was one of his favorite people. He held his biceps in front of him, flexing the muscles. "I could be FlexyBecksy." He forced his pecs to twitch. "Or PecsyBecksy. NecksyBecksy? Too bad I'm not from Texas or it could be TexyBecksy."

"You're ridiculous." A grin took over her face.

"That doesn't rhyme with Becks."

Harrison and Quinn looked at him like they agreed with Nari's assessment of his ridiculousness, but Becks didn't mind. He liked them, thought of them as a sort of family, but he'd never grown as close to the two men as he was with Nari or Avery.

Thinking of Avery brought Nicky to his mind, and his smile dropped. Would it ever get easier to disassociate the two?

The sound producer turned toward Becks. "I think we're done with you for the day. Nari, you're up next."

As Nari stepped behind the glass and slid onto the piano bench, Becks left. Sofie followed him out, holding her phone in front of her. "The label wants to release a single from the new album before we leave on tour."

Becks grunted. "Which one?"

"'Love Me.'"

"Absolutely not."

"Becks." She sighed as if talking to a child. "You don't get to decide these things. It's a wonderful song, and they obviously like it enough to have it be the single."

"Sof." He stopped halfway down the long hallway and turned to her. "Do you know why they want to use that one? I've sent them better songs."

She shook her head.

"Because the entire world will think I wrote it for Nicky."

Her mouth rounded. "Oh. You didn't? The lyrics are beautiful. I guess I assumed he'd inspired it too."

"I wrote it before the kiss at the music festival, before any of this happened. It's not about him. It's not about a romantic love at all." He'd never expected to reveal the truth of that song to anyone. He wrote it when he was a teenager and didn't know what he was thinking when he submitted it for the album. The lyrics spoke of someone just wanting to be seen, to be loved, by the person who should love them more than anyone. He saw how it could be misconstrued and hadn't ever corrected anyone.

Yet, here was Sofie. A girl who cared for him in a way he wished she didn't. But she was also a good friend, had been since he first came to Nashville and signed with the label. Maybe he hadn't seen it because she was his assistant or because she'd been a friend with benefits, but she'd done more for him than he could repay.

"You can tell me, Becks." Her soft voice sank into him.

He rubbed the back of his neck, unable to meet her eyes. "I wrote it about my mom." There'd been a time he wanted nothing more than for his mom to show up on their doorstep and tell them she'd made a terrible mistake abandoning her children.

Sofie reached for his hand, and he let her take it. "Come on." She tugged. "I can't stop the label from releasing that as the single, but I can get you out of here." She tapped her phone and held it to her ear, speaking to someone on the other end for a moment.

By the time they reached the front of the building, a car sat ready to take him home. It had become a running joke how Becks didn't like to drive himself around. He preferred to sit in the back, notebook in his lap, as lyrics ran through his mind on endless loops.

Sofie opened the door for him, and he slid in, giving her a sad smile before closing the door. "Take me to Skylar's, please."

It was late afternoon when the car left Becks at Skylar's house. Saturdays were her day off, so he hoped she'd be home.

When she opened the door in pajama pants and an oversized sweatshirt, he laughed.

"You're one to talk," she snapped. "You've sweat through your shirt."

He walked past her, peeling his shirt off over his head. "I'm going to shower. I think I left some clothes here a few weeks ago. Can you find them?"

"Sure, Becks. Make yourself at home." Sarcasm dripped from her words.

"Why have you put your pajamas on this early, anyway?" he called from the bathroom.

"You're implying I ever took them off. It's Saturday. I was in bed until some jerk made me get up."

"Who would do that?"

"Oh, just shower. I'll make your highness some dinner."

"Don't go to any trouble on my account."

"You're always trouble, Becks. But before you got here, I was considering getting up for food, anyway. You only forced the issue."

"Okay." He stepped into the shower, yelling back to her. "Just don't put anything gross in mine." He couldn't hear her response as the warm water slid over his tense muscles. He rubbed his shoulders, trying to ease the pain.

It wasn't the first time he'd shown up at Skylar's unannounced. In fact, he'd made a habit of it over the last two years, usually when Nari and Avery weren't around because Becks hated being alone.

He washed himself before shutting off the water and toweling off. Skylar left a stack of clothes outside the door. Quickly pulling them on, he walked into the kitchen where she was removing two plastic containers of instant mac and cheese from the microwave.

"Gourmet." His grin didn't quite reach his eyes. Pulling two beers from the fridge, he tossed one to her. "We're such grownups."

They carried their food to the living room and sank into the oversized leather couch. Skylar studied him for a moment, and her scrutinizing gaze made him want to retreat into himself. "You saw it, didn't you? That's why you're here."

Confusion flickered across his face. "Saw what? I've been in the studio all day."

Skylar pressed her lips together, lost in her own thoughts, before she shifted her eyes to his. "I don't want to hurt you, Becks. I never do. You know I love you, right? We've only really known each other for a few years, but you're family."

"Of course. You're family to me too. Now, tell me why you look so sad." He set his bowl on the coffee table and turned to face her.

With a sigh, she reached for her phone on the table and pulled up a gossip site, turning the screen toward Becks.

He didn't understand what he was seeing at first. His brain couldn't comprehend the image. Nicky stood next to the pool in his backyard kissing some man. No, not just any man. Becks recognized him. Kenny Montgomery. The douchebag whose actions started this entire mess.

The flash of the camera reflected in Nicky's wide eyes, and it was all Becks could stare at until he saw the headline of the post.

"Country star's lover caught in a secret affair with Ohio senator's son, Kenny Montgomery."

Lover. That term sounded ridiculous. As if what they'd had was meaningless physical interactions. But it was meaningless because it hadn't been real at all. At least for Nicky.

Becks' pulse pounded in his skull louder than any drumbeat. Water dripped from his wet hair down his cheek as if mocking him for his lack of tears. He sat emotionless, feeling nothing but an empty void.

"Becks." Skylar took the phone, but he didn't respond. "Beckett." She put a hand on his cheek to turn his face to her. Her lips moved, but no sound reached his ears.

Sharp pain exploded across his cheek, and he jerked back from Skylar's slap. "Dude, that wasn't cool."

"No, what's not cool is you sitting here like some sort of zombie because your fake boyfriend kissed someone else. Yes, this is going to be a media nightmare. The picture hit this site an hour ago, so it's only a matter of time. But we can handle it. You'll look like the wronged figure and come out with even more fans than before."

When he didn't say anything to her, she sighed. "All right, it's time you tell me the truth of everything. I've covered for you enough with the label. A week ago, you hopped a plane with Asher Brooks to Twin Rivers, and I know it wasn't just to see your dad. Are you in love with Nicky?"

"Love?" he scoffed. "No." Beckett Anderson didn't fall in love. He had feelings for Nicky and wanted to see where they went, but love? He got it then. Why Nicky said no to him. Becks couldn't be trusted not to break his heart when he didn't know how to love someone. "He's better off without me." But with Kenny? Hell no. How could Nicky go back to that asshat?

Sky sighed. "You told him how you feel, didn't you?"

Becks leaned back, lifting his eyes to the ceiling. "Sort of."

"It didn't go well?"

"You could say that. He told me he couldn't be with me. He doesn't trust me."

"I'm sorry."

"I don't even... Everything is so messed up, Sky. I'm about to go on tour for the first time in my life, a big arena tour. This is what I've always wanted. Beckett Anderson is a household name. My music is played all over the radio. I've made it. Reached my dreams. Yet..."

"It's not enough?"

"Not even close."

"So...are you gay?"

"Asher told me I'm pan because Nicky is the only guy I've ever wanted. But I'm not even sure what that means."

Sky typed into her phone. "Let's Google it." She read for a moment. "Says here pan is Greek for 'all.' It means you can be attracted to a person regardless of their sex or gender identity." Her phone buzzed in her hand. She pressed to answer the call and put it on speakerphone.

"Hello."

A man's voice came through. "This is Stephen Yang at the *Country Chronicle*. As a member of Beckett Anderson's PR team, do you have a moment?"

She raised a brow. "Hi, Stephen, what can I help you with?"

"I'm running with a story on the Nicky St. Germaine affair. Would Beckett like to make a statement?"

Before Skylar could respond, Becks leaned forward. "Hello, Mr. Yang. This is Beckett. The only thing I'm going to say is that Nicky and I have had a mutual parting of ways. We realized we wanted different things." Not a lie. "And our priorities didn't match." He couldn't help his final words. "I wish him well in his new relationship. It seems to suit him better than ours—"

Sky cut him off. "Thank you, Stephen. That is all we have to say." She hung up, staring at Becks in consternation. "You gave him perfect fodder for his article. And that, cuz, is why you let your PR team make all your statements. From now on, you will have no comment on all things Nicky St. Germaine."

Becks dug into his dinner, stuffing cardboard-tasting macaroni into his mouth to avoid telling Skylar how he really felt about it. He knew the moment the words left his mouth he'd messed up.

Becks groaned as sunlight filtered in through the large living room windows. It was all so familiar. Passing out on Skylar's couch only to wake with a headache that had nothing to do with consuming beers the night before.

His phone dinged, and he grabbed it off the table, finding a list of texts he'd missed throughout the night.

Asher: I saw it. I'm sorry.
Wylder: I doubt it's as bad as it looked.
Asher: Want me to send my secret service to scare him?

Becks cracked a smile at that.

Asher: I'm serious. They won't actually hurt Nicky. Kenny on the other hand... I still can't tell if it was him in the picture. It almost looks photoshopped and we all know the media is good at twisting things around until they no longer resemble the truth.

But Becks knew it in his gut. Even if the headlines were a load of crap, he'd have known Kenny anywhere.

Wylder: You've got to respond so I know you're okay.
Dad: Son, he doesn't deserve you.

He half-expected his dad to spout off about how there were many more fish in the sea. He was cheesy like that. Becks typed out a text to Asher.

Becks: No to the secret service... at least for now. Let's hold that option on the back burner.

Next was Wylder. He didn't respond to the words she sent; instead, he said the one thing that might eclipse this in her mind right now.

Becks: They're releasing Love Me as my single.

She was the only person who'd known about the song before he sent it to the label. The title was hers even. She responded immediately.

Wylder: Maybe that means it's time to go see her?

He stared at the text for a moment before switching over to his dad's.

Becks: Plenty more fish, right?
Dad: Took the words out of my mouth, kid.

He knew his dad too well.

Once he dealt with all their worries, he pulled up "Love Me" on his phone and hit play. The lilting melody wrapped him in a cocoon of warmth, and he sang the words along with the demo recording, feeling every one of them deep in his soul.

Dusty roads.
Empty porch swings.
And all the little things
That remind me you're gone.
Love me
Want me
When you return home
I promise I'll be right where you left me

His voice drifted off, and he lifted his eyes to find Skylar in the doorway of her bedroom watching him with tears in her eyes. Suddenly, it didn't matter anymore what he said to a meaningless reporter or if the love story—as Asher called it—didn't have a happy ending.

A different kind of story could. He'd fought so hard against the idea that his mother could change. She'd abandoned him and his sister, giving up her own children. They'd been lucky to have their father and stepmom, but that didn't negate the crushing loneliness she'd instilled in them as children.

"I need to see her."

Skylar nodded. "We can go today. Wylder gave me the address last time she was here."

"She knew I'd eventually change my mind."

"She hoped."

He stood and folded the blanket on the couch. Skylar retreated to her room to get dressed as Beckett made them fresh coffee and poured it into two travel mugs. He fired off a text to Nari.

Becks: I have to take care of something today.
Nari: No worries. We still have to finish some instrumental parts. You okay?
Becks: I think so.
Nari: Okay… Becks, I need to ask you if you really said it.
Becks: Said what?

Nari sent him a link to a *Country Chronicles* blog post titled "It's over, folks: Country's favorite couple calls it quits in cheating scandal."

He scanned the article detailing Becks and Nicky's breakup. That was fast.

Beckett hopes Nicky is happy in his new relationship despite the way it started. Sources close to him says Nicky St. Germaine broke his heart when he decided to break his trust.
"His new relationship suits him better than ours ever did," Beckett said. "We had different priorities. I wanted to focus on my career, my fans, and he was never supportive, having goals that I didn't agree with. I'm hurt, but I think I'll be better off."

Becks couldn't breathe. They'd completely twisted his words, even adding some he'd never said.

Nari: Becks…
Becks: No. I mean, I said some of it, but… you know what, Nars. I can't worry about Nicky today. I have bigger things on my mind. I'm sorry, but he can't be my sole focus. Not anymore.

Becks slid his phone into his pocket, not wanting to see Nari's response. The article created a whole new mess he'd have to fix later, and not when he was about to see his mom for the first time in years. Excitement buzzed through him. Would she recognize him? What would she say when he showed up? Wylder had already been there a few times, so having her children in her life wasn't a shock anymore, but she hadn't seen Becks.

He imagined she'd smile, the act lighting up her entire face. Her arms would reach out, pulling him into the kind of hug he'd craved long after she'd left.

Sky bounced into the kitchen, snatching her coffee off the counter along with a banana. "You ready?"

"As I'll ever be." He didn't know why he'd resisted this for so long. Whatever the woman had done in the past, she was his mother. He knew how addiction worked. Was it fair to blame her for the disease?

Probably not.

It took just over four hours to get to the tiny town she called home. Ramshackle houses lined the winding roads in the hills just outside Cincinnati. By the time they arrived at a blue house with peeling paint, the sun was high in the sky.

Along the walkway, a beautiful garden with flowering bushes and yellow and white flowers spread out before them. Someone obviously spent an enormous amount of time keeping it up.

The gravel driveway radiated summer heat as Becks slammed the car door behind him.

"Do you want me to stay out here?" Skylar asked.

He shook his head, swallowing heavily. "Please. Come."

She slid out of the car and rounded it to grab his hand. A beat-up red sedan sat farther up the drive. They passed it on the way to the front door.

Becks couldn't force his arm to raise or his knuckles to rap against the door, so he stood there still as a statue.

"It's going to be okay." Sky smiled sideways before knocking.

When no answer came, she knocked again.

Panic stabbed through Becks. His mother could be out somewhere, but he couldn't shake the feeling that something was very wrong.

He banged against the door, pleading for it to open, for his mom to pull him into her arms like he'd dreamed of so many times.

"Hey, can I help you?" An older man with a bald head crossed his yard to approach them.

Becks turned to him, taking in his sad expression. "The woman who lives here is my mother."

His eyes softened. "You're Beckett. She told me about both you and your sister. Wylder's visits meant so much to her. I truly think they prolonged her life."

Something cracked inside Becks, and his knees threatened to give out. "What do you mean?"

"I'm sorry, son, I thought you knew. Sadie died two days ago. She was sick for a very long time. Cancer comes for many of us, I'm afraid. After I lost my wife, your mother helped me through it. She was a good friend." The man kept talking, but Becks couldn't hear anything over the ringing in his ears.

Sky tried to wrap an arm around him, but he pushed her away, running down the driveway. Wind from the cars speeding by slapped him in the face as he bent over just trying to breathe.

He was too late. She'd wanted to see him before she died, and he hadn't come.

Instead, he'd focused on a stupid career and a stupid fake relationship. None of it held any meaning if he couldn't be there for the woman who gave birth to him. If he'd known she was sick... He dropped to his knees. When his mother left him as a child, he'd always assumed she'd come back. It was a kid's fantasy.

This time, her leaving was permanent.

Arms wound around him, and he didn't push his cousin away again. He didn't have the strength.

"I need to tell Wylder," he whispered, the words clogging in his throat. How was he supposed to tell his little sister that the mother she'd just found was gone already?

"Do you want me to do it?"

"No." He got to his feet, wanting to be strong for the person who'd need him most. "It needs to come from me."

They said goodbye to his mother's neighbor and sat in the car, silence settling over them. Skylar retrieved his phone from the cup holder and held it out.

Becks' hand shook as he took it. His breath shuddered as he dialed Wylder's number.

And when she answered, the tears finally came.

They'd never truly known their mother. And Becks was the one who had to break his sister's heart. The crack inside him widened, and for a moment, he wished it would swallow him whole.

Nicky:

Nicky sat on the floor of his bedroom amidst a dozen half-empty boxes. He was supposed to be spending his day off packing for school. He still had several weeks before his new life at Vanderbilt University would begin, but his parents wanted to get him settled with the move to Avery's apartment ahead of schedule. They were taking a much-needed vacation at the end of the month. Nicky didn't have the heart to tell them he wasn't so sure moving to Nashville was what he wanted anymore. With a week left before the move, Nicky felt trapped.

He scrolled through the gossip sites on his phone—a terrible habit he'd developed recently, but he couldn't stop looking at Becks' final words on their non-relationship.

> *"His new relationship suits him better than ours ever did. We had different priorities. I wanted to focus on my career, my fans, and he was never supportive, having goals that I didn't agree with. I'm hurt, but I think I'll be better off."*

Nicky didn't understand how Becks could throw him under the bus like that. Not when this whole thing started as a favor to help him save face when he'd lost his mind and kissed Nicky in front of thousands of screaming fans. He scrolled through the comments from the fans, unable to tear his eyes away from the screen. It shattered him all over again to see how much they hated him for breaking Beckett's heart.

Chin up #SexyBecksy. Unfortunately, there will always be guys like Nicky who just get a kick out of breaking hearts. He's not worth it. Your #Fandersons are all behind you!

#SexyBecksy just chose the wrong guy. Fame seekers are the worst. Nicky should be ashamed of himself. And that poor senator's son better watch out for the #BlackWidowBoy.

#SexyBecksy I'll be your boyfriend. You'll never catch me kissing other dudes. #BlackWidowBoy is a gold-digging attention whore who just needs to get a job and stop trying to ride coattails.

#BlackWidowBoy do us all a favor and go back to Twin Rivers and take a dive off Defiance Falls.

#BlackWidowBoy stop trying to turn straight guys into boyfriends. There are plenty of us gays out there for you to date—if any of us would even be interested at this point. What are you trying to prove? The LGBTQ community doesn't need someone like you speaking for us. Go home.

Angry tears rolled down Nicky's cheeks, but he couldn't make himself stop reading the comments. He'd tried so hard to help his friend, and now, the whole world hated him.

After he left work last night, he found his car covered in a mess of rotten eggs and fruit. It was so disgusting he couldn't bring himself to get inside and drive it to the car wash. He could have called Wylder to come get him or asked Julian for a ride home, but he didn't want to face anyone, so he'd walked the seven miles home. This morning, he'd asked his pop to take care of his car. He just wanted to do what most of Beckett Anderson's fans wanted him to do—disappear.

A text from Avery flashed on the screen, breaking Nicky's focus on the comments. His brother had been texting him all day, but Nicky didn't know what to say.

Avery: Are you okay?
Avery: I'm sorry, Becks is an ass.
Avery: Want me to kick his butt for you?
Avery: Nari might beat me to it, she's ready to kill him.
Avery: Nicky, tell me you're okay?
Avery: Little man?
Avery: Dad told me about your car. I'm so sorry, Nicky. Something's not right about this. I don't believe Becks actually said those things. The whole statement didn't even sound like him. I'm here for you, little man.
Nicky: I'm okay.

It was all he could manage. Tossing his phone aside, Nicky stared at the boxes he was supposed to be packing. At the beginning of the summer, he couldn't wait to move to Nashville to be near Avery and Nari. And a part of him had been anxious about living near Becks again. After years of crushing on his brother's best friend, it all came crashing down on him, and he'd made a mess of it. Now, Nicky didn't know where he belonged. He brushed at the tears still burning his eyes.

"That boy is not worth a single one of your tears, son." Grayson St. Germaine's wide frame filled the doorway, the concern in his eyes did nothing to quell Nicky's tears.

"I'm okay, Pop." Nicky scrubbed at his eyes, trying to convince himself he really was okay.

"Listen, Nicky." His father came into the room and sat on the corner of Nicky's bed. "I know I haven't always been the supportive father I'm trying to be now."

"It's okay, Pop. That stuff is behind us now." At the height of his father's addiction, Nicky and Grayson didn't get along. His father was a mean drunk, and when Nicky came out, he hadn't supported him. After rehab and with nearly two years of sobriety behind him, Grayson St. Germaine was a different man. The kind of father Nicky was damn proud of.

"Well, I'm with Avery. That Anderson boy needs a good ass kicking." His pop crossed his arms over his chest. "You deserve better than that train wreck, one-hit wonder."

A laugh burst through Nicky's lips at the look on his father's face. "Thanks, Pop."

Grayson looked around the room at how little Nicky had accomplished. "You got a long way to go if you're going to be ready to move soon. Need some help, son?"

"I don't know." Nicky sighed, tossing a stack of folded sweaters into a box. "I guess I can't get excited about this move right now."

"I meant it when I said you could live in the dorms next semester. It's too late to make that change for this semester, but I don't want to see you give up this opportunity because a boy broke your heart. No man is worth that. I know living across the hall from him won't be easy, but from what your brother tells me,

Becks will be on tour soon, and you won't have to see him as much."

"I know. I just don't think I can face him at all." Nicky threw a pile of jeans into a box.

"Nicky, are you thinking about not going to Vanderbilt this year?" Grayson tried to hide his disapproval.

"No. Yes. I don't know." Nicky leaned back against the wall, pulling his knees up to rest his elbows on top. "I was so excited about going to school with Avery and living with them in Nashville. Now, I just don't know if it's worth it."

"Of course, it's worth it, son. This will all blow over in a few months. I know it won't be easy starting school with the whole country music world talking about you, but this won't follow you forever. Now, if you want to take a semester off and find another school you want to go to in January, your mother and I will support your decision, but I don't want to see you delay your education because of this drama."

"If it was any other relationship that failed, I wouldn't let it affect me like this." Nicky picked at his fingernails, avoiding his father's gaze.

"But it happened in the media, and everyone thinks they have a right to stare at you in your misery when it's none of their damn business. Believe me, son, I know what it's like to have the media's attention for all the wrong reasons. But this is Becks, Nicky." His voice grew soft. "You've had a crush on him for ages. It kills me that this didn't work out for you, but I can't stand to see you stuck in this small town where your options are so limited. You deserve so much more than Kenny or Becks. You deserve a better man, and you will find that someday. I just don't know if you'll find it here in Twin Rivers."

"I know. I'm just so tired of trying. So tired of these boys who don't know what they want."

"Go to Vanderbilt, Nicky. I want you to have the real college experience. Hang out with friends. Go to football games and have the time of your life. And maybe, you'll find a great love out there just waiting for you, but don't stop your life because it didn't work out this time."

"Thanks, Pop." Nicky smiled. "You're absolutely right." Facing Becks and the whole Nashville scene wouldn't be easy, but he didn't want to hide anymore.

"That's my boy." Grayson's wide grin stretched across his face. "Ignore what the media is saying about you because they don't know you. Half of them should just bend over and flap their butt cheeks at the cameras because they're just talking out of their asses. Anyone who really knows you won't believe this Black Widow Boy nonsense."

Nicky threw his head back and laughed until tears leaked out of his eyes. "I needed that." He wiped at his eyes. "I love you, Pop."

"Love you too, son. Now get busy packing up this room. We're leaving at the end of the week and you need to be ready."

Nicky stood in the bathroom at the Main, staring at his ridiculous reflection in the mirror. He'd always made fun of Becks with his disguises, and here he was about to do the same thing. Granted, his disguise was a lot less elaborate and consisted of a black wig from an old Halloween costume—from the year he'd gone as Elvis—a baseball cap, and dark sunglasses. He'd borrowed some of Avery's clothes too. Dressed in too-large basketball shorts and a ratty old Twin Rivers High T-shirt, he definitely didn't look like himself.

"What do you think?" Nicky turned to face Julian. "Am I trying too hard?"

"You look like any other Twin Rivers kid. They shouldn't recognize you. At least not right away. You might want to run as soon as you get past the cameras."

"All this just to walk across the damn street." Nicky wiped his sweaty palms against his shorts and headed for the door. "Wish me luck." He needed to talk to Wylder. She wasn't answering his texts or his calls. He was afraid she'd sided with Becks—he was her brother after all—but she was Nicky's best friend too. He didn't want to face the possibility that he'd lost her and Becks all in one fell swoop.

"Good luck. And be careful," Julian said. "Those guys are getting vicious."

Nicky nodded and started toward the alley exit.

"Go out the main door, Nicky," Julian hissed. "They expect you to use that door."

"Right." Nicky turned around and made his way toward the front of the restaurant.

"Let me ring you up." Sofia Callahan made a show of reaching for his non-existent ticket at the counter. "The vultures are watching." Her eyes danced in amusement as she pretended to charge him for a meal he didn't eat.

"I'll be back for my evening shift." Nicky smiled. "You know, unless they tear me apart when they realize this disguise sucks."

"You look like a young Avery. Just be careful. If I see them gang up on you again, I'm calling the police, and then I'm coming out there with a fire extinguisher to hose them down."

"Thanks, Mrs. C." Nicky turned toward the door, making a show of tucking his wallet back into his pocket.

The line of reporters had grown throughout the day. They were desperate to get his comment on the breakup. The things they shouted at him were maddening, but Nicky had learned they just wanted to piss him off so he'd say something harsh. If they could turn this into a mud-slinging contest between Beckett and Nicky, it would just prolong this media storm and make them more money selling their photos and articles. He refused to give them the satisfaction.

Nicky smiled in relief when he made it past the paparazzi lying in wait for him. They never gave him a second glance. Crossing the street, Nicky felt the first stirring of nerves. What if Wylder refused to talk to him?

The familiar tinkling of the bell at the front door to Anderson's Hardware set him at ease. There was no way Wylder would believe anything the gossip sites claimed. She wouldn't throw their years of friendship away on a misunderstanding.

"Nicky, is that you?" Mrs. Anderson asked.

"Oh, sorry." He pulled the hat and wig off. "Just trying to cross the street these days is impossible. Is Wylder here? She's not answering my texts."

"She didn't tell you?" Mrs. Anderson stepped out from behind the counter, her face a mask of concern for her stepdaughter.

"What's wrong?" Nicky frowned.

"It's her birth mom." Mrs. Anderson's shoulders slumped.

"Has she started using again?" Nicky ran a hand through his messy hair.

"No, Nicky, I'm afraid it's worse. She had cancer. Sadie died a few days ago. She never told Wylder she was sick."

"She died?" Nicky took a step back, his mind reeling. "Is Wylder okay?" This would kill her. After so many years apart, she'd finally reconnected with her mother only to lose her again?

"No. She's not handling it well. She's at home. She won't come out of her room. I thought she'd at least talk to you."

"I'm so sorry, Mrs. Anderson. I... Can I go see her?"

"Oh, Nicky, you don't need to ask. You are always welcome in our house. Wylder needs a friend right now."

Nicky dashed out of the store and back across the street before he realized his hat and wig were still clutched in his hand.

"Nicky!" The cameras flashed, and their prying questions flew at him, but Nicky kept running, ignoring their incessant chatter. He slid into the front seat of his car and gunned the engine as he fled the parking lot, forcing the reporters to get out of his way.

The Andersons lived just a few miles from Main Street, but Nicky's heart was nearly beating out of his chest by the time he pulled into the driveway. The media vultures had followed him and would likely show up any minute. He didn't want to bring this to Wylder's doorstep when she was dealing with such a loss.

"Nicky? What brings you to Beckett's childhood home?" The cameras flashed as several news vans arrived.

Rage boiled inside him. The violation of his privacy was one thing, but Wylder and her parents didn't need this. "You need to leave. Now." Nicky glared at the reporters staring blankly at him, waiting to capture his every word. "This isn't about me or Becks. The Andersons are having a difficult time now, and they need their privacy."

It was like he hadn't said a word. They continued to fire their questions at him.

"At least wait across the street. You all know you can't be on private property. So just move back."

"Will you make a statement before you leave?"

"If it will get you to leave the Andersons alone, yes." It was a lie. He had nothing left to say to them, but he needed to get them away from the house. Nicky took the steps up to the porch two at a time. The reporters retreated to their vans along the street. Knocking on the door, Nicky waited, wondering if anyone would even answer.

"Hey, Nicky," Mr. Anderson said as he opened the door. "My wife called and said you were coming to check on Wylder." He stood back, letting Nicky inside. "I appreciate it."

"I'm so sorry about all of that out there." Nicky waved at the swarm building across the street.

"Oh, we're used to it by now. They're always interested in anything they can find out about Becks and his family. I just don't want them to know about Sadie."

Nicky nodded. "This is none of their business."

"Wylder is in her room. She won't come out and hasn't eaten anything in days. I'm worried about my daughter, Nicky. She's had a rough year, and meeting Sadie again was helping. If I'd known she was sick... Hell, I don't know. Wylder needed this time with her mother, but I'm so angry with Sadie for not preparing her for this."

"You and me both. It's too much for any kid to handle. Last time I saw Sadie, she looked perfectly healthy...and so happy to see Wylder again." Nicky shook his head. "Let's hope Wylder will let me in."

"Hey, Nicky." Wylder held the door open for him after he'd knocked a dozen times. She looked terrible with dark circles under her eyes, and her cheeks had thinned from her refusal to eat.

Without a word, Nicky folded her into his arms, resting his chin on top of her head. "I'm so sorry," he finally said. With dry eyes and a faraway look, she pulled away from him.

"I'm okay. You don't have to check on me."

"It's kind of my job as your best friend to make sure you're okay. I'm always here for you, Wylds." He sank down onto the corner of the bed where she'd flung herself.

"Don't make me talk about it." Her voice was muffled among a pile of pillows.

"Of course not." Nicky crawled up beside her. "But I am going to make you eat something."

"I'm not hungry."

"That doesn't matter. You need to eat some soup or something."

"Whatever."

"And you need a shower. You stink." Nicky smiled when she hit him with a pillow.

"What in God's name are you wearing?" She finally looked at him. "You look like you're trying to be Avery."

"I kind of was." Nicky glanced down at his outfit. He normally dressed a little more fashionably than his brother, preferring skinny jeans and fitted T-shirts to his brother's more sloppy-sporty attire. "Hiding from the cameras." He shrugged.

"My brother's a jerk for making a statement at all. He should have known they'd misuse his words and fabricate more." Wylder pulled her head out of the mountain of pillows and looked at Nicky. "He didn't say all that. He cares too much about you to throw you to the wolves. Don't believe anything the press says he said—not unless Becks says it to your face."

She was right. Whatever Becks said to the media didn't mean anything in their reality. "I just wish they'd leave me alone." Nicky turned onto his back to stare at the ceiling.

"He's the one who found out," Wylder whispered.

"What?" Nicky frowned.

"Becks went to see Mom. Sky said he'd decided he wanted to see her. But it was too late. The neighbor told him." Wylder's eyes filled with tears. "Becks won't answer my calls. I don't think he's doing much better than me."

Nicky sighed, rubbing a tired hand across his face. If he knew Beckett Anderson at all, this loss was going to hit him hard, and he wouldn't know what to do. For so long, Becks held an armor in place between himself and the woman who gave birth to him, the woman who'd abandoned him for drugs. If he'd reached out to Sadie, he'd finally let that armor down only to get hurt again by her absence.

Despite all the insanity of the last few months with Becks and their fake relationship, Nicky wanted to see him. To make sure he was okay.

"I'm leaving for Nashville in a few days. Are you going to be okay, Wylds?" Nicky reached for her hand.

She curled against him, laying her head on his shoulder. "I have Mom and Dad. Go be with Becks. He needs you."

Becks:

Becks didn't need anyone. Life had taught him that. Growing up, he'd been the person people leaned on. His sister, his friends. They all needed him.

But now… Now, he just wanted someone to tell him none of it was real. He'd talked to his sister every day since learning of their mother's death and tried to comfort her as he always did. Wylder was the dramatic Anderson sibling, always had been. That wasn't a bad thing. It just meant she felt everything so much deeper than Becks ever did. And she never even tried to cover up her emotions. Sometimes they were volatile, but still, she let them show.

Unlike her brother. His cool mask settled into place as he sang the last line of the last song for the album. It felt good to lose himself in the music, to let his body sway under its own power.

He held the last note, lowering his voice to give it the breathy quality his fans loved. As the music faded and the red light above the door flickered off, Quinn and Harrison burst into the room to congratulate him. Together, they'd made a killer album.

Yet, Becks wasn't satisfied. He waved them off. "I want to record that one again."

Their producer's voice came over the speaker. "Beckett, this song was perfect ten tries ago. Now, you're just being ridiculous."

He shook his head. "Again."

Harrison removed his glasses and cleaned them on his shirt while studying Becks. "I think you need to go home, bro."

Becks scowled. "No. What I need is to get the song right."

Harrison held up his hands in front of his chest.

Quinn sighed. "Whatever the man wants. It's his song."

"Damn right, it is."

A fourth voice joined theirs. "Actually, it's my song." Nari crossed the room, planting her feet in front of Becks. She wasn't wrong. As a songwriting pair, they both shared credit in each song on the album.

"We need to get this right, Nars."

Her expression softened. "And you have. The album is amazing. Why can't you see that?" She handed him a hand towel and a bottle of water.

He wiped his face before taking a drink. "It's not good enough."

"It's not good enough? Or you're not good enough?"

"Don't twist my words." He walked around her, leaving without so much as a wave to the rest of the guys.

Nari ran after him. "It's not like you to feel sorry for yourself."

Outside, a black town car idled at the curb. The driver got out and opened the back door for Becks. "I'm fine, Nari. Stop worrying about me."

She gripped his arm to stop him from getting into the car. "You're not fine."

Pasting on a bright smile, he turned to her, leaning in to press a kiss to her cheek. "I appreciate the concern. You're a good friend."

She didn't look convinced, but she let him slide into the car.

His phone buzzed, and he answered without looking to see who it was.

"Beckett." April sounded tired. "We need a meeting."

"Well, hello, April, darling. It's a pleasure to speak to my lovely PR specialist. Thanks for the warm greeting." He glanced at the time on his phone, smiling as he heard April's sigh through the phone. "I can be there in twenty."

"Good." She hung up.

Leaning forward, Becks spoke to the driver. "I need to go to the label's office." It was never good when his PR team summoned him on such short notice, but Becks didn't know what else could go wrong in his life right now.

He still held his phone in his palm when it vibrated again. This time, he glanced at the screen. Asher Brooks. If anyone told him months ago that the president's son would have his number, he'd have made some joke of it.

Now, though, after getting to know Asher, he realized maybe the kid just needed a friend.

And maybe, Becks did too, one who wasn't team Nicky. One who didn't know Becks before he'd started questioning everything about himself. He held the phone to his ear. "Brooksy. What's up, man?"

"You call me that, I'll call you SexyBecksy." He chuckled.

Becks groaned. The hashtag had taken on a life of its own, and there was no way to run from it now. "No amount of secret service can protect you if you say that again."

"Yeah, yeah. There's a reason I'm calling. You've been MIA recently. Won't return my calls or my texts."

"Feeling like a jilted lover?"

"We aren't lovers, but we are friends and I like to make sure my friends are okay."

Becks grinned. "Then I'm a lucky guy. I promise, I've just been swamped. I leave for the tour in eight days. We barely got the album done in time."

"You sure career stuff is all that's going on?"

No, he wasn't. He had a dead mother he never got to reconcile with, and he was in love with a dude. One who didn't love him back. Life was just peachy.

But no one really wanted that kind of answer. All they wanted to hear was that he was okay.

"Yeah," he finally answered. "Just music. You know me, dude. I don't let anything but the music get to me."

Asher couldn't know that yet, but it was what Becks wanted him to see. The car stopped in front of the tower housing the offices he'd come to know so well.

"I've got to go, Brooksy." He nodded to the driver and climbed out of the car.

"See ya, SexyBecksy." Shaking his head, Becks ended the call and slid the phone into his jeans pocket. He wasn't dressed for a meeting with the bigwigs, but it wasn't like he really cared.

Sending a smile to the two secretaries by the door, he bypassed them and rode the elevator to the third floor to April's office.

When he knocked on her half-open door, she held one finger up as she finished a phone call. It was only when she set the receiver down that she waved him inside. Kyle rushed in behind him with Skyler on his heels.

His cousin squeezed his shoulder in sympathy. Three days ago, she stood and watched Becks realize he'd been too late to forgive his mother. He hadn't been able to face her since. Every one of Skyler's calls went unanswered.

Now, as she leaned against April's desk, he couldn't avoid her gaze.

April folded her hands on the desk. "Beckett, I'm going to cut to the chase. We have some problems."

He met her stare. "I haven't jumped off any more stages to kiss unsuspecting people, so can't be as bad as that, right?" He smiled as if it was all a big joke. But the biggest joke had been on him.

Kyle grunted. "You told a reporter you and Nicky broke up."

"Well…yeah. We did."

"How can you break up if you weren't dating? The deal was to keep it going at least through the beginning of the tour. The fans love you, Beckett."

Becks face flushed as he tried to hold down his anger. He opened his mouth to refute their words, but it turned out he didn't need to.

"They don't love him because he's gay," Sky snapped. "They love him because he's Beckett."

Kyle glared at her. "We could use some coffee, Skyler."

Her shoulders dropping, she moved to obey, but Beckett stopped her. "Get your own damn coffee," he growled. "And you know what? Get your own damn singing career. This one is mine. From now on, I get to choose who I am." He stood. "What we did wasn't right. We lied to a lot of people. I never wanted it. I wasn't comfortable with it, but I was trapped by this paralyzing fear all of this would go away."

April sighed. "Sit down, Beckett. You too, Sky. Kyle, stop being an asshole. All of us care what comes next for you, Beckett."

He lowered himself back into his chair.

April continued. "The tour begins in eight days. We were hoping the buzz from that could drown out any other media attention, but I'm afraid we have one more mountain to climb."

"What happened?" He rubbed his eyes, suddenly very tired.

"Nicky St. Germaine is in Nashville."

The air left Becks' lungs in a rush, leaving him struggling to breathe. "What?" No. He knew the plan was for Nicky to move in with Avery, but classes didn't start for another month. Becks assumed he'd be long gone by then, traveling across the country on a long tour.

Sky reached for his hand. "Nari told me. Nicky moved in today."

Yet, neither Avery nor Nari had told him. They gave him no warning, no time to prepare.

And suddenly, Becks knew why they'd called him in. "Has the media gotten wind of this yet?"

Kyle shook his head. "It's only a matter of time. It wouldn't be an issue if you hadn't told the world you broke up. Unless you want Nicky's life to be even more of a circus than it is now, we think it's better if you're not seen together."

Becks nodded. They were right. He didn't want to bring attention to the fact that Nicky was in Nashville. Once the tour started, that would be the news.

Sky squeezed his hand. "You can stay at my house. In the guest room. Not the couch you're always falling asleep on."

"Thanks, Sky." He tried to focus on everything else April and Kyle said to him. They handed him a packet that was supposed to help him prepare for press duties on the tour, but he didn't hear their explanations over the rushing in his ears.

The mess he'd made of everything was finally being revealed.

Nicky was in Nashville.

His mother died before she knew he loved her.

His sister was falling apart.

And here he was, planning to go on tour and let music be his greatest companion as it always had been. He just wasn't sure that was enough anymore.

Becks shoveled clothes into a duffle bag, wanting to get out of his apartment and over to Sky's as quickly as possible. He walked into the living room and threw his duffle on the couch, taking one glance at his closed door. Was Nicky across the hall right this moment? Was he worried about seeing Becks?

With a sigh, Becks stepped into his bathroom to grab his toothbrush. He heard the door open but didn't turn as Avery appeared in the mirror.

His best friend looked behind him to where the edge of the duffle peeked up over the couch cushions. "Becks." He ran a hand through his hair, a clear sign of his exasperation. Becks wondered if there'd ever been a time in his friendship with Avery he hadn't been able to read him so easily.

Nari was the same. The two of them never hid what they thought from Becks.

Could they say the same about him? "What do you want, Avery?"

"Why are you leaving? The tour doesn't start until next week."

Becks pushed past him to reenter the living room. "Wasn't my idea."

"You're listening to your PR team? Again? Haven't they ruined things enough for you?"

Becks barked out a laugh. "Says the guy who didn't even tell me his brother was moving here a whole four weeks before he had to."

"He wanted to get settled in."

"Mmhmm. Good for him. But a heads-up would have been nice."

"Why?" He glanced at the duffle again. "So you could leave earlier?"

"The reporters can't see me and Nicky anywhere near each other. I just want them to leave him alone."

"Screw the reporters."

"Easy to say for someone who has never had them dogging their every step, bro." Nicky's voice came from the doorway where he stood picking at the hem of his shirt. "I don't want any more media attention either. It's exhausting."

Avery looked from Becks to Nicky. "So, you're just okay with him leaving?"

Nicky shrugged, and Becks tried not to let the action cause any more pain than he already felt. "I mean…I get it."

Avery clenched his jaw. "You don't know him like I do." He turned to Becks. "When you come back from the tour, someone else will be living in this apartment, won't they?"

The thought had been on his mind ever since finding out his mother died. She'd only had one friend in the end and two children struggling to forgive her. Becks didn't want that. It was time to grow up. He wanted something more to call his own. A home.

And his silence gave Avery the answer he needed. "See, Nicky. You don't know him at all. Beckett Anderson doesn't deal with things. He smiles, and he makes jokes, but he doesn't deal."

Becks stared at the brothers, so alike yet so different. Avery, the golden child with a not-so-golden temper. And Nicky, the quiet one who'd always been on the outside of their friendship.

Or, at least he used to be.

Now, it seemed like every conversation with Avery had these charged feelings because of Nicky. His best friend fell for his brother, and it broke them both.

Until then, Becks hadn't seen just how much harder he'd made this on all of them. It was better for him to go. He'd buy a house once royalties for the new album came in. He needed to let them go. They were a real family and he was just in the way.

Nicky stepped farther into the room, his eyes not leaving Becks. "Avery, back off."

Avery crossed his arms over his chest. "Why? Tell me what's going on. Why has Becks been trying so much harder to seem like the old joking version of himself? Why did Sky refer to you moving here as a 'final straw' for Becks? I know something has happened." His pleading eyes fell on Becks. His anger from moments before was nowhere to be found. "You're my best friend, Becks. I'm sorry I got mad, but you can't tell me you're not hurting. I see it in every excuse you've made to be alone over the last couple days or the way you're running yourself into the ground to prepare for this tour. When we moved to Nashville two years ago, you, me, and Nari became a family."

Becks lifted his duffle onto his shoulder. "But the difference is you three are a real family, Avery." He walked to the door, stopping at Nicky's side. Being so close to him sent a thrill through Becks, but he suppressed the urge to reach out and touch him, to feel the pulse pounding at Nicky's neck.

"Don't go," Nicky whispered.

Becks straightened his spine. He wouldn't let himself be held back by Nicky any longer. "You want to know what happened, Avery? My mom loved me. And she didn't know I loved her back." He couldn't meet Nicky's eyes. "Guess that's going around."

Neither Avery nor Nicky chased after him when he walked down the hall. They weren't there to watch as he slid into the car.

Popping his earbuds into his ears, he leaned his head back, listening to tracks from the new album. The songs spoke for him, of him, to him. And he held onto the words as if they were a lone life raft on a sinking ship.

The room hadn't changed at all. Two years ago, Becks showed up in Nashville with little to his name except big dreams. He'd opted out of college, much to the dismay of every teacher he had, and decided to try to play his music in Music City itself. There were so many musicians in the capital the task seemed impossible at times.

But it was all he wanted.

Luckily, he hadn't been alone.

Nari, finding the courage to realize what she really wanted, followed him. The two of them were in this together. For the first year, they'd lived with Skyler, testing her every nerve. She loved them, but she also loved her space.

Avery, on the other hand, crammed himself into a dorm room with even less space for himself.

And somehow, they'd made it all work.

Now, he was back. In the year since getting his own place, Becks crashed at Skyler's a few times but never in his old room, the same room where he'd sat so many nights wondering if he was on the right path.

Had he been stupid to think he could make it? That he had some worth that raised him above every other white guy with a guitar trying to let their music speak for them in an industry that wanted them to all be the same.

But he was on the way to making it, wasn't he? "Then why doesn't it feel any better?" he whispered to himself as he dropped onto the corner of the bed.

My mom loved me. And she never knew I loved her back.

That was the crux of it, wasn't it? No one could read another's heart; they couldn't control what they felt.

Skyler was out for the night, leaving Becks to an empty house. The silence taunted him.

Scooting farther up onto the bed, he lay back, resting his hands under the back of his head. The LED can lights overhead caused temporary blindness as his eyes adjusted and shifted away from the white glow to the hazy blue walls.

Three days. He found out about his mother three days ago. Only his family knew. And probably Nicky. Wylder told him everything.

Becks wasn't quite sure why he hadn't told his friends or the people at his label. Maybe because he didn't want to see the pity in their eyes. They didn't know the story of his mother—that she abandoned her children after years of choosing drugs over them.

The label didn't know Becks shouldn't love her. That it wasn't like if Avery or Nari lost their moms. It would destroy them.

Becks wasn't allowed to be destroyed, was he? He couldn't mourn her as one mourned a mother. Not after years of hoping he'd never see her again, after months of refusing her phone calls or Wylder's pleas.

"Why does it hurt so much, Mom?" He closed his eyes, willing tears to come. His eyes stayed dry. "You've been gone since I was a kid. I shouldn't miss you." His voice dropped. "I'm so sorry."

For what, he wasn't quite sure. But it seemed like something he needed to say to her. Was he sorry he hadn't gone to her sooner? That he hadn't helped her more when he was a kid?

The bed dipped, and he opened his eyes to find Nicky sitting on the end of it. The way his eyes shifted to the door told Becks he wasn't sure he should be there.

Well, maybe, he shouldn't.

"What do you want, Nick-Nick?" The nickname he'd always used for him slipped out before Becks could call it back. "I don't recall inviting you." In the hours since seeing him, Becks had too much time to think about what Nicky being in Nashville meant.

His conclusion: Absolutely nothing.

They wouldn't have to see each other. Becks wouldn't have to pretend his heart didn't break every time they occupied the same space.

"Are you—"

"So help me, Nicky, if you finish that with 'okay,' I'm going to tell the entire world you hate ketchup."

He crossed his arms over his chest. "There's nothing wrong with hating ketchup."

"Yes, there is. It's sacrilege and un-American. If you think the paps were bad before, just wait till I tell them you're the devil incarnate."

He cracked a small smile, the first Becks had seen on his face in too long.

Becks didn't match it. Instead, he sat up and scooted so his back leaned against the headboard. "You shouldn't be here."

"Why? Becks, you're my—"

"Friend?"

"Yeah, friend." He bit out the word. "Your sister is a mess. I tried to be there for her as much as I could, but she told me it was okay to leave. That she wasn't the only one who needed me. I think she was right."

"I don't need you." His hard façade cracked, just a little.

"Your mom died, Becks."

"No, my mom lives with my dad in Twin Rivers. My mother lost the right to be called Mom a long time ago."

"You don't mean that."

He didn't, but he wasn't going to admit that.

Nicky stood, and for a tiny moment, Becks thought he'd leave. It both relieved and pained him. Instead, Nicky took a seat farther up the bed, pulling his legs up so his head could rest against the headboard at Becks' side.

He dropped his voice. "It's okay to be sad." He reached for Becks' hand, but Becks ripped it away.

"You don't get to do that," he choked out, tears building in his throat. He hadn't cried in front of Avery or Nari or Skyler. Even on the phone with Wylder, he'd been strong, letting her be the one to break down.

But now, with Nicky, he couldn't stop the fat drops from rolling down his face.

Nicky didn't acknowledge the tears. "I want to be here for you. Is that okay?"

All Becks could manage was a nod as Nicky put a hand to his cheek and steered Becks' head onto his shoulder.

Tears dampened Nicky's shirt, but he didn't seem to mind as he let Becks release his strength for once in his life. Nicky didn't expect anything from him. He didn't need him. Becks sighed as he closed his eyes.

When he could finally speak again, his voice rasped out. "I understand, you know."

"Hmm? Understand what?"

"We started with a lie. And it was all my fault. You did so much for me. I never should have asked you to do any of it. The whole fake relationship. I shouldn't have cared what the label said. I'm sorry."

"Becks, I agreed to it. It's not like you forced me. You don't make my decisions."

Becks lifted his head to meet Nicky's gaze. "I'm still sorry. For everything. For the media attention. For my confusion. I'm not even gay. At least I don't think so. But sitting here with you… This is the first time in weeks I haven't felt like I'm standing on the edge of a precipice, just waiting to fall off. You ground me Nicky. My life is insane—as you've seen. I'm not exactly the most down-to-earth guy. But I can be calm when I'm with you. I don't feel that anywhere else."

Nicky swallowed heavily. There was little space separating their faces, and Becks wanted nothing more than to cross the invisible line between them. But he wouldn't. He'd tried telling Nicky how he felt, that it confused him.

Now, it was Nicky's turn.

Instead of moving closer, Nicky backed away, climbing off the bed. "I should go. I just wanted to check on you." He stopped moving. "You know I'm here, right, Becks? If you need me?"

Becks nodded and got to his feet, following Nicky from the room.

They reached the front door, and Nicky pulled it open, revealing a darkness only illuminated by the stars overhead. His beat-up old car sat in the driveway ready to take him away from Becks.

He took one step out the door before he stopped and turned on his heel. He pulled Becks into a crushing hug. "You're going to get through this." He stepped away. As he walked outside, he threw a few more words back over his shoulder. "I'm going to miss you when you leave for the tour."

Becks closed the door, leaning against it. Before, he'd been excited to go on such a big tour, to play music every day. But now, it was more than a job. It was a lifeline. Because if he had to stay in Nashville, he'd never survive Nicky St. Germaine.

A buzz sounded from where his phone sat charging in the kitchen. Then another. Becks walked toward the counter and yanked the cord from his phone before unlocking it.

Text after text had come in the past few hours. Avery and Nari. A few from Quinn and Harrison.

Condolences, mostly. A few "I'm sorries" from Avery. Shaking his head, Becks opened the fridge and grabbed a beer before retreating to the back deck where the sounds of crickets punctuated the stillness of the night.

He set his phone to play his favorite country playlist—songs that were about something more than tractors, beer, and blue jeans.

He hoped one of the songs could tell him how to shove the emotions back in once he'd let them out.

Nicky:

"Now that things are settling down, by the time school starts, people will forget who I am, right?" Nicky gazed over Avery's shoulder at his computer screen.

"Sure, sure." Avery snapped his computer shut with a guilty look on his face.

"What? You looking at naughty websites?" Nicky plopped down on the couch beside his brother.

Avery winced. "Well…no. It's nothing really. Not exactly."

"What are you babbling about?" Nicky didn't think he could take any more drama.

Avery opened his computer and turned it to face Nicky.

His breath caught in his throat at the sight of the headlines.

"Country Music Sensation Beckett Anderson isn't even gay. Was it all a lie?"

"PR Stunt gone awry, #BlackWidowBoy was just a puppet in Beckett Anderson's scheme."

"Will the real Beckett Anderson please stand up?"

"Oh no." Nicky groaned. "Has Becks seen it? Is he going to make it through this?"

"Yeah. The articles broke about an hour ago. Nari and Becks are meeting with the label now. I hope they'll stand behind him since this was all their idea, but I don't know if that's enough to save his career. You two need to talk your shit out together and keep the media out of it."

"What do you think I've been trying to do all summer?" Nicky gave his brother an incredulous look. Did he really think either of them wanted this kind of attention? Nicky clicked on the article with the most hits.

Country music fans everywhere are devastated over the breakup of Beckett Anderson and Nicky St. Germaine—but was it ever a real relationship? Or was it a PR stunt to launch Beckett's new album into the stratosphere right before his first big tour? Our source tells us the real story behind that epic kiss.

"This is not good." Nicky scowled at the screen.

Nari charged through the front door to their apartment. "Fix this, Nicky." She turned devastated eyes on him. "The label is talking about dropping us. Etta Morelli's team is hunting for a new opening act as a backup replacement. Our PR team is trying to do damage control, but this is bad, Nicky. Career ending bad."

"How am I supposed to fix this?" Nicky threw his hands up in despair.

"You two need to have a real conversation about your feelings and you, Nicky St. Germaine, need to trust him. Becks is not

Kenny. You guys need to make some kind of statement to soothe the fans and show them it wasn't all fake."

"But it was all fake," Nicky insisted. "And it's out there now. As much as I'd like to, I can't undo it, Nars."

Nari just gave him a look that said she knew none of it was fake though it may have started out that way. "Just talk to him, Nicky. Even if we can't fix this, Becks needs to know you two can still be friends. If this is really how it's all going to end for us, he needs you to help him get through it."

Nicky thrust his hand in his pocket to keep from running it through his fake hair. He felt ridiculous walking up the steps to Skyler's house looking like an awkward, skinny version of his older brother. But apparently, Nicky would never be able to go anywhere in this town without a disguise. At least not anytime soon.

"Nicky? Is that you?" Skyler laughed as she opened the door.

"Don't laugh." Nicky stepped inside.

She craned her neck out of the door to look for news vans and cameramen lurking in the bushes around her house. "Well, it appears to have worked. No one followed you." She closed the door behind her.

"How did I get to be the center of the country music gossip scene?" Nicky shook his head. "It baffles me."

"It may not seem like it now, but it will blow over. He's hiding in the backyard having a pity party for one. Go see if you can talk some sense into him."

"He's a stubborn guy, but I'll try." Nicky followed Sky through to the back of the house. Nicky stepped onto the small porch, watching Becks sit solemnly beside the firepot in the yard. A circle of Adirondack chairs surrounded the deep stone firepot. Becks stared into the depths of the flames as if they held the answers to his current predicament.

"You look ridiculous." He finally spoke, turning his gaze on Nicky.

"I know." Nicky snatched the dark wig and hat from his head. "Don't ever make fun of my man-bun again."

Nick took the seat beside Becks, rubbing his sweaty palms against the loose-fitting jeans he'd borrowed from Avery.

"You here to try to make me feel better?" Becks took a long sip of his beer. "You should know that's not possible. Even for you."

"You really are throwing a pity party." Nicky sat back against his chair. "Becks, I'm here for whatever you need."

Becks snorted. "Can you go back in time and stop me from kissing you? 'Cause if you can, that'd be perfect."

"No. Unfortunately neither of us can take that back, so we just have to deal with the fallout."

"I'm going to lose everything." Becks turned toward him. "And it's all your fault." His dark eyes were angry and hazy with alcohol.

"No, it's not, and you know it. Don't be an asshole drunk. It doesn't look good on you." Nicky was through with trying to make everyone happy. This all started because he'd wanted to help Becks save his career. And look where that got them? "It's your label's fault. You only did what they insisted, and when it didn't go their way, they didn't step up to support you."

"It doesn't matter anymore." Becks sighed, tossing his empty bottle across the yard toward the garbage cans. He missed and reached for the cooler beside his feet for a fresh beer. He didn't offer one to Nicky, but he knew Nicky didn't drink.

"You can still fix this," Nicky said.

"How?" Becks laughed. "Go back to pretending I'm in love with you? That whole plan was a disaster."

"No, but what if we tried the truth for once?" Nicky suggested. "Give your fans the honesty they deserve. Tell them how you really feel about me and how confusing that is for both of us. And then let the chips fall where they may. Your fans might rally around you and support you or they might not, but either way, you can walk away knowing you did everything you could to save your career—on your own terms and not the label's."

"The truth? I don't think I'm familiar with that version of our story." Becks seemed determined to wallow in his self pity. "Just leave me alone, Nicky. I'm not yours to fix. I never was."

"Knock it off, Beckett," Nicky whispered. "You don't need me or anyone else to fix things for you. You're a big boy now and it's time to clean up your own mess." Nicky stood to leave. "It's up to you to decide what really led you to kiss me that day. Stop lying to your fans and yourself. I can't pretend to know what you're going through right now, but I have always been your friend, and I always will be. You can't get rid of me that easily." Nicky left him to his pity party and hoped that something he'd said would get through that thick skull of his.

"Rising country music star, Beckett Anderson pretends to be gay to garner more fans for his new album, but his PR stunt blows up in his face."

"LGBTQ Community in an uproar over Beckett Anderson's ploy to be one of them.

"Beckett Anderson should be ashamed of himself for exploiting his supposed gay relationship in the media only to 'come out' as straight. His career is over before it really began."

"Nicky St. Germaine—a victim of catfishing? Or a willing participant in this year's biggest celebrity scandal?"

"Nicky St. Germaine was an innocent bystander before Beckett Anderson bulldozed his way into his life, leaving him an outcast with a broken heart."

"This trash has gone too damn far." Avery tossed his phone onto the café table. "They need to leave you out of it."

"At least they're not bashing me anymore," Nicky said. "I just wish they'd leave Becks alone and let this 'scandal' die once and for all."

"He made his bed when he cooked up this whole scheme," Avery said. "It's not like the press is saying anything that isn't true at this point. They've blown this story wide-open and danced on its grave."

"Don't blame Becks for this, Avery. The lie was never his idea."

"That might be true, but he's dragged you through the mud. I don't think I can forgive him for that."

"He was doing what his PR team advised. They're the bad guys in this scenario, and Becks doesn't deserve to lose his dream over this—or his best friend. He's worked too damn hard to get where he is."

"But he used you, Nicky." Avery leaned closer across the table. "He hurt you."

"Avery, don't listen to everything you read about us. Becks was confused. He has all these feelings he doesn't know what to do with. I know better than most how that feels. I was just lucky not to have it all aired in the press when I was struggling with who I was. I don't know how to help Becks, but I'm sure as hell not going to abandon him when he needs us most. And neither are you."

Becks:

Was it ever a real relationship?

That was the answer the world wanted to know from Beckett Anderson. He laughed at the thought, realizing how insane that sounded. The world didn't care what he did. He could disappear, and most people on this planet wouldn't even know he ever existed.

But Nashville was its own kind of world. One where he had to answer to the country gods—the people who signed his checks, booked his concerts, and got his songs on the radio.

Was it ever a real relationship?

Was any relationship in this city real?

Becks knew he should stay away from the internet when his name was trending. This time, there was no hashtag to laugh at like #SexyBecksy. Instead, people didn't write about him, only what he did. As if one action, one lie, determined his worth.

Maybe, it did.

Wylder's name flashed on his phone for the third time in the past hour. Becks set the laptop on the coffee table and scooted across Skylar's couch to reach his phone. If he didn't answer eventually, Wylder would do something stupid like get into her car and drive to Nashville.

"Wylder," he said as a greeting.

Her sigh echoed through the phone. "Do you know who spilled their guts to the press?"

"No." He leaned back. "I've been wracking my brain trying to figure out who even knew. I don't know if there's a way to find out. Besides, I'm not sure it really matters."

"Of course, it does."

He closed his eyes, trying to feel any of the anger his sister held in her words. Instead, he was just tired. Tired of secrets and lies, of doing whatever was necessary for this career he once thought was the most important thing. When he opened them, he wasn't sure he had any fight left in him. "Wylder, finding out who told the press about the fake relationship won't change what I did. It won't change the fact that Etta Morelli will probably decide she wants me off the tour. It won't change the fact that my phone has remained silent all morning except for calls from you and Asher."

"The people from the label haven't called you since the news broke?"

That wasn't exactly what he meant, but for the first time, he realized they hadn't. It'd been a few hours since the first articles appeared, and he knew it was past office hours, but he expected calls from his PR team at least.

His brow furrowed as he tried to remember the last time he spoke to them. Days ago, they'd wanted him to distance himself from Nicky. To let the news of the breakup fade away.

Wylder took his silence to mean something else. "He hasn't called either, has he?"

Becks knew what his sister meant without needed a name. "Have you talked to him?"

"I tried, Becks, but Nicky and I have been missing each other's calls since he moved. He calls me a lot, and I know he just wants to see how I'm doing after Mom...but I haven't exactly been in the mood to talk."

"You called me."

"You're my brother. When the shit hits the fan for you, it no longer matters what else is going on. Mom barely knew us, but I'd like to think she'd want us to be there for each other."

"You're the best, you know that?"

"No, but what I do know is you aren't alone in this. You did something monumentally stupid, brother. I won't pretend you didn't. I don't care if those idiots at the label told you to. You're better than lies. I always knew you'd make it, but I never thought you'd resort to all of this."

Becks rubbed his eyes. "It got so out of control."

"So take back control. The label isn't going to fix this. They're more likely to distance themselves than help you. You need to take care of this yourself."

"How? I don't even know where to start."

She was silent for a long moment before her low voice came through the phone again. "Who are you?"

"What?"

"You heard my question."

"Uhh...I'm your brother."

"And what's my brother's name?"

"Beckett Anderson."

Her voice grew louder. "Who are you?"

"I'm Beckett Anderson."

"Who are you?!"

"Beckett *freaking* Anderson!"

"Hell yes, you are. Now go be Beckett Anderson. You got this, bro."

He smiled. "You should be a football coach, Wylds."

"Whatever."

He could practically hear the smile in her voice before she hung up without a goodbye. He lifted his eyes to find his cousin staring at him from the doorway with Sofie by her side, refusing to look at him.

"What are we yelling about?" Sky asked.

"I'm going to make this right." He scrolled through his contacts until he found the only other number that had been calling him.

Asher picked up after the first ring. "You okay?"

He loved that the first thing out of his friend's mouth was worry and not scorn. "I think I will be, but I need a favor."

After explaining what he wanted from Asher, Becks hung up and walked into the kitchen where Sofie was talking to Skylar.

Sky glanced between the two. "I'll just, uh, give you two a moment."

Sofie watched her leave as if she wished she too could go. Instead, she fixed her eyes on the counter, waiting for Becks to speak.

He stepped toward her, but she put up a hand to stop him. "When you chose not to be with me, I thought it was because you loved Nicky. So, I stayed on. I just wanted you to be happy and if that wasn't with me, so be it. But now—"

"Sof—"

"Now I learn you chose a lie over me."

"It wasn't my doing."

"You're the one who told the lie, Becks. You made everyone root for this false love story. Not dumbass Kyle at the label, not anyone else. You. Stop blaming other people for your actions."

"You're right."

She opened her mouth, looking as if she was prepared to argue further, but shut it when she realized he'd agreed with her.

"I never wanted to hurt you."

"You think you hurt me?" She shook her head. "I'm just trying to figure out if I ever really knew you at all. I used to think you were one of the good ones. I've seen a lot of people come through

Nashville with stars in their eyes and coal in their hearts. But I wanted success for you. Was I just naïve? Are you no better than most of the jerks who think the world owes them?"

"I don't want to be one of them."

She dropped her voice. "Then don't."

"I need your help, Sof. Like always, I can't do anything without my talented assistant and friend. I'm going to apologize for everything tomorrow morning as long as Asher pulls through for me." He kicked his toe against the ground before lifting his eyes to hers. "And I have no idea what to wear."

She covered her mouth to stifle a laugh. "You never do."

"Please. If you don't forgive me after tomorrow, then you don't have to see me again. I'll probably end up back in Twin Rivers playing for pennies in front of my dad's hardware store."

"Beckett." She sighed. "Don't be dramatic. I don't forgive you. Not yet. But whatever you have planned, I won't have you looking like a vagabond." She scanned his ripped jeans and black T-shirt in distaste.

"Thanks, Sof." He tried to slide an arm around her shoulders like he used to, but she turned away from him.

"Don't act like we're friends, Beckett. I'm just doing my job."

Becks didn't sleep that night. Not when his entire career and so many of his friendships relied on what he did in the morning. In five days, he was supposed to leave for the tour of a lifetime, but the silence coming from the label told him how they felt about that.

Maybe that was why Nari, Quinn, and Harrison hadn't spoken to him the day before. He wasn't only screwing things up for himself, but for them as well.

And as much as he said he'd try, he didn't know if he could truly fix it.

In the morning, he dressed in the clothes Sofie had told him to wear and combed his hair. Skylar waited for him in the kitchen, but he couldn't eat when his stomach was tied in knots.

She had the local news on the TV in the living room showing reporters camped outside his place. He imagined them similarly waiting for Nicky outside Becks' old building.

Unplugging his phone from the charger, he fired off a text to Nicky.

Becks: Turn on the local news in two hours.
Nicky: You're alive.
Becks: Could say the same about you.
Nicky: Avery stole my phone yesterday so I wouldn't text you. I was surprised not to have any missed calls from you. Yesterday was…
Becks: Yeah, it was. Look, I'm sorry for everything.
Nicky: I know.

If there was one person who wouldn't hate him after all this, it was Nicky. Knowing that only made it harder. Sometimes, he wondered if he wanted Nicky to hate him. Maybe that would've been better than this friendship dance they did. One where they pretended Becks never said he had feelings for Nicky and where Nicky never said he didn't have feelings back.

Becks pulled a ball cap onto his head and nodded to Sky. She grabbed her keys off the counter before leading him into her garage. As they pulled away from the house, photographers tried to get any picture they could as if they owned him.

The next two hours where a whirlwind of makeup and preparation. Sofie appeared, much to Becks' surprise, to run through questions with him.

As a voice over the loudspeaker called Becks to the side of the stage, he sent Asher a text.

Becks: Thank you.

Asher made calls the night before, and when the president's son called, people listened. He managed to get Becks a spot on Nashville's top morning show, claiming it hadn't been difficult because the fake gay country star was ratings gold.

Becks planned ahead of time what he needed to say, how he could make this right, but as he stepped onto the stage, every word flew from his mind.

Boos came from the crowd, but Becks tried to block them out as he crossed toward Charlotte Keaning sitting on one of two velvet-upholstered chairs, a small table between them.

She stood as he approached, her wide smile for the audience more than for him. She brushed long blond curls over one shoulder and fixed intelligent green eyes on him.

"Beckett Anderson." Her voice held a country twang as she held out a hand.

He took it. "Thank you for having me."

The crowd quieted down as she gestured for him to sit. "Welcome, welcome. Despite the reception from my audience, we're excited to have you here this morning." She laughed as if it was all some joke.

Becks gave her a nervous smile as he fiddled with a fold in his tight black jeans. Sofie picked them out along with a soft blue plaid button-down. She claimed the color was non-threatening and that he could benefit from it in an interview.

Now, he wasn't sure anything could help him.

Charlotte rested in her chair and crossed her legs, studying him before turning to her audience. "Beckett Anderson was one of the fastest rising country stars until it all ground to a halt yesterday." Her eyes drifted back to Becks. "I don't like to bandy about, Beckett." She was known for her brutal honesty. "Did you lie to your fans when you told them you were gay?"

His words clogged in his throat. He'd never told anyone he was gay, only that he was dating Nicky. Did he owe them an explanation? "I lied when I claimed to be dating Nicky St. Germaine." The crowd booed.

Charlotte pursed her lips, but Becks wasn't done. He thought of everything Sofie told him he needed to say about how sorry he was and how it was all a misunderstanding that spiraled out of his control. But none of that seemed right. "Can I ask you a question, Charlotte?"

She laughed. "I'm usually the one asking questions, but sure."

"When you were a kid, what was your dream?"

She was quiet for a moment. "I can't really remember."

"Well, I wanted to sing. I wanted to spend my life making music. There was no other life that ever occurred to me. I grew up in a small town where being different wasn't exactly celebrated, so I chose to be special instead. I put everything I had into music until I didn't recognize myself without it."

"That sounds hard."

"But it wasn't. Not for me. It all came so easily. And the first time I hit a roadblock, I wasn't quite sure how to get through it."

She nodded. "This roadblock was the kiss we've all seen by now? The one from the Cincinnati music festival?"

Becks scratched his jaw. "That's what started this whole mess. After that, I didn't know how to go back." It was on the tip of his tongue to mention his label forcing him into this, but Sofie had been right. It was his decision, and he needed to take responsibility.

"Do you regret it?"

Becks scanned the audience, not seeing their faces with the light shining in his eyes. Did he regret it? "I wish I hadn't lied. I hurt a lot of people. But if you're asking me if I regret stopping my concert to help a friend, then the answer is no."

"Most of us help friends by giving them advice or support, not kissing them." She lifted a brow.

Becks chuckled. "You try seeing the man you love in trouble and not do anything about it." His face flushed as he replayed the words in his mind.

The man you love? The man you love? Shit. He'd just told the entire world the one thing he'd tried so hard to push away.

Charlotte grinned as she leaned forward in her chair, sensing blood in the water. "But the relationship was fake. Beckett, are you telling us that part of it wasn't a lie? Are you saying you're gay?"

"My feelings for Nicky were never fake, but as to the rest of it..." He sucked in a breath.

"Go on."

Are you saying you're gay? No, he wasn't, but that wasn't what came out of his mouth.

He straightened his back, snapping his eyes to Charlotte's. All fear left him as he realized she was just another reporter trying to dig into his private life.

"Whether or not I'm gay shouldn't be a question. It's not information I owe you, Charlotte, or my fans. I love the people who support me. They're the only reason I get to make music. But that doesn't mean they own me or my sexuality. I'm only beginning to understand who I am, and I've started to realize that's okay. It's a journey that belongs to me and me alone."

"And to Nicky if you're with him."

"No. Nicky knows who he is. He has for a very long time. Some days, the only thing I know is that I love him." Crap, he'd said it again.

"So, you're saying you are gay?"

"Do you think gay men are the only ones who can fall in love with other men? I'm not going to sit here on TV and explain to you the vast spectrum of sexuality." He breathed through his anger. "I wish this world would stop defining people based on each person's narrow understanding of love."

She smiled at that, her expression softening. "You're right, you don't owe me answers to sate my curiosity. But yesterday, your relationship with Nicky St. Germaine was revealed as fake, and today, you sit here telling me it was real."

"I never said the relationship was real." His anger dropped away, and he sat back in the chair. "My feelings mean nothing if they're not returned."

The crowd's boos turned to subdued awes. Great, they went from hating him to feeling sorry for him.

Even Charlotte's eyes held a new pity. "You went to great lengths to be here with me today. Why?"

He lifted his eyes to the crowd. "Because I'm sorry. I'm so sorry. This thing snowballed out of control so fast, and I hurt a lot of people. I hurt Nicky. My fans. I just...I wanted people to know I never set out to hurt anyone."

"I think they know that now. Beckett Anderson, thank you for coming onto our show this morning. Now, if I was told correctly, we have a song to play."

Becks told Asher to promise the show they'd get to reveal his new single. The label wouldn't be pleased Becks did it without permission, but he wasn't sure he cared.

Overhead, a song began. It was the best thing Becks had ever written. A long time ago, before he'd even known his sister found their mom, the words came to him speaking of a painful one-sided love. Even though it was about his mom, the words made him think of Nicky as well.

The final words drifted away and Charlotte wiped her eyes. "That was beautiful." She spoke to the audience. "'Love Me' by Beckett Anderson will be available soon on iTunes. As for Beckett Anderson—he'll be performing today at one o'clock at City Park, and admission is free for everyone."

As the show went to a commercial break, Becks made his way to where Sky and Sofie waited for him. Sky wrapped him in a hug, and it surprised him when Sofie joined their embrace as well.

When he pulled away, Sofie pinched him. "I get it now. I suppose you're forgiven, but you didn't tell me you were playing a concert today."

"It was kind of spur of the moment. There's that makeshift stage at the northern side of the park. No one will come anyway, so it'll be me and the pigeons."

"Have you even told your band?"

Becks shrugged. "If they don't come, I'll play on my own. Sof, you don't get it. I just poured every part of me out onto that stage during the interview. I need to play. I need the music to give it all back to me."

Sofie nodded in understanding. "Fine. I have to make some calls. I'll see you there."

As she walked away, Sky led Becks outside to the waiting reporters and fans. He braced for their jeers, but they never came. Instead, they cheered for him as if he was the same country star they'd followed since day one.

No one was going to come. Becks was sure of it. He'd get to the park, step onto the old dilapidated stone stage, and stand in front of an open field to play for the birds. Everything was over, gone. There was no coming back from lying to his fans. Free concert or not, they wouldn't show up to support someone they no longer believed in.

Sky's phone buzzed, and she answered it on the car speaker. April's voice filled the car. "Tell me you two aren't on your way to this insane free concert."

"Sorry, April. Sofie checked Becks' contract, and there's nothing in there saying he can't play music in the park as long as he isn't charging."

"What about releasing the single?" She didn't sound angry, only tired. "There's a section that says we schedule all music releases."

"April." Sky shot Becks a wink. "Sofie and I work for you, for the label, but we care about Becks. Do you really think we haven't combed through every clause? Becks isn't allowed to upload the music online and sell it without the label, but he can give permission for it to be used in a single broadcast as long as no money exchanged hands."

To Becks' surprise, April laughed. "I should know by now not to underestimate you, Skylar."

"What you should know is not to put my cousin in the kind of position you did."

"It was a good idea for you to have him do the morning show. I don't know how you did that so last minute."

"It wasn't me. Becks isn't some idiot you picked up on the side of the road."

"What she's trying to say"—Becks leaned forward—"is that I'm going to be making my own decisions about my image from now on. Now, April, I will speak to you later about what's next, but right now, I have a concert to get to." He hung up without giving her a chance to respond.

Skyler laughed as she pulled into the South lot at the city park. "Where is the guy who tries to please everyone?"

Becks shrugged. "I can't please everyone, cuz." One side of his mouth curled up. "But thanks for taking care of me with the label. If I tried to read my contract and all the legal bunk, I think my brain would break."

"You're not as dumb as you claim. Stop trying to act like some pretty boy airhead, and people might stop treating you like it."

He laughed. "I need you to do all my talking for me." His eyes lit up as an idea popped into his mind. "You should be my manager."

"What?"

"Quit working for the label. You hate it there anyway. Be my manager. If I still have a career after this, I'll need someone as an extra layer between me and those jerks so I don't just do whatever they tell me to next time."

"Beckett..." She shook her head. "Why don't you use your brain to keep yourself from doing stupid stuff?"

"Please."

"We'll talk about it." She opened her car door. "Come on. If I remember correctly, you have some birds to play for."

They crossed the expansive lot, stepping onto the path that wound around various ponds. Shielding his eyes against the sun, Becks lifted his face to the cloudless blue sky. As he walked, he stripped off the short-sleeved, buttoned plaid shirt, leaving him in a simple white T-shirt that was much more comfortable in the August heat.

His jeans clung to his legs in the heat, but there was no helping that. Skylar didn't lead him to the old stage. Instead, she took him to a pavilion out of view of it.

"What are we doing?" He checked the time on his phone. There was half an hour until he had to be on stage; even if no one came, he refused to be late.

Skylar dug through her purse, producing a granola bar. "You haven't eaten all day." She threw it to him. He knew by now not to argue with his cousin. If this was going to be his last performance in Nashville, he wouldn't pass out up there.

The label could drop him, using their morality clauses. That thought had been in the back of his mind, but it wasn't his biggest worry. He still hadn't heard from his friends. Nari. Avery. Quinn. Harrison. Not even Nicky.

Three people crossed the lawn toward them. Becks sat on the end of a picnic table eating his granola bar as he eyed them. Two men stood on either side of a woman in a big hat and sunglasses. Becks almost laughed because he'd worn the same kind of getup many times. He slid from the table as the woman removed her sunglasses. All air left his lungs.

Standing in front of him was Etta Morelli, one of country music's biggest stars.

Etta's eyes shifted to Skylar, and she smiled. "Sky. Thanks for giving me a call."

Becks gaped at his cousin. Etta stepped forward. "Beckett, we haven't had the pleasure of meeting, but I'm Etta."

"I know who you are." He was impressed with himself when he got the words out.

She smiled like he was an adorable child. "I saw your interview this morning and had to come check out your show."

"Well, there'll be a few people here then."

Her laughter was genuine as she looked from Sky to Becks. "Do you know how long I've been doing this fame thing?"

He swallowed. He did. He knew exactly, but how pathetic would it look for him to admit he knew the year her very first single came out? "Eight years." Apparently, pathetic would be a natural state for him.

She nodded. "And in those eight years, I have done a lot of embarrassing things."

"I don't remember seeing them in the press."

"That's because you've forgotten. As your fans will, I'm sure. Our tour will do a lot to speed that along."

"You still want me to come on tour with you?" The label hadn't told him one way or another. Hell, he hadn't even known if they still wanted to back him at all.

Etta pursed her lips. "Beckett… I'm not going to ask you for any explanations. You don't know me and don't owe me anything. But I performed at that music festival in Cincinnati too. I was standing backstage when a rising country star stopped his own concert for a kiss. I know what the media says about you now, but there is no part of me that believes everything was a lie. And anyone who goes to that much trouble for someone they care about is a person I want on tour with me." She glanced behind her. "Now, excuse me. I'm going to go find a spot to watch you perform."

As she walked away, Becks was too stuck in his own head wondering what just happened to realize Nari had arrived.

She stepped in front of him and smoothed out the wrinkles in his shirt.

"You're here," he whispered.

She smiled up at him and pushed her glasses up her nose. "Of course, I am. Where else would I be when my best friend is about to get on stage?"

He crushed her to him, resting his chin on the top of her head. When they first came to Nashville, it had been him and Nari against the world. They didn't know if they'd make it, only that it would be together if they did.

When he released her, she stepped back with a laugh.

"Is Nicky here?" He scanned the park surrounding them, only seeing a few random people walking the paths.

Nari's smile fell. "I'm sorry, Becks. I don't even know if he saw the interview. I haven't been able to reach him today."

Becks knew he saw it. He'd told him to watch, hadn't he? If Nicky hadn't called Nari, it meant he wouldn't be there.

But he couldn't let that disappointment keep him from walking up to the stage. Swinging one arm around Nari and the other around Sky, he started up the hill to the patch of trees separating them from the stage.

Noise reached them before they broke to the other side. Becks sent a questioning look to Sky, but she only shrugged. As they caught sight of the stage and the fields surrounding it, Becks froze. A sea of people spread out before them, all clamoring in excitement.

"What is this?" He could barely get the words out.

Nari grinned. "I think these people want to see Beckett Anderson."

A cheer rose from the crowd as people caught sight of him walking toward the side of the stage. Up ahead, Quinn and

Harrison sat on the steps with Sofie standing in front of him. This was his team, the people who always showed up for him.

No matter what happened to his career, he should have known they'd still be here.

Becks looked down at his drummer and his bassist as he stopped in front of them. They needed no words to explain anything. Instead, Becks only asked, "Are you guys ready?"

They shared a look with Nari.

"Oh, no." Quinn pushed a hand through his hair. "There's nowhere to plug anything in. Harrison doesn't have his drums. It's just you and your guitar, bro."

"don't forget his pretty voice," Harrison added.

"I can't go up there by myself. We're a band."

Harrison crossed his arms. "Should have thought of that before choosing a place with no electricity, douchebag." He paused. "I say that with the greatest affection."

Becks couldn't help but laugh as he considered the crumbling stone stage. They were right. It wasn't meant for musical performances.

"It's an acoustic show." Nari shrugged. "So, ya know, you're all good. I'll go on stage to announce you." She winked as she turned toward the stage.

Becks couldn't remember the last time he'd performed solo or acoustically for that matter. Sofie lifted his guitar and handed it to him. He swung the strap over his head, and the instrument fit him like nothing ever had.

He ran a hand over the smooth curve as he eyed the stairs. He took one step forward knowing this concert wouldn't be his last. Another step and he thought about how soon he'd be playing in arenas as he opened for Etta Morelli. A third step and he glanced back at the people who'd come to support him. As he climbed the stairs, he caught sight of Avery, his best friend, his brother, standing near the front of the stage.

Avery lifted his chin, one corner of his mouth tipping up. That was all Becks needed to know they were okay.

Because families fought, and they loved each other anyway. He thought of his mom, dying with no family surrounding her. Becks never wanted to hurt the people he loved.

But he had.

Nicky hadn't come. After Becks' confession on TV, he knew they could no longer be friends. But it would have been nice to pretend a while longer.

Even though that was what got them into this mess. Pretending. Faking. From now on, Becks wanted to be real.

As his fans chanted his name, he realized this was real. Their love. Their forgiveness.

"The music is real," he said.

Nari lifted one eyebrow. "Of course, it is, Becks. The music has always been real."

Nicky:

Nicky sat impatiently in the back of an Uber, afraid he might miss the most important concert of his life.

"What's taking so long?" Wylder asked the driver. Nicky reached for her hand, glad she insisted on coming with him.

"Traffic is crazy on a normal day in this part of town, but some idiot singer is having an unscheduled concert in the park so traffic's gridlocked." The driver muttered about inconsiderate entitled assholes.

"Wylds, look." Nicky pointed at the crowd making their way to the park a few blocks away. Some carried signs with supportive messages.

We love you #SexyBecksy
We don't care who you love
Kiss Nicky again!

One huge cowboy-looking dude carried a sign that read

"I just like your music. You do you."

"See, no one can resist that lovable doofus." Wylder shook her head.

Nicky smiled, relieved the fans were still with Becks. He'd watched the interview at least a dozen times, and it still didn't feel real.

"It's a journey that belongs to me and me alone." Nicky winced at the memory of Becks' face. The fire in his eyes when he looked at Charlotte Keaning after her intrusive questions.

Nicky's journey to coming out was an easier one than most. He'd always known he was gay, but all his life, people just assumed he was straight like everyone else—like it was a default setting. Breaking free of that life-long label took guts, but his family and friends adjusted, and everything was right with his world. For Nicky, he'd never questioned his sexuality, but when had he forgotten about all of those who were uncertain? What was it like to come to terms with your own sexuality when it wasn't such a clear answer?

Shame filled Nicky as he thought about all the reasons he didn't want to love Beckett Anderson. And it all came down to one issue. Becks wasn't gay. The fear that Becks might leave him for a woman just like Kenny had time and again kept Nicky from seeing what was right in front of him. Becks was in love with him. It didn't matter what label Becks ultimately identified with; he loved Nicky for Nicky. How could he possibly ask for more than that? Becks didn't owe anyone an explanation of his sexuality. Not even Nicky.

What does it matter if a man leaves me for a woman or another man? Whoever Nicky decided to be with could eventually break his heart and leave. That was the gamble with love. A gamble he was ready to take.

"Thanks for the ride." Nicky reached for the door. "But I'm going to run the rest of the way." He didn't wait for Wylder before he shot out of the car. "Come find me up by the stage," he shouted over his shoulder as he left Wylder with the Uber. Running down the sidewalk, he could hear the crowd cheering for Becks, and he only hoped he'd make it in time.

Nicky was sweating in the hot August heat by the time he reached the crowd in the park. Becks' sexy-smooth voice washed over the audience like soft velvet. Nicky stopped to catch his breath and stared at him on the crumbling old stage, just the man and his guitar. The lyrics of "Love Me" hit Nicky hard. The single would be a huge hit, and most fans would think it was about Nicky. But Nicky knew Becks well enough to know what he sang about with his heart bared for the world to see. It broke his own heart to hear how much Becks loved the mother who'd abandoned him. The mother he never got a chance to know. But deep down inside, he wanted the song to be about him—even just a little bit.

Hushed whispers followed Nicky through the crowd as his feet moved toward the stage. He had no idea what would happen, but he needed Becks to know he was there. That no matter what, they were still friends.

"It about time you showed up." Nicky turned to find his brother standing with Wylder.

"What? How did you get here before me?"

"Traffic cleared up after you left." She shrugged. "I've been here for ages."

"Of course." Nicky swept a hand through his sweaty hair. He was a mess in this heat, and his nerves didn't make it any better.

"Well, what now?" Avery bumped Nicky's shoulder. "We just going to stand here enjoying the music, or what?"

"I... I'm not sure." Nicky glanced around at all the staring faces. Becks stood on the other side of the stage, facing his screaming fans. News vans swarmed the nearby parking lot, and a sea of cameras floated through the crowd toward the stage. It was only a matter of time before they reached him, and he didn't want a camera in his face. This wasn't about proving anything to anyone other than Becks, but Nicky was paralyzed with fear.

"Little man, you've got this," Avery said. "I'm not going to lie. The thought of you and Becks together is...weird. But it turns out my best friend is in love with you. If he's your Nari..." Avery's eyes shone bright in the late afternoon light. "Go get your man, and don't let anyone stop you."

Nicky nodded, trying to remember how to breathe. There was a reason he didn't like crowds and being the center of attention.

"Hey, look at me," Wylder said, pulling his face down to her level. "Don't think about the fans, the cameras, or whatever crap they're going to write about you later. This isn't about them. This moment is about you, and it's make or break right now. My brother is in love with you. What are you going to do about it?"

Nicky took a deep breath and looked up toward the stage. His hands were shaking, and the thought of making some kind of grand gesture in front of all these people made him want to hide. But when a pair of sky-blue eyes landed on him, everything else faded. The noise was there, thundering in his ears, but Nicky didn't pay it any mind. The park full of strangers didn't matter. Nicky took one step toward the stage and then another. His feet moved faster than his mind could come up with a reason to stop him. Becks had to know. And he had to know now.

Nicky charged up to the stage, the fans standing aside to clear the way for him. Becks' voice trailed off, and a hush fell over the crowd as the music faded. The setting sun glinted off Becks' hair, casting him in shades of gold. Nicky hauled himself up on the stage, his eyes glued to Becks and no one else.

"I was scared," he blurted. "And I was wrong. I'm sorry." Nicky stopped just inches from Becks, the only thing between them was his guitar.

"Wrong?" Becks frowned at him. "I got us in this mess. What do you have to be sorry about, Nick-Nick?" Becks shoved the guitar behind him and took a step forward, narrowing the distance between them.

Nicky shut his eyes, and goose bumps shivered down his spine. It nearly undid him whenever Becks said his name like that. "I judged you, and I didn't believe you could ever want me," he whispered. "I thought it was just a phase for you, and I swore I wouldn't go down that road again—"

"I don't have all the answers you need, but I'm not him, Nicky. I won't hurt you."

"I don't need answers." Nicky grabbed the sweaty front of his shirt and tugged him closer. "I just need you." He stepped into Becks' arms, and their lips met in a searing-hot kiss. For a moment, it was just them. Then tension between them melted as Nicky's hands explored Becks' chest through his fitted T-shirt.

Becks' thumb swiped at the tears escaping Nicky's eyes. "Don't cry, Nick-Nick." Becks wrapped his arms around Nicky's waist. "I don't have the words to explain how I can feel the way I do about you. All I can say is I love you." He smiled down at Nicky, reaching to cup his face.

The thunderous screaming and applause hit Nicky, reminding him they were not alone.

"Gay, straight, bi, pan, however you want to define yourself doesn't matter to me, Beckett Anderson. I love you for you." Nicky reluctantly pulled away. "But I think you have a concert to finish." He turned toward the audience cheering them on. Red crept up his neck to his face, his ears burning under the scrutiny of so much attention.

"Oh my God, you're adorable." Becks laughed, taking his hand with a gentle squeeze. "Don't go too far." Becks leaned in to whisper in his ear. "I haven't kissed you nearly enough yet."

Nicky wasn't sure he could handle what Becks did to him with just his words, but he managed to wave to the crowd and made his way off stage without tripping over his own feet.

"My boyfriend, ladies and gentleman," Becks shouted, sliding his guitar back in front of him, his eyes alight with a fire Nicky hadn't seen in a long time. "And would you look at that." Becks pointed to the roadies arriving with speakers and equipment behind the stage. "Looks like my label sent over some backup with a generator. Narisaurus, where's the rest of our band? It's time to turn this one-man show into a real concert!" Becks turned toward the crowd while Quinn and Harrison joined him on stage with their instruments.

"You know this all started out with a kiss I couldn't explain." Becks spoke to the hushed crowd hanging on his every word. "But it means the world to me you've all stuck with me through one of the most confusing times of my life. I still have lots to figure out, but right now, let's make some music!"

Nicky wanted to rush the stage with the rest of the fans by the time the concert was over, but he restrained himself. His boyfriend was enjoying his impromptu concert, and Nicky was content to just watch him.

My boyfriend, the country star. Nicky smiled, ignoring the cameras eager to get his picture. He'd never get used to that, but for Becks, he would find a way to deal with the attention.

"I'm so excited I could die!" Wylder slammed into his side. The label sent security to the park to help get Becks and the band out safely. They'd roped off an area behind the stage where Wylder and Avery joined him. "My best friend's dating my brother. I can't wait to hear all the juicy details!"

Nicky's brow raised in surprise. "You sure you want to hear about how your brother makes my toes curl when he kisses me? Or how ungodly sexy he is when he takes his sweaty shirt off and plays his guitar?" Nicky couldn't help himself; he couldn't take his eyes off shirtless SexyBecksy on stage.

"Ew, no, la-la-la-la-la, I need to unhear that. I want to know the cute adorable stuff, like when he brings you flowers the first time, your first response should be to text me immediately."

"Yeah, sure, Wylder." Nicky laughed, throwing his arm around her.

"Look at us, bro." Avery shook his head. "How did we get here?" A deep frown creased his forehead.

"You say that like it's a bad thing." Nicky waited for Avery to say something ridiculous. He'd been best friends with Becks for too long.

"You realize what we are, right?" Avery scratched the back of his head.

"What?"

"Groupies, man. We're country music groupies." His voice held a hint of disgust. Few people knew he hated country music.

Nicky threw his head back and laughed. "As long as he doesn't start singing songs about his truck, I think we're okay."

Avery tugged Nicky away from Wylder, ruffling his hair in that annoying brotherly way of his. "I'm damn happy for you, Nicky. For both of you."

"I know it's weird, but you sure you're okay with this? Me with your best friend?"

"It's weird because it's new and unexpected. But it's not bad weird. It makes sense. Me, you, Nari, Becks, and Wylder are family."

Nicky linked his arms around his best friend and his brother, happy Avery included Wylder as part of their little family.

"They're leaving soon," Avery said, his voice sad. "It's hard when they leave, and this time, it's a full tour."

"Hey, we've got each other and school to keep us busy until they get back," Nicky said.

"I can't wait to get you out of this insane country music world and back to the real world at school. You're going to love it."

Nicky was looking forward to life at Vanderbilt University and living with his brother, but he had a month of summer vacation left. A month he intended to enjoy.

"Good night, ladies and gentlemen!" Becks raised his fist to the sky and charged off the stage, handing off his guitar to one of the stage assistants.

Nicky's breath caught in his throat as Becks cupped his face in his hands, his kiss gentle and sweet. It was the first time his kiss didn't take him by surprise.

Becks pressed his forehead against Nicky's, his eyes closed and his breath warm in Nicky's face. "I don't think I'll ever get tired of doing that." His eyes flickered open as they stood there, the rest of the world fading behind them. "I want you to know you are not a phase, Nicky St. Germaine. I feel more like myself in this moment than I ever have before."

Nicky couldn't help the huge smile plastered to his face. He'd once thought he loved Kenny, but they were never right for each other. Nicky hadn't known it could be like this.

"I'm just sorry I have to leave so soon. April texted during the concert. Everything's back on. I'm leaving with Etta next week for an eight-month tour. It's everything I've ever wanted for my career, but I'm not ready to leave you." Becks took his hands, worry filled his eyes.

"That's probably a good thing since I'm about to invite myself on tour with you." Nicky squeezed his hands. "I'm not ready to leave you yet either."

"You're coming with me?" Becks' blue eyes lit up.

"I have a month off until school starts, so what better way to end my summer vacation than traveling with my boyfriend?"

"Yes!" Becks grinned and grabbed Nicky, whirling him around. Setting Nicky back on his feet, he whispered, "I love you, Nick-Nick."

Nicky would never get tired of hearing those words from his lips.

Becks: One Year Later

What's it like to have country's hottest album?

That was what she'd asked, right? Becks stared at Charlotte Keaning, remembering the last time he sat on this very couch, baring his soul, nearly a year ago.

"Beckett." She smiled as if she couldn't quite figure him out.

"Can you repeat the question?"

"Your album has been on every country top ten list since it released earlier this year. That has to be exciting."

A grin spread across his face. "I'm very thankful to everyone who loves these songs."

"And humble."

He laughed. "Charlotte, I think you're probably the first person to call me humble. The truth is, it never really sinks in. Every day, I wake up and wonder just how I got here. That's not me being humble. I know I'm good. And I'm definitely SexyBecksy." He flashed her a smile. "But I'm also a small town kid who formed a band called *Anonymous* in high school because none of us wanted our classmates to know about it."

"Why not?"

"Well, if you tell someone you want to be a performer, that you want to be famous, they think you're ridiculous. I mean, how many people are lucky enough to get this far? The odds are against you. But then if you manage to catch a shooting star, to get lucky, those doubters pretend they believed in you all along."

"Did you have a lot of doubters?"

"It's the age of the internet, Charlotte." He lifted a brow, not finishing his answer. "But my support was always louder. That is how I got here. Well, that, my insane talent, and ridiculously good looks."

"I take back my humble comment." Her smile crinkled the corners of her eyes. "You've just returned from an eight-month tour with Etta Morelli. That had to be a wild ride."

"It was more than I could've imagined." His eyes drifted to the side of the stage where Nicky watched with a proud smile on his face.

"You even got to play at the president's son's birthday party."

"Asher Brooks is a cool dude. We're bros."

"Beckett." She set aside her notes and leaned forward, her gaze meeting his.

Becks only responded with a smug grin. He knew exactly what she wanted him to say, what the viewers wanted to hear. There'd been rumors but no announcement yet.

"Fine." Becks crossed his arms and leaned back. "You want me to reveal my big secret? Nicky is pregnant."

Confused chatter wound through the audience, and Charlotte only gaped at him, unsure how to take his joke.

Becks didn't get to enjoy his joke for long because Nicky charged onto the stage, his brown hair swept back from his forehead. "For God's sake, we're engaged." He froze as he reached the chairs, realizing for the first time he was on live TV with an audience cheering for him.

Becks watched the red creep up his neck and into his cheeks in the most adorable way. Before last summer, he'd never imagined spending his life with Nicky St. Germaine. Now, he wanted nothing more than to make him blush every day.

With more calm than Nicky currently showed, Becks turned back to Charlotte. "It seems Nicky has told our secret to the entire world. Our relationship played out in the press, so it only seems fitting."

"Beckett." Charlotte's lips tugged up as she stared at Nicky who stood completely still, unable to move under the bright lights. "If you don't get off your butt and kiss that boy, someone from my audience will."

She was right. The cheers for Nicky were louder than they'd been for Becks. He was America's sweetheart, the guy who proved nice guys could win.

Becks reached for Nicky's arm and tugged, pulling him toward the chair. When Nicky didn't resist, Becks yanked him down onto his lap. He leaned in until his lips were inches from Nicky's. "We've got to give them what they want." As he kissed his fiancé with the crowd whistling and cheering them on, Becks realized he'd always been his own biggest doubter.

But Nicky washed all doubt away.

WANT MORE FROM TWIN RIVERS?
CHECK OUT DATING WASHINGTON,
AVAILABLE ON AMAZON

Asher:

I live in a fishbowl. Sometimes I call it a prison.

The White House is the only home I've ever really known. Yeah, that White House.

The entire world idolizes my family. And me? I'm the president's gay son, Asher Brooks. Some people cheer for me, others only want me to go away.

I wish they'd all just see me, Asher.

I come with a lot of baggage in the form of a team of secret service agents following me wherever I go and a codename that reminds them all just who I am.

It's no wonder I've never been kissed.

Now it's my birthday and my present? A huge, stuffy party, Washington style.

I didn't expect my former best friend, Kenny, to show up. I didn't plan to escape my own party with him. I've hated him since the day he decided he couldn't be friends with the gay kid.

So, why did I let him kiss me?

And why do I want to do it again?

Kenny:

Hockey is life.

Well, I want it to be. I have a three letter goal: N-H-L.

Focusing on my dream helps me tune out my parents' constant disapproval.

Because I'm that guy, Kenny Montgomery, son of the conservative senator. Only months ago, every media outlet posted pictures of me kissing another boy.

Yep, outed in epic fashion. Go big or go home.

I'd rather just go home.

Now, here I am at the White House of all places, forced to sit through a party for someone I once considered my only friend. But that was before. Before I abandoned him, afraid people would assume I played for his team (News flash. I did.)

He's become this tall, insanely talented artist. Even if it was possible for me to leave every doubt behind, Asher Brooks is out of my league.

It's better to focus on that three letter goal.

G-A-Y.

No, not that one.

N-H-L.

Yeah, I'm screwed.

AVAILABLE ON AMAZON

FREE IN KINDLE UNLIMITED

Don't forget your free Bonus Chapters! Download now at http://bit.ly/DNBonus. Along with the chapters, you'll receive occasional emails with special deals, giveaways, and new release alerts for all of our upcoming Twin Rivers books.

ABOUT MICHELLE MACQUEEN

Michelle MacQueen is a USA Today bestselling author of love. Yes, love. Whether it be YA romance, NA romance, or fantasy romance (Under M. Lynn), she loves to make readers swoon.

The great loves of her life to this point are two tiny blond creatures who call her "aunt" and proclaim her books to be "boring books" for their lack of pictures. Yet, somehow, she still manages to love them more than chocolate.

When she's not sharing her inexhaustible wisdom with her niece and nephew, Michelle is usually lounging in her ridiculously large bean bag chair creating worlds and characters that remind her to smile every day—even when a feisty five-year-old is telling her just how much she doesn't know.

ABOUT ANN MAREE CRAVEN

Ann Maree Craven is an Amazon bestselling author of YA Contemporary Fiction and YA Fantasy (her Fantasy fans will know her as Melissa A. Craven). Her books focus on strong female protagonists who aren't always perfect, but they find their inner strength along the way. Ann's novels will appeal to audiences of all ages and fans of almost any genre. She believes in stories that make you think and loves playing with foreshadowing, leaving clues for the careful reader.

She draws inspiration from her background in architecture and interior design to help with the small details in world building and scene settings. (Her degree in fine art also comes in handy.) She's a diehard introvert with a wicked sense of humor and a tendency for hermit-like behavior. (Seriously, she gets cranky if she has to put on anything other than yoga pants and t-shirts!)

Ann Maree enjoys editing almost as much as she enjoys writing, which makes her an absolute weirdo among her peers. Her favorite pastime is sitting on her porch when the weather is nice with her two dogs, Fynlee and Nahla, reading from her massive TBR pile and dreaming up new stories.

www.ingramcontent.com/pod-product-compliance
Lightning Source LLC
Chambersburg PA
CBHW020552310726
48979CB00008B/1186/J
* 9 7 8 1 9 7 0 0 5 2 0 3 9 *